TELL ME NO LIES

C. MORGAN

BRIXBAXTER PUBLISHING

Tell Me No Lies
Copyright © 2020 by C. Morgan.

All rights reserved. This book or any portion thereof may not be reproduced or used in any manner whatsoever without the express written permission of the publisher except for the use of brief quotations in a book review.

The novel is a work of fiction. Names, characters, places and plot are all either products of the author's imagination or used fictitiously. Any resemblance to actual events, locales, or persons – living or dead – is purely coincidental.

Editor: Eric Martinez
Cover Designer: Ryn Katryn Digital Art

DEDICATION

To my readers - Thank you for picking up a copy of this book! And to Mary, the one person that has pushed me into writing and never seems to give up on me, even when I want to give up on myself!

C. Morgan

CHAPTER 1

ZANE

As I entered the trailer at the Clover Oil Field on the outskirts of Williston, North Dakota, I dusted off my boots. "I'm taking a break," I yelled at my crew in my gruffest voice. "Don't bother me unless someone is on fire."

I slammed the door so hard the walls rattled, stirring up the fine layer of dust that clouded the air and the office. It was impossible to keep the place clean. Everything was dusty, and it was so thick you could write your name on every surface.

I often wondered what was getting into my lungs, but there were worse hazards to worry about in the oil field I'd called my home for the past ten years.

I'd worked my way up to foreman after starting out as a floor hand, and while I had one of the best crews of damned fine men, there were always a few bad apples to make my morning rough. Like the lazy ones, the careless ones, the homesick ones. But worse than those guys were the types who liked to run their mouths. The big talkers, the prideful. Those were the ones who usually got the raw ass the easiest, and after an early morning, I just needed a break from them all, especially since we'd all been living on top of one another without a woman in sight for the past two months.

What better way than to call home and talk to my little girl, Mila? She was the only girl in my life other than my mother, and at five years old, she was the center of my universe.

Before I even dropped my ass into the chair, which again caused a cloud to rise around me, I pulled out my phone and hit the magic button. As I waited for my mother to answer the phone, I closed my eyes and imagined what my life would be like if I didn't have my parents to help me.

Lord knew my sorry ex-girlfriend, Heather, wasn't going to help. Not that she could do anything from a prison cell. She had gotten herself in a string of trouble. Drugs—both using and trafficking—writing hot checks, and even shoplifting. All while she was supposed to be caring for our daughter. While I worked hard to make a living, putting myself in danger so she didn't have to, she chose to anyway. I guessed the life I had to offer wasn't the excitement she wanted.

Who knew a one-night stand with the girl I'd crushed on in high school could lead to so much drama? When she ended up pregnant, I tried to do the right thing, and for a while, I thought it might work out. I'd go through it all again, the lying and the cheating, just to have my daughter.

It turned out that I wasn't the only man in Heather's life. Not that it shouldn't be expected from a woman who blew her dealer just feet away from where our infant daughter was strapped into her car seat. And as if that wasn't enough to make me want to kill her, she had to get caught doing it, becoming the talk of the town and the shame of my parents. That was when the cops found the pills in the car, the pills she had driven all the way across the border to get for her boyfriend, using my daughter's car seat as a hiding place.

Before I could get another sick thought about killing the woman, my mother's sweet voice came to rescue me from hell. "Zane!" she said, sounding surprised as if I didn't call every single day at least twice. "How's your day going, honey?"

"It's going, Mom. Where's that little angel? I sure need to hear her voice." It had been a long stay at the man camp, and even though I wasn't but an hour away, I couldn't leave my post. Not until the job was done.

"She's trying to talk her Pop-pop into giving her real paints. He's trying to figure out a way to get out of that one without caving in and making you mad at him."

I laughed. My Mila could drive a hard bargain. "Tell him good luck. He'll need it." He didn't stand a chance.

"I think he's hoping you'll be the bad daddy and tell her no so he won't have to. He's already given up on Bad Nana."

"I'll talk to her about it." I could already hear Mila giggling in the background.

"Here she is," said my mother.

Mila got on the phone, and her sweet voice was like the clouds parting on a rainy day. "Hey, Daddy. Are you taking a break?"

I scratched my stubbly chin. "You know it. I had to call my girl and make sure she's not trying to talk her Pop-pop into buying her real paints when she knows she's only supposed to use crayons and finger-paints."

"But I drew a masterpiece, and my finger-paints didn't come with magenta."

"What do you know about magenta?" I asked. Shouldn't her color options be limited to primary at this stage in life?

"It's like hot pink, only a little darker. And I need it for the flowers."

"Why don't you just paint them pink?"

"They aren't pink, Daddy. They are magenta. Trust me. It's going to be a masterpiece." Everything she painted was a masterpiece in my eyes, but as her skills advanced, so did her desire for better instruments.

I ran my hand through my hair and closed my eyes, imagining her in her favorite pair of sparkly leggings and the princess costume she'd gotten too tall for. She wore them nearly every day unless we could talk her out of it. "Can't you just use your crayons? I bought you the big box you wanted."

"Yes, but masterpieces don't come in crayons, Daddy. They are painted." Her voice wasn't whiny at all. It was very matter-of-fact, which made it even harder for me to keep from melting even though I had to disagree.

"That's not true, honey. Art comes in all kinds of mediums."

"Well, I'm sick of mediums. I am ready to move up to larges."

I laughed at her confusion and could imagine how serious she was about her art, and at such a young age. What did I have to look forward to when she got older? She was going to be a handful. But so worth it. "We'll talk about it when I get home."

"Okay. When are you coming home?"

"When the job is over." It was supposed to be a few months with only a week break in the middle, but I didn't want to make her unhappy. I never wanted to do that. "I love you, Noodle. Put Nana back on the phone."

"I love you too, Daddy." She raised her little voice. "Nana!" I could hear her footsteps as she scurried away.

But it wasn't my mother who got back on the phone. "Hey, son," said my father. "Did you ever make up your mind about that trip we wanted to take Mila on? It's only for a week. She's restless here. And with her school letting out in a few days, we just thought it would be good for her."

I had forgotten all about them wanting to take her to the Animal Kingdom amusement park a few hours away. My mother had mentioned it the last time I called, but I wasn't sure anything was definite. "Yeah, I think it will be okay. Just the amusement park?"

"Well, there's a smaller preserve on the way. We're talking about doing the drive-through tour, but we'll keep the windows up. I won't let any lions eat her if that's what you're worried about."

There were other predators to worry about, but I wasn't afraid of anything. My father would keep her safe, and Mom managed to keep me alive as a kid. Somehow. I was a rambunctious boy, and some might say I never outgrew it.

"Just have fun. I wish I could come with—"

A ruckus occurred at that moment, and from the sound of the wailing, I could tell it was bad. "Emergency! I have to go!" I ended the call and rushed out of my chair and to the door, where I could already see the men gathering through the window.

"What is it?" I shouted to one of the men nearby.

"I'm not sure," he said as we both made our way over to the rig in a hurry.

He stopped behind the other men, but I pushed myself through. "Back up!" I shouted, the crowd parting as I peeled them away.

As the men parted, I could see the newest floor-hand's face as he tried to pull his arm free of the machine it was stuck in. "Help me!" he cried. "It's broken, I can feel it." The young man's name was Lee, and he had just turned twenty-one a week ago.

"Don't move!" I said. His arm was wedged in the inner workings of the machine that I couldn't even see from the outside. "Where is the medic?"

"He was across the field. He's on the way."

"Tell him to hurry the fuck up!" I wasn't going to have someone sit there and die on me while that pompous-ass medic was taking his sweet time.

"We hit the emergency shut off," said my best driller, Jake. "I think we stopped it just in time. I told him not to reach in there."

"He stuck his hand in there to get a tool that fell in," said Pete, the oldest of my roughnecks. He had been around the fields longer than anyone in the camp. "He's going to have to take the damned thing apart if he wants to get that arm out in one piece."

"Crack it open," I said, wishing I'd used better words. The man began to panic. "It's going to be okay, Lee. Don't panic."

The motor hand, whose name was Hank, came running over with his tools. "I'm going to need your help, Boss," he said to me.

The medic arrived, taking immediate action. "We're probably going to need a tourniquet," he said. "I have one. Let's get it around his arm before we undo anything. The pressure is most likely keeping him from bleeding out."

I nodded. "Can you see what's going on?" I asked Hank, wondering if he had gotten a better look. I didn't want to look into that machine. What I had seen already was enough to bring any man to his knees.

"I have a pretty good idea." He popped open the safety shield, which did fuck all to help, and we could see the blood and twisted bone.

I winced, trying to keep a straight face as not to upset the man any more than he was already. He had turned pale and was beginning to fade out on us.

"Stay with me," said the medic. His name was Tony. I didn't have the best relationship with him, but at times like this, I was glad we had him handy.

"Ambulance is on the way," said one of the men from the back. "They said they're five away."

"That's good," said Tony. "How long until you can get him free?"

As the man began to sag, putting pressure on his already fucked up arm, Jake held on to him.

"Someone is going to have to pry this," said Hank. "I'm not sure I'm strong enough, and I have to make sure this piece here doesn't shift."

"I can't," said Tony. "I've got to get the arm free while you do it."

"I'll do it," I said. "Give me some fucking air first."

I had the men back away as I prepared to help Lee, hoping we'd keep his arm intact in the process. It had damn near been ripped off. If not for the fast action of the other men, it would have been.

"Okay, on three." Tony, Hank, and I exchanged nods.

"I'll count." I prepared myself and took a deep breath as we worked together to get the job done. "One. Two. Three." I pried the part as Tony pulled the man's arm free, and thankfully, all went as planned. The men hurried to lay him down in the break station as they waited for the ambulance.

Letting loose a long breath, I got up to dust off. I had to call my superior and let them know about the incident.

I went to the trailer for some privacy. I hit the call button and wiped my gritty brow where the sweat and dirt had combined, making me my own mud mask.

"Zane Ballard," said Earl Douglas before he even said hello. "I do hope you're calling to tell me that progress and production are up."

I clenched my jaw. I hated to tell him what had happened but I knew the best way was to just say it. No beating around the bush like a pussy. "Actually, sir, there's been another accident."

"Another one? That's two this month."

"Yes, sir."

"How is he?" His stern tone was his way of asking if the man was dead.

"He's alive. It's serious, though. He's probably going to lose his arm if he makes it."

"Who is he?"

"Lee Reynolds. He's a rookie roughneck. He put his hand in a machine to fetch a tool that fell in it."

"Jesus Christ," said the man under his breath.

"Yeah. It's pretty bad. One stupid decision, and he's messed up for life."

"Was the machine up to date on its maintenance and inspections?" All Earl really cared about was a lawsuit.

I always made sure my field was working in tip-top shape. "Yes. We had to crack it open to get him free. It was a stupid mistake on his part."

"A mistake that is costing us time and production, not to mention however much else in a settlement. His fault or not, we get to pay for his stupidity."

And arms, I wanted to say, but why would the man give two fucks about my crew? They were my responsibility.

"It's been a long job. The men are pent up, and they need a break. I'll see to it they have one." I was about to go out and shut the entire operation down for the day. There was no way we could start up again.

"Give them the rest of the day off. I'm going to send you a replacement. Go home. Come back in a few weeks."

"A few weeks?" I wondered for a moment if I was about to lose my job.

"Make it a month. And then I want you to come back and make sure this never happens again on your watch. I know it's not your fault. But I have to take action."

I breathed a sigh of relief. My daughter couldn't have an unemployed father. And I didn't want to have to move her. Williston was where it was at in the industry and I wouldn't make the kind of money I made anywhere else this close to home.

"Yes, sir." I hung up the phone and wiped my brow. The only light in the darkness of the day was the fact that I could go home and see Mila. She would make everything better.

CHAPTER 2

TARA

I had just set out the last of the flower arrangements at the Golden Flower Hotel's morning breakfast buffet when Ben, my boss and resident pervert, came up to me with an insinuating smile as he looked me up and down.

"You look like a rare rose today," he said as he approached the waffle station. "Did you make sure to put the little packets of food in the arrangements this time? I don't want those wilting by lunch."

"Yeah, Ben, I know the drill. Keep the flowers fresh and the food fresher."

"Hey, when are you going to call me Benny? I like the ladies to call me Benny Vinnie, you know. It brings me back to the days when I was a high roller. Keeps me young." He wagged his brows at me the same way he always did.

"Sorry, Ben. I'm just not that type of girl."

"Speaking of that kind of girl, where's your friend? She was supposed to be here thirty minutes ago."

"Don't ask me." I shrugged, though I had a pretty good idea. My friend and favorite party girl, Karen, was usually doing her walk of shame this time of the morning. Why Ben had just now cared to ask about her showed how much he really cared.

Karen was his favorite, and not only because she called him Benny. But because she was the type who could draw in a crowd and work it. She could make you feel good with a smile and talk you into just about anything if and when she wanted. It was her gift, and Ben saw the profit in it.

She usually got away with murder. I wasn't so lucky.

About that time, the kitchen door swung open, and she sauntered out as the first customer walked in and made his rounds quietly, piling the waffles onto his plate.

"Where have you been?" asked Ben with a tone so hard the customer glanced up and made a face before going on with his business.

Karen looked like she had stuffed her uniform in that beach bag she called a purse and dragged it all around the city last night before putting it back on this morning.

"Take it easy. I didn't have time to iron my uniform." The white cotton blouse, which was designed to show off her rack, was rumpled and full of creases, as was the black skirt.

"It smells like you didn't have time to wash it either," he said. "You smell like booze."

"That's me," she said. "I'm still riding the last wave of drinks from last night. I haven't had much sleep."

"Then maybe you should go home early and get to work earlier. I have a buffet to run." His tone was steeped with disappointment until she pinched his cheek.

"Come on, Benny Vinnie. You know you aren't mad at me." She gave him a wink. "You wouldn't know what to do without me around." She had a way of working people, a way I'd never had. And while I worried about her sometimes, she never let anything slow her down.

"Maybe that's true." He gave a shrug and hurried to the back when the phone rang in the kitchen.

When Ben was gone, I walked up to her to get the real scoop. "So? Where were you really?"

She gave me a big smile. "I met these guys last night, two of them.

They were in town and wanted the grand tour. Well, who does that better than me?"

"Two of them? Are you talking about those guys who were at the back table last night? The ones you called nerdy?"

"Yeah, well, nerdy equals money, honey. I know I've told you that."

"And you spent the night with them both?"

Her grin got bigger. "You really do think the worst of me, don't you?" She gave me a playful slap. "Not hardly. I waited for them to pass out and left."

"Just like that? You left?" There had to be more to the story, but somehow, Karen always managed to surprise me.

She laughed. "They were nerds. I outdrank them. That's why I'm still a bit buzzed."

"I don't see how you have the money to do all of that."

"You really need to go out with me sometime. I keep telling you that I can teach you the ropes, including getting the men to pay for everything."

She claimed that she never had to pay for so much as a drink but I found it hard to believe. But then, money didn't come easily to me, so I wasn't looking for extra ways to spend it. "So, those nerdy men paid for your night?"

"Every drink, every morsel of food. Even gambling. I won three hundred dollars."

"I wouldn't have that luck."

"You're the only person in this city who doesn't enjoy it. I swear, to live in Vegas and not gamble? I think you need your head examined."

"Not everyone here is a gambler. Some of us are just trying to make it." I had ends to meet, not money to throw away. I lived in a simple economy apartment with one bedroom and a bathroom that was just big enough to be functional. I had stayed in motels that were bigger when I was a kid with my mother. But it would do. It suited my needs and would until I could find a way out.

"You want to leave. The one place in the world people want to go, and you can't even appreciate living here."

I was more of a nature girl or wanted to be. One time when I was younger, my mom and I took a road trip and stayed in a camp in the forest. When we finally settled in Vegas with her boyfriend, we never went anywhere again. It had been my dream since to go back. And I didn't even really know where it was.

"Want to go to the pool later?" She knew I loved the pool, and that was one of the perks of working in the hotel. That and the free food from the buffet leftovers.

I ate pretty well for someone who was barely getting by. Admittedly, I was mostly roughing it to save money and I tucked away all I could. Although it wasn't much since I had dipped in to buy the little Nissan that got me to and from work with great gas mileage.

"That does sound good." I always kept a bathing suit and towel in the car, and we used it quite a bit.

"Okay then. It's a date. Maybe we'll pick up some hotties." No sooner than she had the words out of her mouth than two older men walked into the buffet. One had salt-and-pepper hair, and the other was balding, but to Karen, they were a sure thing. They caught her eye immediately, and she caught theirs, earning a big smile.

"Oh, lucky me. Look who just sat down in my section. Those look like winners to me."

"They're a little old for you, aren't they?"

"I swear, you don't know anything about men. Men like that love to spend money, which means free dinner and drinks. I'll see you later." She hurried across the room to them, and I went over to check on the first customer who was making slow work of his waffles.

"Can I get you anything, sir? Refill? Extra napkins?" He had syrup on his fingers, which he proceeded to lick off.

"No, thanks. I'm good, miss." He went back to stuffing his face while reading through his phone.

After looking around the room for comparison, his behavior seemed to be the norm. If they weren't working on a plate of food, they were lost in the hypnotic glare from their own phone screens.

I went back around to stir the gravy and made sure that everything was presentable while the customers filed in.

The line grew longer as, table by table, they filled the place up.

After about thirty minutes of flirting, Karen walked back into the kitchen as I was getting refills on the waffles and fruit.

"Hey," she said. "About later. I got invited to go out with those guys. They asked if I had a friend and said they'd love to show us a good time."

"I bet they would. They are old enough to be our fathers. What happened to lounging by the pool?" I knew the prospect of having two men falling all over her was much more appealing, especially by the look she gave me.

"You cannot be serious. This is a perfect chance for you to come out with me and see how it's done. I can train you, Grasshopper. I'm a master. And these two? They're harmless. Just looking for a nice girl to show them a good time in the big city."

Some of her behavior scared me. I waited for the day she would end up dead in a dumpster somewhere or buried in the desert. "Nah, you go on ahead. I'll just go to the pool alone or see if one of the other girls wants to hang with me."

"Sorry, Tara. It's just that the pool will always be there. These guys? They are once in a lifetime, and look at the tall one." Her eyes lingered on Mr. Salt and Pepper, who was actually really good looking for his age. "Dear Lord, that daddy can give me a spanking anytime." She gave a sultry growl and licked her lips.

My eyes widened as my face turned red. "Karen! He's probably someone's husband."

"Calm down. I'm not going to sleep with him if he's married. And besides, I've told you it's not always about sex. These men want attention—a little flirting, something to slap, grab, and tickle for a few hours. And if they throw their money at me in the process, lucky me. It's all in fun. I let them know where I stand."

"It's just not for me. I'm sorry, but no." I had never wanted to be with that kind of man and certainly not on a whim. I wanted someone who was strong, a working man, not some old man wanting to slap and tickle me. He could keep his money. I didn't need a man wanting to make it big in the city either, ready to strike it rich. I needed a man who, like me, wanted to get out of the city. "I go for the more rugged, outdoorsy type."

"You want a redneck," she said, making a face. "No thanks."

"More like a working man," I corrected. "There's nothing wrong with that kind of man. My grandfather was that kind of man." From what I remembered at least. I also thought he probably would want better for me than one-night stands and pimping myself as some sort of tagalong escort.

It wasn't that I thought I was better than Karen, but men who wanted girls like that, they didn't like girls like me. I wasn't flashy or glamourous enough.

"You should just try it once. Let go now and then. Trust me. You'd thank me if you followed my advice. You'd get the bug, and then you'd never get enough of the Vegas nightlife." She wagged her brows, and she went back out to their table.

As I walked out and spotted them glancing over, neither seemingly disappointed that I couldn't come along and both looking at Karen like they'd share, I felt like I'd never find my place in the world.

But I could rest easy knowing one thing. I wasn't going to be an old man's one-night stand.

CHAPTER 3

ZANE

When I showed up at my parents' house in the late afternoon, my father met me at the door.

"Are you okay?" he asked. "I didn't tell your mother what happened this morning." He glanced down at my arm that was still bandaged from my afternoon trip to the hospital.

I had left him hanging and only briefly called back to tell him I was on my way after shutting things down for the day. It turned out I'd been on the phone with the hospital and even went to donate a pint of blood to the poor kid after finding out I was a universal donor.

"Yeah, just had a kid lose his arm today. He stuck it in the machine, and I'm still not sure how he managed that. I gave him a pint of my own blood."

"Damn, son. I'm sorry to hear that. You think they can save it?"

"It was so mangled. I doubt it." I took a deep breath. I didn't want to repeat that image all day. "Where's my girl?"

"She's in the house with her nana. She's still trying to convince me about paints. I think there has to be a compromise somewhere."

My father had bargained with her before. "Dad, she can't have paints because she found some of Mom's, brought them home to her room, and painted her headboard. She had paint from one end of the bedroom to the other by the time I found it."

"You should have been paying attention to her." My father was never going to blame his precious angel.

"It was after lights out." I wasn't going to stand there, debating it with him. I headed into the house. "Is there anything left over from dinner?"

"Might be something. Ask your mother. She'll feed you." As I started in, Dad stayed on my heels. "I just think you're going to squash her creativity. She's a good girl, and this is a healthy outlet. Set some rules, and she'll follow them."

"I'll think about it." I wasn't giving up on the paints.

I walked into the kitchen and found Mila with her back to me. She stood on the step stool, making cookies with my mother. The brown curls that normally went down her back had been tied up out of the way.

I had intended to sneak up behind her, but hearing my footsteps, she thought I was my father. "Pop-pop! I made a bird." She turned around with the cookie dough in her hand. "Daddy!" She jumped down and hugged my legs, then held up the smashed dough. "See!" Her big brown eyes that were just like my mother's stared up at me.

It didn't look an awful lot like a bird to me after she squished it, but I wasn't going to disappoint her. "I see that."

She had on her sparkly leggings, but instead of her princess costume, she wore a T-shirt with a unicorn in rain boots with them.

"I'm glad you're home, Daddy. I have to show you something. Look at the fridge." She pointed across the room.

I walked over and looked at the picture on the door. The drawing of the birdhouse on a tree branch had amazing detail. It seemed almost a little too good for her age, and for a moment, I wondered if my parents had helped her. "This is really advanced stuff, Noodle."

I had called her Noodle since the minute she was born. She wiggled like one and was just as slippery. Heather had done the whole water birth, and I was eager to entertain her whims back then when she was clean.

My mother turned around, wiping flour from her hands. "Yeah, she's been improving a lot since I let her use the app on my phone. It teaches kids to draw."

"I told you," said my father. "Not something you want to waste."

Maybe he was right. "Okay, okay. I'll find a compromise. But let's keep it under wraps for now." I gave my father a pointed look. I didn't need her getting too excited.

"Okay, okay." He held up his hands, mimicking me.

"So, what are you baking? Dessert?"

"Cookies. The sugar kind. I wanted to make funny shapes."

"We're supposed to be making a farm scene," said Mom. "I thought she could play with the animals once we make them."

"She's got a toybox full of toys in the next room, in case you forgot buying them."

"But you can eat these when you're done," said Mom.

"When you tell me to clean up my toys, I'll just eat them. Chomp. Chomp. Chomp." Mila pretended to eat the raw dough.

My parents had spoiled her terribly from the moment she came into the world. It was like they were making up for the time they had missed with me, being working parents. My mother was a retired school teacher, who after three years of retirement still missed her classroom, and my father was a semi-retired electrician, who still wished I had gone into his line of work.

Mom laughed, and they put the dough on the pan, and she took it to the oven. When she walked back over, she leaned against the counter as Mila ran off with my dad to the living room.

"Guess who I saw the other day?" She gave me a grin and waited for me to guess.

"Tell me." I hated guessing games.

"Clay Whitmore. He looked pretty rough. He had a black eye. I asked him what happened, and he said he got thrown out of the piano bar he was working in downtown."

"That's Clay. Always in trouble." The man just didn't take the world as seriously as he should.

My mother nodded. "He's always been the most rambunctious and immature of your friends. You might want to go over and check on him. He needs a good friend, someone like you with a good head on your shoulders." She had said the same thing to me when Clay announced that he was going to join me at college. He was my oldest friend and the closest thing to a brother I'd ever had.

"I wouldn't go calling my life perfect, Mom." It wasn't that in any way, but I was trying my best.

"No, but it's better than his. He's got to grow up. I heard Beth kicked him out."

"Seriously? I thought they just had a kid." I couldn't believe what I heard. Beth and Clay were like salt and pepper. You rarely saw one without the other close by. "How's he taking that?"

"Well, he had a black eye, so you tell me."

"I should go see him." Clay had been there for me when Heather had gone off the deep end. "I'll put Mila to bed here and head out if that's okay?"

"Sure," she said. "Your room's all made up. I'll put her in there. Just don't wake her up when you get back. You should just stay the night. I'll make a big breakfast before you go home."

"Sounds good." I owned my own house about two miles away, and while it was nice to have, I felt like I didn't spend enough time there. Most of the time I was home, I spent at my parents' and I would only go home to clean up to go downtown. I wasn't going to go anywhere dressed in my work clothes, though my daily attire was not much different.

Mom lowered her voice. "We could postpone the trip tomorrow, now that you're home. We understand if you want to spend some time with her. What happened must have been pretty bad if they sent you home. I assume that was the protocol?"

She knew what was up. She was a smart lady. "Yeah, but no, I think you should go. I've got some work to do around the house."

She gave me a concerned look. "You should get out, maybe take a nice woman out to dinner."

Mom had only recently started to hound me about dating. She

didn't necessarily want me to get too serious, but going on a date now and then seemed healthy to her.

"I'd have to meet one first."

"Exactly. And I'm sure she's not hiding out in your house."

"That would be convenient," I said while wagging my brows.

Mom rolled her eyes and walked away, giving me a moment to myself.

I went down the hall to the bathroom, stripped off my work boots, and cleaned up a bit. Then I found something to eat while I searched for better options than "real paint" for Mila. I finally settled on watercolors. They even had watercolor pencils available, which sounded even better.

I tucked Mila into bed and read her a story. I hadn't gotten off the first page when she nodded off. After I kissed her goodnight, I sneaked out to go home and change.

I couldn't wait to get a drink and see my old friend. Maybe I would meet someone, but then, it wasn't likely in Williston, where most people knew Heather. Women didn't want to date someone with baggage, especially when my baggage included a crazy ex who was in prison.

After a short drive into town, I found Clay down at the club, the one my mother had told me he had gotten kicked out of and the only one in town that had the right kind of feel for a smart-ass piano player with a drinking problem.

He was a few sheets to the wind by the time I arrived and, between sets, bellied up to the bar for another fix. "And don't water this one down, sweetheart," he called to the bartender, who was a busty, tall blonde who looked like she'd had enough of his shit.

"Fuck you. I don't water my drinks." She poured him another and slid it to him. "Now fuck off, Piano Man."

"Still making friends wherever you go, I see."

Clay turned around, and his brown, bloodshot eyes widened as he saw me. "No fucking way! Zane Ballard, you son of a bitch." He grabbed me and hugged me close. "It's been months. Where the fuck have you been?"

"Working in the oil fields. What about you? Mom told me that you got kicked out of this place." I looked at his eye, which was still a nasty shade of yellow peeking out from under his shaggy brown hair. He also had stubble I'd never seen, another sign that all was not the same in his world.

"Yeah, but they let me back in. I guess they realized I'm worth the trouble. Either that, or it's because I'm the only true talent within a hundred miles of this place." He tasted his drink and made a face. "Hey, I've meant to get in touch. Guess who I heard from?"

"I'm not guessing." I followed him as he took his drink and went to a table near the piano.

"Fine, because you never would. And I'd tell you anyway." He smirked, his cocky grin making me feel like I wanted to punch him in the face. I probably would have if I didn't love him like a brother. He took another drink, and I thought I was going to lose my fucking cool wondering. It had to be one of the old crew from college—The Five.

"Are you going to tell me or nurse that drink?"

Clay chuckled. "Easy, big fella. It's Grady Black. He sold his software to some company for millions, and now he bought a big house in Vegas. He wants us to come out. He said he wanted me to call you, but I didn't know how to reach you out in the field. You've been a stranger lately. I don't like it."

"Yeah, it's not easy. We had an injury today, though, and it bought me some time off."

Clay's eyes widened. "Oh, fuck yeah. We have to go then."

"Go? I don't know, man." I thought about leaving Mila, but then it dawned on me that she would be leaving for her trip too. "When would we leave?"

"Tomorrow. He wants to show the place off and take us out on the town. You know, he's got that pact to fulfill."

Pact? I thought for a moment, trying to remember which pact he was referring to. "We made so many."

"You know. The first one of us to a million had to pay for a Vegas blowout."

I was pretty sure at the time, we all just wanted a blowjob in Vegas, but I nodded like I remembered the same as he did. Maybe it had just been too fucking long since I had the company of a woman? Regardless, I was in.

"Sure, I'll go."

"Really?" He grabbed me and tried to hug me but ended up slapping my back and laughing instead. I was more like a mountain. He wasn't going to move me. "Damn, you're solid, you big son of a gun. God, it's so good to see you."

"It's good to see you too, friend." Now I just had to see Mila off and pack for Vegas. I was long overdue a break, and getting to see my old gang was going to be the perfect way to unwind.

CHAPTER 4

TARA

The next day, after having worked the early shift, I decided to hit the pool before going home. Mondays were always fairly private at the pool, and I was content to soak up some sun in peace outside in my favorite lounger.

This particular seat was in the corner on the side with little traffic, near the waterfall, and in the breeze. If I closed my eyes, I could imagine I was out on a beach somewhere.

"I thought I'd find you here," said Karen. "Are you still mad at me?" She gave me a big-eyed stare with her baby blues and a pleading look that was irresistible.

I hadn't had much of a chance to speak with her while at work, and I guessed she thought it was because of the incident with the older men the day before. "I'm not mad at you, Karen. Why would I be?" And if she thought I was, didn't that say a lot about her conscience? You'd think.

Her shoulders loosened up as she relaxed. "Thanks Matilda," she said, never wanting to take the Lord's name in vain. "I thought you were upset with me for being a bad girl." She took the lounger next to me, her usual spot as well, and popped on her shades.

She looked like a blonde goddess in the sunlight, and I was ever envious of her tan.

"You're not a bad girl. You're just a bit more adventurous than me." There was nothing wrong with that. "Honestly, Karen, I just worry about your safety more than anything. It's a dangerous city."

"And I love you for caring. But I won't live a life of fear. But if you're so worried, why don't you join me sometimes and keep me safe. What's that old adage about safety in numbers?"

"I doubt I'd be able to do anything to protect us both but nice try."

She shrugged it off as she glanced over beside my chair. "You don't have a drink? They look so delicious." She spotted an older couple at the bar ordering drinks with tiny umbrellas. "Let's get one."

"Nah," I said, shaking my head as she called the waiter over. "It's okay. I've got water."

"Water? Boring. Let me get us something." She turned to order the drinks, ignoring my protests. "I just love anything with fruit and an umbrella. We can pretend we're in Hawaii or on a beach in the Bahamas."

"You don't have to," I said, trying to get her to not order me yet another drink I'd never be able to pay her back for. She took care of me way more than I was able to take care of her, and that made me feel bad.

"Nonsense. We're best friends. I'm buying you a drink. Besides, it's just mimosas, and this is last night's winnings."

"Fine." I didn't feel like arguing, especially since she already thought I was upset with her. "You just know how I feel about you paying my way."

"Relax. Don't think of it as me. Think of it as that tall graying hunk from last night buying it. I won a ton of money off of him. He wanted to challenge me. It was cute. Then I won another hundred all on my own."

"I still can't believe you went out with them." She had gotten more and more addicted to the night scene, and I missed the days when it was just the two of us enjoying shopping or a movie. Now, it was damned near impossible to get her to do anything but party.

"Sorry, Mom," she said as she rolled her eyes. "I didn't mean to disappoint you."

I gave her a sideward look. "It's not that, Karen. It's just this is two nights in a row. Don't you think you should slow down a bit?"

"Those two nights are helping me pay the bills, and I didn't even have to take off my clothes. It's just for fun. There's nothing against meeting new people and making new friends. Even if it's just for the moment. I swear you're going to die alone if you don't start putting yourself out there."

Those words hurt a lot more than I expected them to, but I had to defend myself. "It's just that you used to want to fall in love and have a boyfriend, and lately, it's more about who you can get to buy you a free dinner. Don't you still want to fall in love?" We had talked about our dreams a lot when we were younger, and never once did she let on that she wanted to lead a party life.

"Love is just an illusion anyway. We trick ourselves into believing it's real, and then we get let down."

I pointed to an older couple who were walking hand in hand out to the poolside across the water. "Tell that to them."

She smiled at the sweet couple. "Okay, maybe for some people, assuming he's not some scam artist hoping to steal her dead husband's money. Or she's not blowing him for his pension."

I glanced back at the old man, who didn't seem to have anything but love for the woman next to him. I had a feeling I knew where this attitude was coming from, but I wasn't going to mention her last relationship.

She had dated a man named James and thought it was going to be forever, but James dragged his feet and never would pop the question. He was a loser anyway, but she had been devastated. She hadn't had a boyfriend or a real relationship since.

She began to laugh. "The look on your face. I'm sure he's a sweet old man."

"I guess I'm just old fashioned. I want true love, a love to last me when I'm their age."

"Haven't you ever just saw a hot guy and wished you could walk right up and kiss him?"

The thought of it had my cheeks burning. "No, I couldn't do that." I wasn't about kissing strangers.

"You need more confidence. You're a gorgeous girl, with perfect skin, teeth, and I'd die for your hair." She reached over and brushed my hair off my shoulder.

"You're supposed to say that. You're my best friend."

"It's the truth. So I'd say it even if I wasn't." She took the drinks from the waiter and passed me one. They were orange with a dash of grenadine and two cherries hiding beneath a colorful umbrella.

I sipped it and closed my eyes, enjoying the first taste. The champagne made me smile.

"You should really take me up on my offer. You need to meet someone and lose that V card. Take a chance."

"I'll think about it." I did want to get out now and then but on my own terms, in my own time.

She laughed and shook her head like she would believe it when she saw it. "I won't hold my breath." She made a face that made me want to muster up the courage. "One day, I hope you see a man that you want so badly that you throw all caution to the wind."

"And I just hope that if I do decide to do something that harebrained, I don't fall on my face at his feet and get my heart trampled." No one was going to notice me the way I noticed them. At least, they hadn't. But part of me hoped that she was right. I would love to meet my dream man. And maybe if I was lucky, he would take me away from Vegas. But things like that just didn't happen in the real world.

We finished our drinks and sat talking for at least an hour more while more and more people came.

"Well, this is getting a little too busy for my tastes," I said as a little boy ran past me and jumped in the pool, splashing water all over my feet.

"No running or diving, little man!" shouted Karen. She turned to the kid's mother and gave her a dirty look.

"I'm going to go too," she said after the woman took her son aside and yelled at him. "Do you want to go hang out later?"

"I'm not sure. I've got a lot to do." I had put off doing my daily chores for days but only because I'd been trying to pick up extra shifts whenever Ben would let me.

"Like what?"

"Laundry for one, and I have to scrub the oven. I cooked a frozen lasagna, and now there's black stuff on the bottom. I think it must have bubbled over."

"That's really exciting," she said as she faked a yawn. "And those are all things you'll have done by tonight. So be ready. I'm dropping by to get you."

"Karen, I—"

"No protesting. We're going to have some innocent fun. Besides, it's Monday. What kind of trouble could we possibly get into on a Monday night?"

The magic of Vegas was that it didn't adhere to the regular day of the week logic. "Tell that to the tourists." They didn't care what day it was. They were just trying to forget their regular life for a while.

She let out a sound of frustration. "Fine, we'll do something boring if you want. Maybe you will meet Mr. Right at the Cineplex."

"Ha ha. You make it sound like I don't know how to have fun."

"I'm not sure you do anymore. But how about proving me wrong?"

"Maybe I will," I said. On second thought, maybe I wouldn't.

CHAPTER 5

ZANE

As a tough man, as most people said I was, it still pained me to see my little girl getting into the car to go on her first long trip without me. She was all ready to leave with her little suitcase packed and a big smile on her face.

"Don't forget my travel pillow, Pop-pop," she said as I put her in the booster seat behind my dad.

I knew she was in good hands. My father handed her the pillow, and she hugged it close with her stuffed unicorn.

"Now you're all set," I said, securing the seatbelt. "You be a good girl for Daddy and mind your grandparents."

"She'll be fine and so will we," said my mother. She had been handling classrooms full of children for over thirty years, so I decided to take her word for it.

"I'll miss you, Daddy. Are you sure you can't come with us?"

I felt my heart tug, but my mother shook her head as if to tell me not to change my plans. "I can't, sweetheart, but when you get back, we'll be together. And Daddy will be home a while with you."

"Good. I like my room and miss my toys."

I knew being between two houses hadn't been easy on her. And with all of the time I was gone after losing her mother, that had been rough too.

"Your daddy needs to go and see his friends while he has the chance." My mother gave me a look like she was worried I might change my mind and stow away. But after all that time in the man camp, I needed a lot more than just my friends' company. I needed the company of a woman. And I had a pretty good idea that I'd find one in Vegas.

After they drove away, I went back into the house I hadn't spent more than two hours inside over the past two months.

It had been so closed up, it needed a good airing out, and while I had popped in to get ready the night before, I had gone back to my parents' house to sleep in my old room.

When I got to the airport where Clay was supposed to be waiting, I glanced at the time and looked around the terminal. "Where the fuck is he?" I mumbled.

If he stood me up, I was going to be so pissed, but before I could really get angry, I spotted him coming in the main entrance with his overnight bag in tow. At least I hadn't been the only one to pack light.

"Hey, Insane Zane, waiting on me?" He had a big personality and was dressed just as nicely as if he was performing.

"Don't call me that," I said, giving him a hard look. "Unless you want me to remind you why I was given that name in the first place."

Clay laughed. "Oh, I remember, and I'm pretty sure that guy you went off on remembers it too every time he looks in the mirror."

"He shouldn't have put his hands on my woman." I didn't like people trying to take what was mine.

"Well, I guess you wouldn't care now, would you?"

"No, now he could have her. He can go bust her out of the pen for all I care." She'd be his problem then instead of mine.

"So is there anyone else you're talking to?"

"Nah. I haven't even flirted with a woman in months. No time for it with Mila, you know? What about you? I heard about you and Beth."

"Yeah, well, hasn't everyone?"

"Well, you know you can talk to me, right?"

"Yeah, I know."

"It's just, you're a father now, man. It might be time to calm down and stop fucking around. You can't do that forever. You have to think of your son." He and his wife had a little boy he had named Jack after his grandfather.

"Bethany hates me, so I'm pretty sure that's over. It's time to move on, and I'm hoping that Vegas at least helps me move on."

I hated to hear it, but I knew how he felt. The feeling of being unwanted was a total headfuck. "Well, I've been in the fucking oil field too long, so maybe we'll both get lucky."

Clay laughed and patted me on the back. "That's my boy," he said. "I've already been assured that Grady knows all of the hot spots for the hottest chicks."

"I bet he does." Grady Black had been the only one of us men who hadn't found love, had a kid, and ended up in a terrible relationship. The rest of us were on a losing streak, and all he could seem to do was win.

It made perfect sense that he had hit a million before the rest of us. There was nothing and no one holding him back.

And I wouldn't trade my life with his for anything because I had Mila.

"He's hosting a little welcoming party at his house, and then he's got us all suites at The Golden Shower. You know, in case we get lucky. I guess no one can fuck in that big house of his but him."

"The what?" I knew he was just fucking around. There was no way there was a real place with that name. "You mean the Golden *Tower*?"

"No, it's the Golden Flower actually. Don't ask me. I've never heard of it, but it's supposed to have the best accommodations, and I think Grady said he knows the owner. Nick's company built the place, so he said he'd been there before. We're in good hands. I hope that means we'll get a *happy ending*."

I sighed. It was going to be a long trip.

We boarded the plane, and as it took off, I prayed to make it back down to earth to my child. It wasn't that I was afraid of flying, but with so much going on in the world, it was better to be safe than sorry.

"I can't wait to see everyone. It's been a while since I saw Nick. His construction company must be doing well because he's as busy as you are. Rylen, he's been so busy caring for animals that I'm pretty sure he lives in the back room of the clinic now. That awkward fuck." Clay laughed, and I couldn't help but think of my old pals.

We had all gone to college together and shared a house off campus. Since none of us belonged to a fraternity, we called ourselves the Five.

"Hey, do you remember that time when Rylen got drunk and pissed in the neighbor's bushes. She found his BVDs there a week later. And he couldn't even deny it because they had his name written in them." He gave a belly laugh that was earning us strange looks.

I was the strong silent one of the bunch, and I didn't really like people gawking at me, especially when he didn't know how to act. He ate it up, though, and the more attention he got, the better.

"Why don't you take the window seat?" I said, hoping to contain him. Knowing Clay, he would stand up and start singing mid-flight. And then, I'd have to beat his ass.

"Thanks, man. Don't tell me you're still afraid of heights." He chuckled. "Remember that time when—"

"Yeah, I remember. Now that's enough. I don't think all of these fine people want to relive my college days." I glanced around and caught a few people smiling, including one woman I'd seen around Williston. No sense in showing off for the home crowd.

I managed to contain him for most of the flight, but he still managed to flirt with the flight attendant and get her number.

I wasn't sure how Beth was going to like him fucking around. Even if she had told him to beat feet, it was probably just a scare tactic or a test, and if so, he was failing miserably.

Halfway through the flight, he leaned over and whispered to me. "Do you think there's time for a quickie in the bathroom?"

"A quickie? You mean with the attendant?" I couldn't believe the guy. He had absolutely no self-control.

"Well, I certainly don't want to fuck you, big boy, but yeah, she's hot. Do you think she'd lose her job? I bet no one would even notice. I mean, look around. They're all about to nod off."

I glanced around. "If you make them land this plane, I swear to God I'm going to mop the tarmac with your guts."

"Why are you always so violent?" he asked. "I know your parents didn't raise you that way."

"Maybe it's from being your friend all of these years," I said, giving him a smirk. Although we liked to taunt each other, I would never really hit the guy, unless he hit a woman. Then I'd knock his teeth loose. And that was better than knocking them out. At six foot one, he was three inches shorter, but I packed on more muscle in the field than he had behind his piano or that pretty boy gym.

We joked with each other until the idea of banging the flight attendant was a distant memory, and he finally settled for her number and a smile every time she passed.

Before we got off the plane, he nudged me. "I hope she calls me up next time she's in town."

"That's just what you need," I said. "A woman who can get the fuck out of town in a hurry. Especially when Beth hears about her."

His face fell. I could tell he didn't want to think about his baby mama. "She made her choice. She can live with the consequences."

"Can you?"

The question was a little too deep. He turned to get his bag out of the overhead compartment and didn't respond.

When we walked out of the airport, there was a huge limo waiting. The driver was holding a sign that read, Black, Party of Five.

"I think that's us," I said. "I can't believe that fucking car."

"Let's hope it has a minibar. I could use a drink." He gave me a devilish grin and strutted to the car. I picked up the rear, and the driver stepped over and opened the door. "Your ladies await," he said. "Compliments of Mr. Black."

Before I could react, Clay turned to me and wagged his brows. "Now that's what I call service." He rubbed his hands together and climbed in the back.

When I stuck my head in, I nearly busted my gut laughing. There was a cardboard cut-out of Grady sitting in the seat, holding a drink with a stupid smile on his face. And by his side, two blow-up dolls both with gaping mouth holes.

"That motherfucker." I laughed.

Clay looked too disappointed to laugh. I was in for one hell of a trip.

CHAPTER 6

TARA

As I stood at the kitchen sink waiting for hot water to come out of the tap, I thought of how many times I'd reported it to the landlord and how many times he had promised to come and take a look at the water heater. My apartment had been economy size in the eighties, and its last update was just as long ago. Everything was in working order, barely functional, but it was all I could afford.

I kept it clean and had scrubbed the yellowed walls white when I moved in and even had given them a fresh coat of paint.

I turned off the faucet, giving up, and went to get the kettle to boil some water so I could wash the few dishes I'd dirtied. It wasn't like my dishwasher was going to work. Nope, it had been my designated drying rack, but that was the only way it functioned.

I had just stepped away from the stove when I heard a knock at the door. "Open up," called Karen. "It's party time, sexy. We're going out tonight."

I couldn't believe her. She had already earned me a couple of noise complaints, and now she was probably going to get me thrown out.

"Hey," I said, opening the door with a hard look. "Thin walls, okay? Thin walls."

"Right," she said. "Sorry. So are you ready?"

"I've already told you, no. I'm not ready." I had called her an hour before, telling her that I wasn't feeling like getting fixed up to go out and that I was going to have to pass.

"You're not getting out of it this time. I can't let you keep doing this. You need some attention, girl, and I'm going to see that you get it."

"I don't need attention."

"You're starved for it, and you just don't know it. Come on. When are you going to stop fooling yourself? It has to be lonely."

I looked to the floor. "I have no hot water, okay? I've been trying for an hour to get water to wash dishes. And I don't feel like taking a cold shower just to go out."

"So take a hot bath." She walked over and stroked my hair. "Look. You need to get out of this apartment now and then. It's depressing. It's already bringing me down. And I'm in the same boat, so I know what I'm talking about."

She didn't have it any better. Her apartment unit was the next one over, and while it was owned and managed by a different man, he wasn't that much better about keeping things up as my own landlord. But at least her place was newer and nicer.

"My clothes are still in the dryer, and I don't have anything to wear."

"We can find you something."

She looked over to the kettle. "Draw a hot bath, and I'll find you something. I know you bought that cute little top I showed you the last time we went out. You should wear that."

"It doesn't fit right." I hated wearing anything that showed off my breasts. She had talked it up in the fitting room and talked me into it, but once I got it home, I decided it was a bit more revealing than I was comfortable with.

"What do you mean? You loved it in the store."

"I do love it, and it's just not me."

"It's so you. Not everyone has your curves to pull it off."

"You should wear it then." It would look better on her anyway. Most things did.

"Again, not everyone, including me, can pull it off. You have the body of a goddess. You'd give men whiplash if you ever found the confidence that went with that figure of yours."

"I have confidence." I was strong, just more conservative. "And to prove it, I'm going to wear the stupid blouse."

Karen smiled big. "That's my girl. And we're going to have the time of our lives."

After a cold shower, I dressed in a pair of my favorite dressy jeans and put the blouse on with some heels that Karen insisted I wear and the right amount of jewelry.

By the time I got to the club, I was feeling good and actually loved the outfit.

The music pulsed with the lights, and the crowd moved to the beat. Karen and I made our way through to a table.

"We should get a drink," I said. I had brought enough money for a couple, but that was going to be my limit.

"Wait," she said. "Put your money away." She glanced over her shoulder and smiled. "See those men over there?"

"No way. I'm not having them buy me a drink."

"You don't have to." She smiled when the man flagged the waitress, and after their exchange, he smiled and waved.

"He's actually good looking," she said. "But I don't know. He looks like he's full of himself, doesn't he?"

I glanced over to the man, who winked.

Karen giggled. "Looks like you're the lucky one."

About that time, the waitress came back from the bar and placed a drink on the table in front of me.

"Oh, I didn't order this," I said.

"It's from the gentleman," she said as she put one down for Karen as well.

"I wonder if he thinks he'll get a threesome," she said, making my cheeks burn.

"No way. I'm not accepting this."

"Go for it. He'll come over and talk and then we can thank him and move on."

"Shouldn't I at least dance with him or something?"

"Not unless you want to," she said with a smile. "Do you want to?"

Before I could respond, a couple of men walked over to the table and sat down in the extra chairs. "Ladies, how are we doing tonight?"

"Just fine until you came along," I said. Who did they think they were? They just barged right up and sat down. I didn't like anyone who was that pushy.

"Oh, wow," said the one guy. "Someone's got PMS. What about you, darling?" The man turned his attention to Karen. "Are you in a better mood?"

"No, I'm afraid I'm not. You see, we're besties, and so our menses have coordinated."

The man who was sitting across the way at the other table got up and walked away, and Karen cursed.

"Great," she said. "Now you've totally fucked up my game. You can go now. Run along, shoo."

The men exchanged a look and shook their heads. "Your loss, bitches."

"Charming men," I said.

"Yeah, you're one to talk. You don't have to come out swinging, you know? I could have gotten us free drinks all night with those two clowns."

"Look, Karen. I'm not going to sit here and be treated like a piece of meat for attention and alcohol. I just want to have a good time with a nice man."

"Well, the good catch ran away with the bait."

"I'm not baiting anyone." I saw her eyes glance down at my chest. My eyes followed, making my cheeks even redder. "I wore this because you said I looked good in it, not to dangle a carrot."

"Call them what you want, but I'm pretty sure that you're going to get another bite soon."

No sooner than she said it, another man walked over to the table. "Hello, ladies," he said. "There must be a meteor shower in here tonight because I see two stars from heaven."

"Did you just make that up?" I asked, giving him a sideward look.

"Off the cuff. Did you like it?" He laughed and searched my eyes as the smell of his cheap cologne penetrated my nose.

"I'm pretty sure you could do better if you rehearse." It was hard to keep a smile when the man's eyes were stuck on my chest. He hadn't even seen the look I was giving him.

"Why don't you let me take you somewhere for private lessons?" He licked his lips and leaned in on the table. "I've got a nice car. It's roomy."

"Roomy? Is it your grandmother's? Because you look like the kind of man that lives with your grandmother."

He glanced at Karen, who was trying very hard not to laugh and failing miserably, and he walked away without another word.

"And another one bites the dust," she said. "I have to say. This is kind of fun."

"Maybe I'll teach you a thing or two," I said, taking a sip of my drink. Karen had nearly finished hers, but then, she'd had a lot of time to drink with most of the attention on me.

It must have been some strange cosmic phenomenon because usually, she was the one draped in attention.

"No, I doubt that. But it's humorous."

"I'm glad you're having a good time. And don't even try to say that you could have gotten anything out of Mr. Stars from Heaven. He only had one thing in mind."

"Oh, no. You were right about him. He's a total douche. He's here all the time, and the lines only get worse. I just wondered how you'd handle him."

"Oh, thanks. So you know the crowd?"

"Some, not all. But that's the beauty of our great city. Always a new face in the crowd wanting attention."

Finally, some attention came her way, and by the time her first drink was gone, she had another one waiting in the wings. She raised the glass to the gentleman across the room, whom the waitress indicated, and a moment later, he walked over to the table.

He was a good-looking man, with dark hair, deep-set eyes, and an expensive suit, but there was some underlying creep factor to him that made my skin crawl.

"Hello, beautiful," he said in a thick French accent. "I couldn't help but notice you from across the room. What is an angel like you doing in Sin City tonight?"

Karen smiled. "Just having a drink. How about you?"

"Admiring the view. It's almost as nice as the one from my hotel room." He cocked a brow. "Maybe you and your friend would like to come up for a drink? I have a hot tub."

Karen glanced at me, and I was already shaking my head. I wasn't going up to any rooms with any of the men there.

She gave him an apologetic look. "I'm sorry," she said. "I'm waiting for my boyfriend. He's the bartender." She turned her head and gave the bartender a little wave. He waved back, giving her a cocky grin. She obviously knew him.

The Frenchman looked at me as if Karen never existed. "We could go alone if you'd like?"

"No thanks." I kept my voice stern and took another sip of my drink as I looked away. Hopefully, when I looked back, he'd be gone.

As he walked away, I looked over at the bar. "Do you know him?"

"Yeah, he used to work at the Golden Flower's bar. I always sit here close to the bar, and he keeps an eye on me."

I breathed a sigh of relief. "Well, at least I don't have to worry so much."

"Hey, I'm not crazy. And I use my intuition. If anyone seems out of line, I don't entertain. You can tell the harmless from the scum. Or at least in my experience. The point is to talk to men."

"I don't think these are my type of men."

Karen giggled. "What do you want? A biker bar? Or how about a saloon?"

"A man who is smart and attractive, as well as a hard worker. Someone who knows how to treat a lady."

"You're husband hunting. Have you ever thought about just having a good time? You can have sex with someone and it not mean anything. It can just be a one-night, one-time thing."

My mother had had her fair share of those, all while we were traveling across the US. It wasn't a good time in my life. The type of men she brought around—the lazy ones who had everyone taking care of them while they laid up on their ass—weren't anything I wanted to return to.

"I don't want to be my mother."

"Again, your final choice can be better, but you aren't going to meet Mr. Right unless you go through a few Mr. Wrongs."

Maybe she had a point. But I still didn't see one man around me who I was even remotely attracted to.

After a few hours of sitting and dancing with Karen, which only got us even more unwanted attention, I knew it was time I bowed out. It was getting late anyway, and I had a headache from the cheap cologne and alcohol. "Hey, I should go. I need to rest up for tomorrow morning."

"Aww, really? It's just starting to pop here. Are you sure?"

"Yeah, I'm beat."

She gave me a disappointed look and downed the rest of her drink. "Fine. But I think I'm going to stay. Do you mind?"

"Just be safe and call me when you get home. I'll see you tomorrow." I hugged her and left, hoping it didn't take too long to get home.

I needed another cold shower to get the funk off of me.

CHAPTER 7

ZANE

We had gotten to Grady's house as the sun was setting, and we spent all evening having dinner in his mansion, which was a lot more grown-up than I expected, even though it had a huge game room and a theater that would fulfill any kid's dream.

His billiards room was the place we hung out the most, and as we started a round of eight-ball, he explained that he had designed it to have a speakeasy feel.

It was good to reminisce about our college days, but as it got later and the tournament ended up between Grady and Nick, I couldn't help but wonder how my little girl was. I checked the time.

"I didn't know you were taking medicine," said Clay, who was propped up on a bar stool nursing his umpteenth drink.

"I'm not. I'm just thinking about Mila. I hope she's okay in a strange place. Mom and Dad were taking her to Animal Kingdom. I don't think she's ever stayed away from home in a hotel before."

"Well, I'm sure she's fine and getting spoiled, man. Your parents are good with kids. But Daddy needs to get laid, and so do I, so I wish we'd get this party moving." He raised his voice across the room so the others could hear. He had been anxious to meet a woman the whole evening.

"Relax," said Grady, taking another shot. "It's Las Vegas. The party is just getting started."

"Yeah, well, I'm about to deflate one of those blow-up dolls if you don't get me to the clubs, and I'm not talking about pulling its plug." He turned to the barstool beside him where we had put the dolls from the limo ride. He turned one around and bent it over the barstool, working his hips at it like he was fucking it in the ass.

He had already told everyone that getting laid was his goal because of how terrible Beth had treated him, and he hadn't slowed down with the drinking since we had gotten on the plane.

"Hey, man, don't you think you should take it easy?" Rylen asked. He was always socially awkward and the most reserved out of the bunch, and when someone was getting out of line, he was worse than me about telling them to calm down.

I didn't let things bother me, but Rylen, who was the Five's intellectual, was the most conservative of us all.

So naturally, Clay, who was his exact polar opposite, wasn't going to let that go. "Aww, did you want me to stop? Go ahead, buddy." He worked his hips, acting out a slow grind on the blow-up doll. "I'm sure her friend won't mind. Seriously, Poindexter, take a stab because it's all the pussy you're going to get tonight."

"Don't call me that, you twat. Just because some of us don't want to see you act like an idiot."

"And idiot? I'm sorry, man. We're not all as smart as you are. Oh, wait. Turns out, someone is." He gestured to the room around us. "Where's your million-dollar mansion, smart ass?"

Rylen turned a bit red, as did Grady. "Whoa, we can't all be superior gamers like me," he said as he gave Rylen a pat on the back. "Who could have guessed skipping class to play video games all day would come in handy? Come on, brother. I know the best clubs, and you're going to love it."

Everyone knew that Ry's record of being the smartest was still ongoing, and Grady did his best to make sure everyone felt welcome. He had shown them his home being as humble as he could, and that only made Clay look even more like an ass.

"That's enough of that," said Nick. "We came to have a good time, and I, for one, am ready to go. I don't want to sit here looking at you ugly bastards all night."

"I agree," I said.

"Yeah," said Clay, turning his attention to me. "Big papa misses his little bear cub. We need to take him out to meet some cougars." He gave a sound like a big cat's screech as he raised his hand like a claw in my face.

I grabbed his wrist and squeezed it tight.

"Still got those cat-like reflexes, I see," he said, wincing from the pressure.

"You better worry about the little cub you have back home," I said. "You're going to be cut off the minute you order your first drink at the rate you're going."

"I can hold my liquor, my good man. I'm used to the club scene, remember? It's my livelihood."

"Come on," said Grady. "Before we have to kill Clay, let's take him out and see how long it takes him to pass out."

"Fine, I'll settle down," he said. "Excuse me for being the life of the party." He got a pouty look, and I could tell that he wasn't himself. Something more was going on inside Clay's mind, something he was trying to either drown in alcohol or flush out. Either way, he was going to end up hurting himself if he didn't sort it out.

"Come on, man." I let go of his wrist and put my arm around his neck. "Get your date, and let's go."

He grabbed the blow-up doll and dropkicked her across the room. Everyone laughed as she landed face-up on the lounger.

"Look, Clay," said Nick. "She's ready for more."

After another limo ride down the Strip, this time seeing it in all of its spectacular glory at night, we made it to the club where Grady had us set up with a private section that had private accommodations and its own dance floor.

I had never been to anything like it and couldn't believe the women who were all scantily dressed and giving us attention.

Although there were some knockouts, I just wasn't feeling the vibe.

Then a hot little redhead in a black dress sauntered up. "Excuse me, but could you help me with this?" Her dress, which had a strap that tied at the back of her neck, had come undone. She turned and lifted her hair, peeking back over her shoulder at me as she licked her lips.

I obliged, but to be honest, she was such a little thing, no bigger than a twig compared to my mighty oak, that I was afraid I might break her.

"There you go," I said, giving her a smile. "You're all set." It was the exact same thing I'd said to my daughter after tying her shoe, and I regarded the young woman no differently.

Only she didn't take the hint. "Thank you," she said as she turned around and stumbled into my lap. "Oh, sorry. Wow, you're strong." She put her hands around my bicep and looked up into my eyes.

She was pretty but wore far too much makeup for me and seemed a little too young as well. "Yeah," I said, not really knowing what to say.

"My throat is so dry," she said. "Do you think you could buy me a drink?"

"Um, sure," I said. "Have you met my friend, Clay?"

Clay had already run off several girls with his come-on-strong attitude, so I only thought it fair that he met his match.

"I like you," she said. "Not that your friend isn't hot too. I mean, I guess what I'm trying to say is I don't mind both of your company as long as you are there."

Clay moved closer and put his arm around the girl, untying her dress that I'd just tied. "I'm open to anything," he said.

She caught the front of her dress, where she didn't have much to hold it up. "Hey!" She turned to me. "Your friend is an asshole," she said as she ran to the next victim.

"What the fuck is wrong with you?" I asked.

"You wanted her gone. Why? I have no idea, but I thought I'd speed things along. You're welcome."

"Yeah, well, you're not wrong there, but why didn't you want to fuck her? She's cute. That skinny-butt type you like."

"Hey, Beth wasn't a skinny butt." He turned and gave me a sideward look. "Don't tell her I said that. But she's got a nice ass. Plump and gorgeous, ripe as an apple." He sighed. "I used to love taking a bite out of it. You should see it now. Even better. And her tits? Motherhood looks damned good on her."

"Why aren't you with her instead of here, drunk off your ass and trying to put your dick in anything that will accept it?"

"She wants me to settle down, and I'm just not there for some reason. Every time I think about settling down, I just get scared." He played with the olives in his drink, poking them with his toothpick. "I just don't want to get old, I guess. Turn into my father."

"You don't have to. Look at my dad and me. We're a good team, but we don't act and think just alike. And your kid needs a father, a man who is settled down."

"I guess I just feel like I'm running out of time, you know?"

"I get it. But time's up. He's born now. He's here. And he needs you."

"I just need something more for myself. I'll figure it out by the time he's old enough to know better."

"Well, for the record, I think you're an idiot. You could have something really nice, but you're fucking it up. I didn't have a choice when it came to Heather, and fuck, I tried harder than you are."

Clay sighed and took another drink. "Yeah, fuck me. I'm such a piece of shit." As a pretty blonde walked by, his attention turned to her. "Mmm, speaking of fucking me, I'm going to go see if she will."

I didn't have time to say a word, and he was already on the move. I stayed at the table and polished off a few more drinks. I spoke with a few more ladies, not one who was worth leaving with, though I did have a nice conversation with a rodeo queen for nearly three hours. She was in town for her sponsor, and while she was sexy, she just wasn't my type either.

But I did invite her up to one of Grady's friend's suites in a hotel across town. I eventually ended up on the balcony alone after putting the rodeo girl in a cab hours earlier. It was easy to feel that my first night in Vegas wasn't at all what I thought it would be. Maybe I just wasn't cut out for this type of life. All I really needed was my daughter and a job to keep her fed.

It was the wee hours of the morning when I decided to be a good guy and made sure the others—especially Clay, who had almost left with the blonde—got in the cab when the party ended.

After a long drive back to the hotel, I turned to see Nick, who looked like he had his own agenda. "You coming?" I asked him.

"Nah. I'm starving. And I don't feel like calling something up. Do you want to come with?"

"Okay, sure." I was hungry too and hated for Nick to have to hang alone.

I turned to my old pal. "Where to?"

"The hotel has the best breakfast buffet in the city. Biggest fluffiest waffles I've ever had in my life. I mean, hands down the best."

"Sounds good to me." I walked with him, hoping the whole trip wouldn't be like last night. Waffles were one of my favorites, but I didn't think they were going to work miracles.

CHAPTER 8

TARA

I was glad I had gotten home early and had rested up for the hectic morning at the Golden Flower Hotel's buffet. "I need another pan of waffles," I said, telling Ben who was standing around watching the floor.

"Where's Karen?"

"I have no idea." I wasn't about to get into it with him about my friend. He had hired her first, and why he was keeping her on if he hated her lack of work ethics was beyond me. I just knew the days were a lot longer without her around. "She's probably stuck in traffic."

Ben gave me a hard look. "Don't you ever get tired of covering for her?"

"She's my best friend. And besides, you're the one who keeps giving her second chances, so don't blame me." I gave him a hard look. "Are you going to get those waffles? Please?" He technically didn't have to do anything but manage, but with the hoard of kids who had shown up with their parents, we were busier than expected.

Ben didn't say anything but went back to the kitchen.

"I told you not to do that," said one of the mothers to her child, who was touching everything within reach. "I'm not buying all of the biscuits because you want to touch them all."

I reached over and moved the ones the child had handled.

"You shouldn't have made him come down here," said the father. "I asked you to come and get our food and bring it back up. How hard is it to do that?"

"How hard is it for you to sit down here with your family for a nice breakfast for a change? All you've done is run off to play slots."

The man gave his wife a narrow stare. "I'd rather pull a crank than spend all day with one."

"That's real nice," she said. "I don't know why you even brought us at all."

"Me either."

I cleared my throat, and a voice from behind me said, "Excuse me, could you at least please take your argument to your table? You're holding up the line."

I spun around to see Karen tying on her apron. Her hair was perfect, and she looked good, but it was probably from the extra sleep she'd gotten.

The woman, who looked like she could mop the floor with Karen, put her hand on her hip. "We're waiting on more waffles. Apparently, you don't know how to run a buffet."

"Hot waffles coming through," said Ben as we stepped out of the way.

"Here's your waffles." Karen waved her hand over the tray. "Help yourself."

The woman looked at Ben. "Are you the manager here?"

"Yes, ma'am. What can I do for you?"

"This girl is rude. She needs to learn some manners and how to treat a customer." The woman got her child's waffles, and she and her family stormed away, cursing the entire time.

"Poor kid," I said, hating that the boy had to put up with his parents who probably only noticed he was there when he did something like touch food he wasn't supposed to touch.

As I mumbled to myself, I turned to see Ben had pulled Karen aside. "What's your problem?" I heard him ask.

"I don't have one. But clearly, the woman does, and frankly, I don't know how she can be married to him."

"If you think you're funny, you're not."

"Damn. I was hoping to quit and become a comic. I guess I should just keep my day job." She glanced over at me, and I shook my head, trying to discourage her.

"Keep it up, and you won't have it either."

"Come on, Benny Vinnie." She used her flirty voice, but he wasn't buying into it today.

"Don't you Benny Vinnie me. You're taking advantage. And not only of me but of Tara, who had to wait on your tables. I'd think you'd treat your friends better, but you're not a good one."

I could see the light go out of Karen's eyes at that point. That was when I felt like I had to step in.

"Actually, Ben, she's letting me take on some of her tables so I can make a few more tips. I kind of need it for rent."

"Well, that's still not an excuse for her showing up late, and if it happens again, I'm going to have to let you go. And before you go telling me I can't make it without your charm and personality, let me remind you that this is Las Vegas, honey. There's a girl like you on every corner." He stormed away, and I turned to go back to the buffet to make sure it was in order before I stepped away to check the tables.

Karen came up to me. "Thanks for speaking up. He's right. I've been a shitty friend. But hey, if you really need to keep a few of my tables today, go ahead."

"Thanks, and don't beat yourself up. Ben is just in a mood. It's been crazy around here." I looked across the room, which was thinning out a bit. "You missed the mad rush of kids."

"Yeah, there's a beauty pageant in town."

"Oh yeah, I forgot about that." I tried to imagine the little boy in a pageant and decided that wasn't the case for his family. "Some of these parents… the way they talk to their kids…" I shook my head. "It's a wonder they ever stopped fighting long enough to reproduce."

"Make-up sex is a bitch. That's what got my sister, and now's she's expecting her third." All of a sudden, she glanced up. "Oh, baby. Look at those two."

I turned to see two men who were being seated in my area. "You're not kidding." I turned and flashed her a smile. "Lucky me."

Both of the men were handsome, but the taller of the two, who had to be at least six-three, was absolutely gorgeous. His hair was cut short, and he had a little stubble that gave him a rugged look.

"Didn't you say you wanted to trade some tables?" Karen asked.

"No way," I said, not taking my eyes off of him.

"Oh no, I think you're in love."

My cheeks reddened. "Shut up." I had to go over and wait on them, and I didn't want the man to think I was weird.

As they talked across the table to each other, I made my way over with a nervous smile, hoping the guy wouldn't be a jerk.

"Hello, and welcome to the Golden Flower. My name is Tara. We are currently serving our breakfast buffet if you're interested, or you can order from the menu. Can I get you started with something to drink?"

"We'll have the buffet," said the other man. He was good looking too, but his friend was tattooed and downright sexy. "I'll have orange juice and a cup of coffee."

"I'll have coffee." The tattooed man looked up at me with the most amazing olivine eyes. They were sparkling like peridot, and his dark hair and thick lashes made them even more vibrant somehow.

"Okay." I nodded, my tongue suddenly feeling heavy in my mouth as he mesmerized me. "Is that all?"

"For now," he said. His eyes lingered down my body. I felt my face burn and my pulse quickened.

He smiled. *Sweet agony. He's hot.*

"Do you know if there's a newsstand around?" asked his friend. "I'd like a newspaper."

"I think there's still one in the hotel lobby," I told him. "But there's free wi-fi, so most people just use their phones."

"He's a bit old-fashioned when it comes to technology," said the hot one.

"Nothing wrong with being a little old fashioned." It had always been appealing in some ways, especially when it came to having relationships.

"See?" said his friend as he got up from the table. "That's what I say, and yet, I never hear the end of it. I'm going to grab that paper. I'll be right back."

"So what about you?" asked the hot one. "Are you old fashioned too?"

"In ways, I suppose. But newspapers? I'll stick to my cell phone." I laughed and realized that something about him made it easy to talk to him. I was still a nervous wreck, wondering what he thought of me, noticing the way his eyes lingered on my body, all the while unable to tell if he liked what he saw.

Of course, he doesn't. Don't overreact and don't get your hopes up. You don't even know his name.

"I'm Zane Ballard," said the man. "Tara's a pretty name. Old fashioned as well but in a good way."

"Unlike Zane. I like it, though." I smiled, feeling my cheeks grow warm again. "Well, I should get your coffee. Your friend will be returning soon."

As I walked away, I glanced back over my shoulder to see him staring at me.

I went to the kitchen, and Karen came around the corner after me. "Oh man, he was so looking at you."

"What?" I knew he had been, but I was scared to death that he was laughing at me on the inside. Fuck him if he was, but I wanted him to like me.

"Come on. You can't tell me you didn't notice. He was practically undressing you with his eyes. He's definitely into you."

"I barely know him, Karen." I fixed their coffees and put them on the tray.

"Well, what the hell are you doing hiding in here?" she asked. "Get back out there."

"I'm not hiding. I need to pour some juice." My hand was shaking so badly that I made a mess and had to wipe the side of the glass.

Karen felt bad for me and helped me out, only to rush me along. "Get his friend's name and their room number and see if they want to hang out later."

I shook my head as I walked out the door. I wasn't about to let her try and take advantage of the men. Neither looked like the type she usually worked, and both seemed to be pretty reserved.

I carried their drinks and found his friend had already returned. He had the newspaper open and was squinting to read it.

"Thank you," he said.

"Thanks," said Zane, who was now angling in his seat to face me.

"Thank you. And enjoy it."

I stepped away as he rose from his seat. "Tara?"

"Yes?" I stopped and looked up at him, towering a good head taller than me. *He's perfect.* And I felt perfect next to him—as if I was made to fit.

"What do you recommend?" he asked.

"The waffles are a favorite here."

"Are they *your* favorite?"

"I like them, but honestly, I like biscuits and gravy. I guess I prefer my morning foods a little savory."

"Biscuits and gravy? I had that when I worked in Texas." He acted like he had never seen them other than that.

"Yeah, my mother and I used to stop at different diners while on the road and compare who had the best. There was this one place down in Nacogdoches that won, and ours are pretty close."

"Hmm. Well, I might have to give them a try."

I smiled, and when I turned to go check a few of my other tables, I noticed him still looking at me.

I tried not to read too much into it, even when I noticed it again as he was eating. Each time I went to the table, he struck up a conversation, even if it was just to tell me how good the food was.

Unfortunately, I had to tend to another family table, and by the time I finished getting their four kids' orders straight and listening to their parents bicker and make things worse, Zane Ballard and his friend had left.

I walked over to the table, and when I went to remove the plate, I found a hundred-dollar bill stuffed under the plate. "Holy shit," I mumbled. I tucked it into my pocket and smiled to myself, still not letting myself read too much into it.

If he liked me so much, why didn't he ask for my number?

Because he was only being nice or showing off to his friend?

Either way, I could pay the rent.

CHAPTER 9

ZANE

As Nick and I left the Golden Flower Buffet for a quick run at some slot machines, I couldn't help but wonder if I should have gotten the waitress's number.

"Why did you leave that waitress such a big tip?" asked Nick as he stuffed a dollar in the machine.

"None of your business," I said, giving him the side-eye and a smile. I didn't need him ragging on me about it.

"She must have made an impression while I was gone."

"Her name is Tara, and she made her impression just walking up to me." The woman was a knockout, and she was probably the prettiest woman I'd seen since arriving. But she was probably married or seeing someone. I should have found out.

"Really?" Now he was giving me a sideward look. "She was pretty."

"She was a babe. Are you kidding me?"

"Yeah. Hey, it's cool. I mean, I was just shocked you threw that kind of money for tips. Business must be good."

"It's oil. It's always good."

Nick laughed. "You got me there."

"I bet you can say the same for construction, the way you were tossing the money around last night buying drinks for everyone. How are you doing?"

"Okay. I'm just keeping busy. Probably the same way you are. Did the whole Heather thing ever work out?" I knew that before the trip was over, everyone would ask about that situation. I had kept it private, even from them, but now that we were face to face, it was expected I face it.

"She's still in prison, so it's working for me. She's where I don't have to fucking worry and look over my shoulder every five minutes, wondering if she's going to try and come take Mila."

"I can't imagine what you're going through. How's Mila doing with all of it?"

"She's perfect. She is growing like a little weed. She's going to be as tall as me if she doesn't stop growing. But I tell you, I don't know if I want to do this alone forever."

"Did you get the waitress's number? Maybe she likes kids." He gave a chuckle as he put in another dollar.

"No, but I should have."

"They serve dinner too, my friend. You can always check back."

"She probably wouldn't want a man with so much baggage. I've not only got a kid, but with Heather's bullshit, no one wants to get involved with that. It's just not fair to ask."

"So? What then? Do you just stay a bachelor for the next twenty years until she's grown up?"

"If that's what it takes. It's just going to take a pretty special person to be all in with me. And what are the chances of that?"

"You're talking like a man who needs to get laid."

"God, it's been so long, I'm about to propose to my right hand."

Nick laughed. "There were women all over you last night. You talked to that rodeo queen so long I thought you were looking to hogtie someone. I bet she would have let you."

"She was nice, but she'd have hogtied me. She just wasn't my type. And I guess I'm a loser, but Mila makes me want to be a better man. I can't just sleep around like a man whore." It just didn't feel right.

Nick chuckled as he lost again. "You're overthinking it. You're just getting laid, and you don't have to introduce them to your daughter. Hell, you don't even have to tell them about her. Especially if it's just while you're here in town."

"I guess you're right," I said, sitting on a stool next to his machine and putting in a dollar. "I just miss my little girl, and it's tough to scout women for sex while I'm wondering if she's okay." I pulled the lever and watched as I lost my money.

"I get it," he said, trying again to win. "You're a good father. Just make sure you take care of your needs. It's okay."

As he finally hit a small payout, I eased back in the seat, wondering if my parents and daughter had made it to the Animal Kingdom park and if they were having fun.

I pulled the lever again and, this time, hit a winner. "One hundred dollars," I said. "I guess it's my lucky day." I had just won back the money I'd given Tara.

"You son of a bitch. I only won ten."

We both laughed and played some more, moving on to blackjack until I lost half of my earlier win. "I'm beat. I'm going upstairs."

When I got up to my room, the others were still sleeping, and I was just getting settled into my bed after a long hot shower when my phone rang.

It was a call from my mother's phone, and I expected it to be Mila. But my mother's voice greeted me. "Hey, honey. Sorry to bother you on your trip."

"Is something wrong?" I asked, sitting up in bed with my pulse racing.

"No, honey. She's fine. But I wasn't sure if sending you a video chat this time of the morning was a good idea. You know, since you're in Sin City."

"I'm alone, so yes, video call me. I need to see her and hear her voice." I couldn't believe that even my mother thought I'd be in bed with someone. I hung up the call, and a few seconds later, the video chat request came through. I answered and smiled big as Mila waved to me.

"Hi, Daddy!" Mila sounded as happy as ever.

"Hey, Noodle. I miss you. How do you like your trip?"

"It's fun. And I miss you too. I get to go to the park today. They have rides." She had wanted to go to an amusement park with rides since she saw one on TV.

"That's awesome. Be safe and have fun, okay? Are you behaving?" I could see my mother in the back, nodding.

"She's been good," said my father from somewhere off-camera. "But she has a question for you."

Mila gave me her puppy eyes, and I laughed, knowing it was going to be hard to tell her no. "Is it okay if I have cotton candy, a candy apple, *and* a funnel cake?"

My eyes widened. "Wow, that's a bit much, don't you think?" I tried to imagine her eating all of that sugar. She would be wound up, and I was pretty sure by the way my mother was looking at me, she wanted me to say no. "Can't you just pick two?"

"That's what Nana said, but Pop-pop said to ask anyway."

"How about this? You and Pop-pop can share. That will make me and Nana happy. But I don't want you bouncing off the walls. You behave yourself."

"I don't know how to bounce off the walls, Daddy. I'm not even sure that's real." I was certain I'd used the phrase with her before.

"It's real. Believe me. It means I want you to behave, and don't get wild and hyper from all of those sweets."

"I won't. I promise."

"Okay. I miss you."

"You already said that. You must miss me a lot."

"I do. Do you miss me a whole lot?"

She nodded. "Yes, will you ever have to go away again?"

"It's how I make a living for us, Noodle. You know I will. But I promise I'm giving you my full attention when I get home, and we're going to have lots of fun things planned." I had to start making a list of things other than cleaning out our closets. She still had clothes that she'd outgrown a year ago.

"I can't wait."

Finally and all too soon, Mom spoke up. "Honey, we need to get going if we're going to make the park by opening. I want to get a good spot in line."

"Okay. Have fun. I love you."

"I love you, Daddy," said Mila.

After a collective goodbye from my parents, I ended the call. I looked around the room, realizing I was too far away from her and promised myself just a few more days.

As I lay back in bed and closed my eyes, I thought about the waitress and wondered what time she would get off work and if I'd get to see her again.

After that, I must have drifted off because the next thing I knew, Clay was pounding on my door.

"Rise and shine, you tattooed bastard. We're going down to the pool."

"Fuck you," I said, peeking out the door. "It's too early for the pool. I'm going back to bed."

"You've slept through lunch as it is. It's nearly two."

"Two? Shit." I didn't want to sleep all day either. "Fine, I'll get ready and meet you down there." I slammed the door in his face before he could say anything else.

It might not be too early for the pool, but it was still too early in the day to deal with Clay.

CHAPTER 10

TARA

After our shift was over, I was in the ladies' room putting up my hair when Karen came in.

"God, I swear Benny is really pissed off at me this time," she said. "And I'm sorry, Tara. I don't really try and make it hard for you."

"I know, and don't worry about Ben. He'll get over it. I really did like the extra tables, so thanks for that. I did really well today."

"That's good. Are you going to the pool?"

"Yes, it's the only time I get to relax, and besides, I'm almost finished with that novel I started reading the other day."

"Reading a book like that would take me months, and you're done in a matter of days."

"I could finish it in one night if I didn't have bills to pay, but thank goodness we get pool access."

"Want some company? I could use a cocktail."

"I'll buy it. I did really well today."

"Sounds good to me. I've got my suit in my bag." She went into one of the stalls to change, and by the time she came out, I was ready for the sun and water.

We went out to our usual spot by the fountains, and I pulled our chairs back from the edge of the pool. Once we were settled, I noticed the couple with the boy, still arguing. "There's your friend."

"Yeah, she's yelling at him for staring at us," said Karen. "He's been gawking ever since we came out, and I'm pretty sure he nearly broke his neck when you bent over to move the lounger."

"Ew. In front of his family? What a scum. Now I really feel sorry for his kid." I took out my wallet and flagged the waiter over to order us drinks.

"What about his wife? Poor woman."

"She's as bad as he is. They have no business raising kids if they can't behave in front of them." I had watched my mother and her boyfriend arguing enough to know it wasn't pleasant for the boy.

Karen rolled her eyes. "You're acting as if it should be a law who gets to be a parent and who doesn't. If that were the case, we probably wouldn't have been born, and what a waste that would be."

"I just wish they'd stop exposing him to their nonsense." He was probably already scarred for life. The damage had been done.

"Another solid opinion formed from having parental problems."

She should know. She'd had the same problems. And it was part of our bond. Not that my mother had always been horrible, but once she got to Vegas and met her boyfriend, I ceased to exist.

Once we got our drinks, Karen eased back in her chair to get some sun, and I began reading my book, hoping to finish.

Just as I was enthralled, about to figure out who the murderer was, a voice came from behind me. "Don't you know that paperbacks are old fashioned? I've heard that you can read them on your phone now."

I looked up and saw Zane standing next to me. My heart nearly leaped out of my chest. "Zane," I said. "Hi." I didn't know what else to say. I hadn't expected to see him again.

"I hoped I'd get to see you around. Do you live near the hotel?"

"Yeah, not far from here. Using the pool is one of the perks of working for this fine establishment."

"Well, that's a pretty good perk if you ask me."

Karen cleared her throat, begging to be introduced.

"Oh, this is my friend, Karen. Karen, this is Zane Ballard." I thought I'd keep it simple.

"You remembered my full name," he said. "I'm impressed and flattered." He turned his attention to Karen. "It's good to meet you."

"And you as well. Are those your friends?" She waved across the water to where the man from breakfast and two more hotties sat by the pool.

"Yeah, those are my buddies. They're about to order drinks. Could I get you two something?"

"That would be so nice," said Karen. I cut her a warning look, hoping she wasn't going to try and use them like she did everyone else.

"What about you, Tara? Another cocktail?"

Karen gave me an urging look.

"Yeah, sure. I'm running a bit low."

He ordered our drinks with the waiter as I put my book away. I hoped to talk to him more, and that was the only reason I let him get me a drink.

"Thank you," I said. "And thank you for the huge tip." I hoped this wasn't the time he came to collect whatever he thought he was paying for.

"Don't mention it. I like to do that from time to time, is all. And I won it back like an hour later playing slots, so I guess it really does pay to be kind."

I liked that philosophy. It was just hard for me to be on the receiving end of a gift like that. "So, what brings you to the Golden Flower?" I asked.

"My friend bought a house out here, and we all haven't seen each other in a while, so we came out. We're all staying here for a few more days and just taking a break from life."

"Oh, I see. That sounds like fun."

"Vegas is a lot of fun," he said. "But I don't have to tell you that. You live here."

"Yeah, lucky me. I actually meant the break from life part. I can't tell you how long it's been since I took a vacation. Honestly, I'd rather live someplace greener."

"Greener? As in you don't want it to leave a huge carbon footprint?" His eyes widened, and he suddenly looked like the cat who ate the canary.

"No, not green like that. I mean literally green. Like a place with more trees and not as much desert."

"Ah, I live in Williston, North Dakota and work the oil fields. So for a minute there, I thought we might end up in a disagreement."

I laughed. "No, it's fine. My grandfather used to work in a refinery."

"I see. And I know what you mean about missing green. Our landscape is similar in many ways, but we still have a lot of that old-town charm too. It's a boomtown, though, so it's changing daily. But then, the economy is great there. I still hate to see it growing too fast."

As he spoke about the place, there was a sparkle in his eye. He might not like being there all of the time, but that place he spoke of was home to him.

"Hey, it can't be any worse than all of the palm trees and neon we have here," I said.

"It's beautiful here at night," he said, and I got a warm feeling, as if he was looking into my eyes. He licked his lips. "Do you mind if I sit down?"

I glanced up to see Karen talking to one of his friends.

"She's not coming back anytime soon if she's talking to Clay. He's not quick to let go of an audience, unless, of course, she tells him to piss off."

She'd never do that. Not as long as they were paying her attention and behaving. "You're right. She's not coming back. Have a seat." I couldn't believe that the gorgeous man wanted to sit with me. "Maybe I won't get a pain in my neck from looking up."

"Six-four," he said with a nod as if he got questioned about his height all the time. "I was always the tallest of my friends."

"Do people always ask if you played sports? Basketball?" That was the biggest complaint from every tall person I'd met—that and doorways.

"Are *you* asking me that?" he said with a chuckle.

"Well, I guess so." I didn't really care what kind of sports he played. I just enjoyed the conversation. He was really nice and seemed like he had a good head on his shoulders.

"I did play some sports, and yes, basketball was one of them. Mostly in high school. I prefer leisure sports, though. Fishing mostly."

"Yeah? I'd love to try it sometime. I used to watch my grandfather out at the pond growing up. But my mother wouldn't let me go out there with him. She said it was his alone time." I felt my face go red as I noticed him looking at me like he was in deep thought. He probably wished that I'd shut up. "Sorry, I didn't mean to ramble on."

"No, it's cool. It's good to have a conversation with you. I have been stuck on the job for so long with nothing but a bunch of men, and it's refreshing to talk to a woman."

Now it made more sense. He had been stuck with a bunch of men and was probably just talking to me because any woman would do. I was just the first one who held a conversation. It was all out of politeness and boredom.

"No women? None?"

"No, we call it the man camp. And it's not glamourous at all. I'm the foreman, and we had an accident, the second one in a month, and so they made me take off for legal reasons. But I needed the time anyway."

"That sounds terrible. I'm sorry that happened. I hope the man is okay." It had to be a man. There weren't any women. "But I bet it is nice to take a break."

"Yeah. He'll live but most likely be a limb short." He went quiet for a moment.

In the silence, I could feel the conversation had been about to shift.

"So, what do you like to do besides read?" he asked, glancing down to the book which I'd left sticking out of my bag. "Surely, you know how to have fun in a city like this. It's your city."

"It's not my city. Never has been." I had never wanted to claim the place and always knew that I'd leave as soon as I got the chance. It had never been home to me. Home was a place I'd left a long time ago, a place that no longer existed, but I'd always hoped to find it again somewhere.

"Do you want to come out later?" he asked. The invitation came out of nowhere.

"I'm not sure." I shook my head. "I have to work tomorrow." I couldn't just go out with him. Not after that big tip and then him telling me he'd been locked up in a man camp. He surely only wanted one thing from me. And I wasn't sure I could give it away, not even to him. "I'm sorry."

He looked disappointed but not devastated. "Oh, okay." He nodded as if he understood. "I just thought we'd have a good time." He shrugged his broad shoulders and looked across the pool to his friends.

"Oh, I'm sure we could. It's just not a good time for me."

"Maybe I'll see you again at the buffet," he said with a smile.

"Maybe. I work a lot." I wasn't opposed if he wanted to say hello again, but the problem was, my heart was already yearning for more.

The conversation, which had gone well up until the invite, lulled. I sat there nervously looking across the pool at Karen, who had abandoned the group of his friends to talk to some of our coworkers.

"Well, I guess I'll see you around," he said, bailing now that I'd turned down his invitation. "It was good talking to you, Tara."

My heart sank. "You too, Zane." I so wished his invitation wasn't steeped with suspicion, but I wasn't going to be used by a tourist. There were thousands of others in the city he could pay to do that kind of thing for him. He obviously had no problem throwing his money around.

I watched as he walked away, going to the door where he waved his friends over. My face burned with jealousy, just thinking that he would move on to another as if I were nothing.

Karen stormed over to me. "Well, what happened?" She gave me a worried look.

"He asked me to go out tonight. I told him no. It turns out he's just looking to score."

"And you're not?" She gave me the most disappointed look.

"No. He's from North Dakota, and he's not staying here long. Why bother getting mixed up with him?" Even though he was perfect, it wasn't like I could win him over, make him stay, make him love me.

"Why bother? I'll give you a number of reasons. For one, he's hot, like manly rugged and perfect for you hot. And two, he's the guy I imagine when you describe your ideal man. Three, I'm pretty sure he's packing a whopper. Did you see the size of his hands?"

"And yet, he's not for me. He just wants to have sex." I glanced up to see he had gone.

"You should have at least had sex with him. Can you imagine? I'd climb him like a tree."

"Hey," I said, nudging her. Someone else would, though. And that thought was making me regret turning him down.

"What? It's true. But hey, if you're not interested and he's only interested in sex, maybe I will go and talk to him. You won't mind, would you?"

"You wouldn't." He was not her type at all, and she wouldn't hurt me that way.

"No, I wouldn't, but the look on your face is telling me you like him more than you're letting on and you should have accepted. You like him. Go for it. What's the worst thing that could happen? Better to sleep with him now than for him to leave town without you ever knowing."

The only problem was, I had already turned him down, and he had already left. "Maybe you're right, but it's too late now, so let's drop it."

I felt my stomach twisting in knots and wished I could turn back time and get a redo.

CHAPTER 11

ZANE

By the time I went back to the pool, Tara was gone, and I was glad that I had gone up to my room instead of sitting there across the pool watching the woman who had turned me down sit there looking like a goddess in the sun.

Clay and Nick were standing on the side of the pool arguing, and Rylen's nose was buried in a book. "Have they been going at it like that for long?"

"Yeah, like twenty minutes. They've already run about six people off." He never looked away from his book, and his tone didn't change much.

"Are you having fun?"

"Not particularly," he said. "I'm ready to gamble."

"Did I hear someone say they're ready to gamble?" Grady asked behind me. I turned to see him dressed to the nines in a suit. "Get your asses upstairs and get dressed."

"It's still early," said Clay. "I'll run out of money by the time it gets dark."

"It's on me," he said.

That piqued everyone's interest. "Well then, fuck it," said Clay. "I'm ready when you are."

"I thought you'd say that."

"You don't have to do this," said Nick.

But Grady held out his hand. "Hey, it's cool. I've got the money, and I want to do it. Besides, we made a deal."

"Yeah, we did, didn't we?" said Clay. "And I want my blowjob."

"It was a blowout in Vegas, not a blowjob in Vegas," said Rylen.

"Dammit, Zane. You got my hopes up."

I hadn't really thought he'd believe me. I shrugged. "It's been a long time ago."

"I'll buy you one if you want, but I get to pick the girl." Grady smiled, and Clay looked a bit scared.

"Fuck it. Okay. I'll have my eyes closed anyway. And I'll be dreaming about Zane's mom."

Everyone laughed, and I grabbed him around the neck and knuckled his head.

"Fuck you," said Grady. "I'm not getting Beth pissed off at me."

"I can't believe you're all against me."

"No more mom jokes," I said, turning him loose. "That shit wasn't funny in college."

"Says you, only because we voted for your mom to win the MILF award."

I gave him a hard look, and Rylen spoke up. "I don't know, Clay. Your mom's latest Facebook profile photo really did it for me."

"That's not funny, Ry," he said, getting pissed off.

"You saw it, didn't you, Nick?"

"Yeah, I got off on it, too," Nick said.

They were never going to stop now. I, for one, was sick of the mom jokes, even if it did serve Clay right.

"Are we gambling, or are you all going to sit around acting like a bunch of high school freshman?" Clay asked.

"Yeah," said Grady. "Get up to your rooms and meet me in the bar."

"I'm coming with," I said. I was glad I'd given up on the pool time and had gone up to change. It would give Grady and me some time to hang out alone.

After twenty minutes of Grady ordering wings and a couple of pitchers of beer, we had a minute to talk.

"Can you believe that bunch?" asked Grady. "They're going to be a handful tonight. And Nick? He's only egging it on."

"He's clashing with Clay over something. They had it out at the pool. I didn't catch what was going on."

"And so why are you so bummed out? You've been sitting here looking like your world is ending."

Had I been bummed? I gave him a sideward look. "What do you mean?"

"You look like you'd rather be anywhere else. Are you upset about me paying?"

I couldn't believe he thought that. "Hell no. It's your money. I'd tell you, but it's dumb."

"That's the kind of shit you're supposed to tell me."

"Fine. I'm upset about a girl." I felt like a kid. What the fuck was wrong with me? I had been pouting ever since she had turned me down.

"Your little one?"

"No, there is a waitress here. She works at the buffet. Her name is Tara. I asked her out, and she turned me down. I thought we'd have a good time after a nice chat, and the last thing I expected was for her to say no."

"It happens to the best of us, man. I wouldn't let it bother you." He gave me a look like he couldn't believe how hard I was taking it.

"Wouldn't let what bother him?" asked Clay as he joined us. He was cleaned up and freshly showered.

"He's upset about a girl."

"That waitress you were talking to? Nick said that you gave her a hundred-dollar tip. Were you trying to tap that? She might not want to feel like you're paying her to fuck you."

I hadn't even thought of it like that. "Shit. And I told her I'd been in the man camp. I guess that didn't help."

Clay laughed. "Man camp. She probably thinks you're a felon."

"I explained it to her. But she probably thinks it's just a come on. Shit." I hadn't meant for that to happen. I hoped I was wrong.

Clay nudged me. "She's just a waitress, isn't she? Fuck it. There are going to be a lot of hot titties—I mean women—out tonight."

I looked at Grady, who shook his head. "What is with you, Clay?" he asked. "Why are you acting like a horny teenager? It's not like you."

"He's having an early mid-life crisis," I said.

Nick joined us, only catching the tail end.

Clay spoke up. "You all sound like that bastard."

"Fuck you," said Nick. "You know I'm right."

Whatever the two had been bitching about, it had clearly come between them. "Fuck off." Clay gave him the finger.

"Okay, so the next one to bitch like a chick is not getting their allowance."

Clay straightened up and was suddenly like a different person. I didn't know what was up with him, but I had a good idea he was struggling with something. A battle with what he knew to be right, his family, and what he was scared of losing: his youth.

After we started the night off with beer and wings, we left the bar for the casino, and Grady wasn't lying. He handed us each stacks of bills so big you could choke a horse.

"Have fun with it, fellas," he said. "I'm going to hit the blackjack table. If any of you want to see how it's done, follow me."

I had to see him in action, and I was eager to get my mind on something besides my bruised ego.

It was an hour into watching him win when I decided to give it a try. I placed my bet just like I had seen him do, and I tried to follow the rules he had told me. He had more experience, and since it was his money, I was going to trust him.

"That's a pretty confident bet," he said when I laid down five hundred dollars.

"Go big or go home. Besides, it's your money, and I'm following your advice. If I lose, it's on you."

But I didn't lose. I won. "See there, ye of little faith?"

"You think I'm much more confident than I am apparently," joked Grady. "I'm just having really good dumb luck."

By the end of the night, we had managed to squander away over twenty grand, and while I had done my fair share of gambling by the end of the night, I still came out ahead.

"Here's your money back," I said to Grady, handing him the original amount of five-thousand dollars.

"No, man. You keep it. Consider it a party favor."

"I'm good. I profited nicely on it." I urged him to take it.

"Not going to happen, brother. Give it to Mila. Put it in her piggy bank for college. Or better yet, let her buy a car when she's sixteen. I'm not taking it back."

"Fine. I'll tell her that Uncle Grady says hello." I stuffed the money back in my pocket. "And thanks for this. You really did give us a blowout."

"Yeah, and don't worry. The night's not over. We're hitting the strip club. It's my favorite place, and I actually own a small corner of it, so you're going to be treated like royalty."

"You own part of a strip club? How come you didn't tell us?"

"Because it's only on paper. I gave the owner a loan."

It kind of scared me that he was so frivolous with his money and was already letting people borrow from him. Not to mention giving it away for us to gamble.

"Do you have someone looking out for you? You know, in the financial department?"

"Yeah, don't worry. My father is looking after it. And you wouldn't believe the shit I have to go through just to get my hands on it. But don't tell the other guys. I don't want them to know."

"Well, it makes me feel better anyway."

"Yeah, yeah. Well, it's okay really. I swear I could wipe my ass with hundies for the rest of my life and never run out."

"You must have really made a good deal."

"Oh yeah. And I don't have anything holding me down. No wife to spend it, no kids to feed. I'm just on my own and living the good life."

"Doesn't that get old? Don't you want someone to be there for you at the end of the day?" He had to get lonely. Hell, everyone did.

"Not really," he said. "If I want company, it's just a phone call away."

That kind of life was soon going to get old. And I hoped he was okay when it did.

I thought of Tara again and realized I wasn't going to let her get away from me so easily. I had to make at least one more attempt and show her that I was a good guy who just wanted to get to know her better. Hopefully, Clay had been wrong, and she didn't think I was trying to buy her affection.

CHAPTER 12

TARA

I had just about finished my shift after a long day of Karen not showing up to work. Ben had said that she had called in sick, and if I didn't already know she was skipping work to catch up on sleep, I might have been worried enough to call her.

As it was, I was busy cleaning up the morning buffet by myself, taking away the empty pans of breakfast food, and making room to phase in the lunch specials. There was a lot of food left, which meant I'd have more frozen waffles and some biscuits to take home as leftovers. I had a freezer full of them already, but it helped when I didn't have enough money to buy groceries.

"You have another table," said Ben while I was in the kitchen, stacking the empties to make way for the dishwasher.

"My shift ended twenty minutes ago," I said, knowing I needed the money. "But okay." It wasn't like I could turn the money down, and he knew it.

He gave me a sympathetic look. "Well, if your buddy wasn't sick, she'd be here to deal with it. I had her scheduled alone for the hour since this is our usual slow time, but I've got Carmen coming in early to make up for it. I'm sure you don't mind staying for the extra tips."

"Sure," I said, knowing that the chances of the tips being worth the extra time weren't likely but knowing every penny counted. "I'll be right there."

I finished what I was doing and washed my hands. Then I hurried out to the floor and past the buffet where the tables began. At the last table, I found Zane, who was sitting alone.

I looked around for his friends, but they were not around.

"Hey," I said, surprised and happy to see him. "You are all by your lonesome today?"

He was dressed in jeans and a nice button down with the sleeves pushed up to show his muscular, tattooed forearms that looked like they'd seen a lot of hard work to get so strong. Not to mention a lot of hours under the needle.

Instant turn on.

"Yeah, I thought I'd come down and say hi. I figured you were working."

"Actually, I'm just finishing up until someone else clocks in. You would have missed me if my friend hadn't called in sick. I'd already be gone."

"Well, I'd say lucky me, but that wouldn't be too nice because of your friend. I hate that she's sick." He gave me a sympathetic look, but he seemed happy that it worked to his advantage.

"Well, she's not really sick," I said in a low voice. "She was out late last night."

He gave me a quizzical look. "Oh? Did you go with her?"

"No, going out to party hard as she does really isn't my thing. She called me early this morning to warn me she wasn't coming in and that she was sorry for leaving me hanging."

"Well, I guess I have her to thank anyway. I really wanted to see you."

He could be really convincing if I let him. "Can I get you something?" Surely, he was there to eat. It couldn't be all about me. He was just polite.

"Um, I really hadn't thought about it. But sure. How about some coffee? And I'm not sure what else you have."

"How about a slice of pie?" It was just a suggestion and the best thing we had on the menu at that hour.

He shook his head. "Just the coffee, thanks."

I hurried away, and when I came back, I poured the cup, feeling his eyes on me. "There you go."

He gestured to the chair to his left. "Would you like to join me? Since technically you're not even supposed to be working right now?"

I looked around. There wasn't another person in the place but us. "Sure, why not? Even though I know you didn't *really* come to see me."

"I did, though," he said with a laugh. "Why is that so hard to believe?"

He sipped his black coffee and pushed it aside.

"I guess I just thought you were here for an early lunch." I'd already turned him down, and surely, that was my one chance, which I'd blown.

"I just said I wanted to see you. I meant that." He looked at the coffee and made a face. "I really didn't want this." He crinkled his nose.

"Well, why did you order it?" I hoped he wasn't looking for another reason to tip me. Things were awkward enough.

He shrugged those broad shoulders, and I couldn't take my eyes off of his perfect build. "I have no idea. I guess the truth is, I was really disappointed you turned me down. I missed you last night."

This was too good to be true. Men like him were never interested in me. "Missed me? You don't even know me." I began to blush and looked away, hoping he couldn't see.

"I want to know you better. Is that so hard to believe? That's why I asked you out." He took a deep breath. "And that's why I came back to ask you again."

There was silence between us as he waited for my response.

"Look, if the tip was some kind of pick-up tactic, it's not going to work on me. I mean, I think you're nice and attractive, but I don't party, and I'm not the kind of girl you can buy." Zane should have gone with Karen. She would love all of the attention and spend his money for him.

He winced. "Shit," he said. "I didn't mean it that way. I didn't even think of how that might come across until my friend pointed it out. I honestly wasn't trying to buy you. I just felt like tipping you. No strings. And if you turn me down again, fine, but at least I go home knowing I tried."

"Sorry for jumping to conclusions, but I guess I just don't have men ask me out often, and especially after a huge tip."

He gave me a sideward look with his glassy green eyes. "Come on. Now you're pulling my leg."

"What?"

"Men don't ask you out? I find it hard to believe." He took another sip of his coffee as if to have something to do. "I figured it was the reason you turned me down, unless I'm just not *your* type."

"No, you're my type," I blurted before pulling my lips into a tight line. "It's just I don't date. I suppose it's my fault. I don't really put myself out there, you know? I guess it's because I don't really feel like I fit in here. The things people do, the gambling, and the clubs? It's not really my scene."

"I get that. It's not really me either. So, what is your scene? It's a big city, and I'm sure we'll find something to do. If you'll go out with me tonight."

I smiled big. I couldn't believe he was asking me out again. And this time, I wasn't going to say no. "We could see a show?" That was something I didn't mind doing, and there would be other people around for the majority of the time. It would be a nice, safe first date for a practical girl like me.

Zane grinned from ear to ear as if my accepting his invitation was the best thing in the world. "Your pick. Any show you want to go see."

"Cirque du Soleil?" I had wanted to go and see that one again since my birthday two years before.

"I've always wanted to see that," he said. "I'd love to take you there. You don't see that kind of thing in North Dakota." He chuckled, and even that was sexy.

I could feel my body responding to him the longer we sat and chatted. Why had I been so stupid and turned him down? What the hell was wrong with me?

"North Dakota sounds good," I said, trying to focus on the conversation. "Anywhere but Nevada."

He met my eyes as if he was trying to figure me out. "One day, you'll tell me why you don't like it here."

I had never had anyone who was that interested without hoping it would lead us to the bedroom. "I'll tell you now if you really want to know." Or at least, I'd give him the abridged version.

He eased back in his chair. "Sure, tell me."

I took a deep breath and let it out. "When I was younger, my mother and I went on a road trip across the States. We left Missouri, hit old Route 66 off and on when we could, and stopped everywhere in between. It was amazing. I had so much fun all that time, and I thought it was just for us, you know? Like a dream vacation. But then, I found out that she was leaving our home behind, and when we got to Las Vegas, this place she made sound so surreal—The Neon City— it was just her boyfriend in a crappy motel. And we never went back home."

"That would be hard."

"Yeah. I mean, I did eventually get to see the neon city she'd promised, but it was tainted by having another man in our life." I never got over it. I was still a bitter mess.

"Was he a bad man?" he asked with a look as if he could fight a bear.

"Yeah, but he seemed nice enough when he wanted to, but after coming here, it was like my mom was different, and things changed."

"Wow, that really sucks. I'm sorry I brought it up." He was cute when he was apologetic. As if all he cared about was my happiness.

"No, it's okay. If I didn't want to share, I wouldn't have."

"Well, I appreciate that." He smiled. "So, why don't you leave?"

I shook my head. "Money. I can't afford to start over somewhere else. And I guess it's because this is all I know. If I left, I'd be all alone."

He took another sip of his coffee and made a face. "I really didn't want this." He gestured to the cup.

I laughed. "Stop drinking it."

"It's horrible," he said with a chuckle in his voice.

"You don't like my coffee?" I pretended to be insulted.

He gave me an apologetic look. "If you made this, I'm sorry, but you can't make coffee."

I giggled. "I didn't. I think Ben did."

"Well, I think Ben washed his socks in it."

"Oh." I covered my mouth. "That's terrible."

"It is." He made a face.

"I'll get you something else on the house. I can do that. I have special privileges for being a valued employee."

"I know I'd never fire you." He looked me up and down, and I smiled, realizing that he might just like me after all.

Slow down, girl.

"I'm good actually. So, what time should I pick you up?"

I got a sinking feeling in the pit of my stomach. He couldn't go to my apartment. I didn't want him to see where I lived. It was more than embarrassing, and just in case he ended up being a really clever con artist, I didn't want him to know where I lived. "Could we just meet here? At the hotel?"

"Sure, if that makes you feel better. But what time is their show?" He seemed like a real easy-going guy.

"Usually they have one at seven-thirty. Unless you need to do something with your friends, I'd totally understand that, since you are here to see them." I wondered if he'd bring his friends along and hoped we'd have more time together.

"No, they'll be fine without me for one night. And honestly, I need a break from them. I've been missing the company of a beautiful woman lately, and I'm really glad I met one to go out with tonight."

"Well, if you'd rather be with her, I understand." I was only teasing, but he made a face.

"Why do you joke like that? Don't put yourself down. You're an amazing woman, and you should have the confidence to show it."

"Thank you." I searched his eyes and could tell that he was sincere. Or a damned good actor. "I just try not to take myself too seriously, is all. I mean, I have confidence, although I'm not exactly the standard for beauty."

"Whose standards?" he asked, making a face. "And no, I don't want you to answer that." He seemed a bit irritated. "I'm sorry. I just wish more women would see how amazing they are. Too many are too hard on themselves."

I felt as if I'd hit a nerve, and I didn't want the talk to take a bad turn. "Well, I'm a rock star," I said. "And you're not so bad yourself." I gave him a wink, and he smiled back at me.

Ben coming out of the back caught his eye, and he glanced over my shoulder.

"Hey, Tara," Ben called. "I need you to help me carry out the fish." The tone of his voice told me he wasn't asking. Breaktime was over.

"Duty calls," I said. "But I'll see you tonight?"

"Yeah, I'll meet you down here at seven?"

"Perfect," I said. "But could we make it in the lobby in front of the elevators? I don't want Ben to see me. He'll try and put me to work."

He laughed. "Well, if he did, he'd have to go through me because I'm having my date with you even if we're standing in that kitchen."

"Oh, I like how sure you are," I said, giving him the side-eye as I stood.

"Mhm. You'll show." He gave me a playful look.

"Will I?" I said in a teasing voice.

He nodded. "Yeah, you will. You like me." His smile brightened, and I couldn't help but reciprocate.

As I walked away, all I could think was, *Yes, I do*. But I wasn't going to give him the satisfaction of saying so.

CHAPTER 13

ZANE

I left that buffet feeling like a winner, even more than I had walking out of the casino the night before with a few hundred extra dollars in my pocket. I really liked Tara and couldn't wait to see her again.

But my friends had other opinions.

After stopping off at the room for a call home to Mila and catching up on some sleep, which happened mostly by accident, I met up with the others at Grady's house. We were supposed to have dinner there, and even though it was early in the evening, they were already drinking and just back from a daily run to the casinos.

"I can't believe you ditched us for that waitress," said Clay, who had just lost three-hundred dollars on the roulette wheel. He had told the others about it when I arrived.

"And he's ditching us tonight too," said Rylen, who was still riding the high of winning fifty bucks during that same trip.

I walked over and stood by the pool table where they were playing, both smelling of booze. "You assholes don't need me, but I need her."

It had been far too long without the company of a woman. It was pathetic. I'd stumbled around the conversation at the buffet like I'd lost my touch, but there was just something about her that put me a little off my game. I hoped to rectify that later.

"You mean you need that pussy," said Clay. "I don't blame you, man. I can't get enough of it too." He took a shot and missed it.

"No, I don't even mean sex. I can't tell you how long it's been since I *talked* to a woman." Not that sex hadn't been on my mind. Hell, I couldn't look at Tara without getting an erection. At least I knew it still worked.

Ry laughed as he lined up his shot. "If all you're doing is talking, then you're doing it wrong, my friend."

The others joined in laughing with him, and before I knew it, they were making fun of me. Good thing I could take it. I found a stool at the bar and listened as they did their best ribbing.

Nick walked over and put his arm around me. "I bet you forgot how to use your tools, Zane. Just remember the train goes in the tunnel."

Grady laughed. "Nah, in his case, it's the pencil goes into the sharpener."

"Nothing's small about me," I said, defending my manhood. That was one department I figured I had them all beat.

"Come on, guys. Be nice." At first, I thought Rylen was really going to stick up for me for all of the times I'd defended him. "Put it in terms he can understand. The thread goes through the needle."

Laughter echoed off the walls of the big room.

"You're all really funny," I said. "And while I'm doing that, you all can stand around and circle jerk."

"Fuck that," said Clay. "I'm buying my action."

"Not if you keep gambling," said Nick. "You've already blown through what Grady gave you."

Clay made a face. "Try double that," he said.

"You've lost ten grand?" I glanced up at Grady. How could they have let that happen? "Fuck, Clay. You have a kid back home."

"It's okay," said Grady. "I fronted it."

It was still no excuse. I looked at Clay. "Man, I hate to be you when your mid-life crisis is over. You keep at it, and you're really going to hate yourself."

Grady spoke up. "Come on. Let's just have fun. That's why I called you all here."

"Tell that to Zane. He's finding his own fun. Abandoning us." Ry nudged Clay to take his turn.

My oldest friend looked up at me. "Good riddance," he said. "I'll make another bet in your honor tonight, my friend. A big one." He pointed his pool cue at me as if he was making a threat.

"Not with my money, you won't," said Grady. "I'm cutting you off again."

Clay took his shot and missed, then laid down his cue. "Who's next?"

"Lunch is ready," said Grady. "Everyone to the dining room. I've got something special for you." He had a sly smile on his face, and I couldn't help but wonder what he'd done.

As we walked into his formal dining room, which looked more like a greenhouse with all of the plants and windows, I glanced at the table and realized there were two women, each spread out on the table, wearing nothing but vegetables and flowers.

"Shit, is this what we've come to? Cannibalism?"

"I'm a breast man, myself," said Clay, rushing over to take a seat, only to find there were place cards.

We all took our seats, and while I was appreciative of her beauty, I couldn't help but think she was someone's daughter.

"For your viewing pleasure, my friends. Tonight, we feast like kings." Grady clapped his hands, and three more women came into the room, each carrying big trays of food, placing them on the table around the nude models.

I had never seen anything like it in my life. I would have thought I was in paradise, but when I closed my eyes and opened them, the guys were all still there. And my heaven would have surely had Tara in it. She would have been in my lap, and I would have been feeding her from my hand.

It was all well and good, but while the guys laughed and talked, entertaining the women, all I could do was watch the clock. I couldn't wait to get out of there.

Before things got too weird and just after Nick realized one of the girls was his second cousin, it was time for me to leave. I bailed out, eager to get to her.

I arrived a bit early at the Golden Flower, so I went up to my room to freshen up my cologne. The last thing I wanted was for her to smell the other girls' perfume on me. It turned out they were belly dancers, and they had gotten a bit closer than expected.

I hurried back down, and when the elevator doors opened, I found her standing in the lobby, her hair pulled back from her beautiful face and tucked and arranged just so. Her dress showed more leg and cleavage than I expected, but I wasn't complaining. I'd just have to poke out eyeballs if I caught anyone staring.

"You look amazing," I whispered behind her, and she turned around quickly, startled and barely staying on her feet. Thankfully, I caught her.

"You scared me!" she said, taking a deep breath.

"Sorry," I said.

"No, I'm sorry. I was just looking for you in the waiting area."

"I went up to my room. I didn't mean to scare you." Her chest heaved as her heart raced, and I could barely peel my eyes away.

"I hope this isn't too much," she said. "I haven't gone out in a while."

"It's perfect."

She smiled, and the flush on her cheeks made my body respond.

Easy. We have to get through the night.

I held out my arm, and she took it.

"Are you ready?" I asked. "We should probably go." I had Grady arrange for tickets, and thankfully, he was able to get them. Apparently, the evening shows were almost always sold out.

We stepped inside the theater of the Bellagio.

"You know, I didn't really think you'd be able to pull this off," she confessed. "It's kind of a busy attraction."

"Yeah, well, I have friends in high places." I realized she must have hoped I'd fail. "And so, if I hadn't got the tickets, then what?"

"We'd just hang out, people watch, or maybe take a drive somewhere."

"Oh, so you didn't really want to come here?" I was curious about what was on her mind.

"Yeah, I did. I just didn't think you'd be able to do it. But I'm glad you did. I've wanted to see the new show for a while now."

We went inside, and I kept my hands on her as we weaved through the crowd. We had VIP seats reserved, and while they were closer to the stage, they were also semi-private.

When the show began, her eyes lit up as big as her smile, and she reached for my hand when the feats became exciting. "How do they do that?" she asked as one of the ladies on the ropes seemed to tumble from the silk ropes. She turned her face into me as if the woman would hit the floor.

I didn't mind the closeness, and I put my arm around her as her hand landed on my lap.

About half an hour later, with the show reaching its climax, another series of stunts left us in awe.

"They are braver than me," I said, glancing up at one of the performers who was perched atop a plank ready to jump off of it. "I don't even like sitting on the monkey board at work."

"What's a monkey board?" she asked with a laugh.

"It's where a derrickman stands on an oil derrick. It's really high. I've never liked it."

"You've done it?" She looked at me as if she couldn't believe it, her gorgeous eyes wide with wonder.

"I tried. But I'm too big and bulky. It wasn't for me, so I worked hard to be a foreman."

Another dangerous feat had her tucking her face at my shoulder. And when she looked up at me, I couldn't help but kiss her.

Our lips moved together with a fervor that said she wanted it as much as I did, and I felt my cock stiffen and my pulse race as her hand moved on my thigh.

"Do you want to get out of here?" she asked in a breathy voice.

"Yeah." I kissed her again and took her hand as I stood. We sneaked out, trying hard not to block anyone's view as we ditched the rest of the show.

I couldn't believe she had wanted to leave and miss the big finish. But maybe she wanted a big finish of her own.

When we got outside, I hailed a cab. "Where to?"

"Don't you have a room at the hotel?"

"Yeah, are you sure?" I didn't want to pressure her into anything.

"Yeah, I'm sure." She searched my eyes and kissed me again as the cab stopped.

I opened the door for her and could barely keep my hands to myself in the backseat on the way back to the room.

When we got to the hotel, we hurried to the elevator, hoping she wouldn't be seen, and thankfully, we were the only ones in it. I put her against the wall and kissed her mouth, her neck, and lower, all while her hands were roaming my body.

As I ground my hips against her, she reached down and cupped my balls through my pants, and I nearly fucking lost it.

Easy boy.

She had needs too, and from the hunger she was displaying, I needed hours to attend to each one. I couldn't wait for the elevator to reach my floor. What the fuck was taking so long?

CHAPTER 14

TARA

I had never noticed the elevators at the hotel were that damned slow until I found myself anxious to get to Zane's room. My body was on fire for him, burning so fiercely only he could tame me.

Not only was I surprised at my own behavior but surprised that I didn't care or have a conscience about what it would lead to. I wanted him, and having him was the only thing I could think about.

As the elevator stopped, we came up for air, our lips parting only long enough to hurry to his room.

I was thankful his friend had the foresight to book them their own private suites, as I didn't want to make excuses for my apartment or scare him away. I really wanted him to like me, and even though I felt it made me a little pathetic, it had been way too long to overanalyze it.

"Your friend must have money," I said when we stopped outside his room. I knew enough about the hotel, and this was one of the nicer suites.

"More money than he knows what to do with apparently. Not that I'm complaining. It's been a fun ride so far and getting better by the minute." He opened the door, and as we walked in, he tossed the key card on the table and turned to me. "Do you want a drink?"

I shook my head and walked over to put my arms arm around his neck. "I just want more of you," I said, my voice cracking. I was actually going to do it. I was going to live a little, throw caution to the wind, and have fun, as Karen had always told me.

"Well, I can handle that," he said in a husky voice. "Ask and you shall receive." He pulled me to him, my back arching as he kissed me down my body, and just when I thought I might hit the floor, he scooped me up into his arms, his muscles flexing as he carried me to the bed where he laid me down and moved over me. As he braced himself with one arm, the other roamed my body as he kissed me.

Zane moved his hand between my legs as if every gesture was carefully practiced and studied for maximum efficiency, and before I knew it, I had abandoned all control and let him take the lead.

"Does that feel good?" he whispered in my ear as his fingers rubbed my mound.

I nodded. "Yes," I said breathlessly, eagerly moving my hips.

"Just wait until I get you undressed." He chuckled and moved down, planting kisses in all the places my skin had become exposed.

He helped me with my dress as I sat up, pulling it up over my head. He took a minute to stand and put it across a chair that was close to the bed. Then he reached for his belt and undid his pants.

He looked super sexy, and I couldn't wait to see him without them. When he dropped them, undies and all, I got a glimpse as he unbuttoned his shirt, which he peeled back from his shoulders in a sexy way that showed off his build.

I tried not to notice the tattoo on his left pectoral, but it was hard not to. The name Mila was stamped there in bold letters as if she were someone very important. I tried to put it out of my head, not wanting to know but hoping he wasn't married. That would be just my luck.

Zane was more than I'd ever dreamed of—that was for sure—and I was still telling myself not to wake up. If it was a dream, I was content to live there a while.

Once I caught a good look at the rest of him, my jaw dropped. His erection was well proportioned to the rest of his muscled body, and I grew a little nervous, wondering if I could take all of it.

"I'll take that as a compliment," he said as he stared down at me.

"Now it's my turn to watch." He licked his lips and gripped his cock, giving it a tug. "Fuck, I don't have a condom. Do you?"

I hoped it wasn't a deal-breaker for him. I knew I hadn't been sleeping around, but a guy like him?

"I'm clean," he said. "I got tested after my last relationship." I wondered if her name was Mila. "But if you want to stop—"

"No." I wasn't going to let that stop me. Nor was I going to let a little ink bother me. His past was his past, and whatever stupid mistake he'd made to end up with that tattoo was his business.

I sat up, reaching between my breasts for the clasp. My breasts bounced as I set them free, and he wasted no time taking me in his arms as he kissed them, circling his tongue as he kneaded them with his free hand.

"Lay back," he said. "Get comfortable." He smiled at me, and I had a feeling that I was going to be very uncomfortable in the days to come—if I'd be able to walk at all—but I couldn't wait to feel him inside me.

My core burned with an aching desire and need for his flesh.

He rose up, hooked his arms under my knees, and pulled me closer, moving me around in a way that made me feel dainty and wanted.

I lay there looking up at him, and he seemed to like what he was seeing, what he was feeling, tasting. He slipped his fingers into the elastic of my panties and pulled them down over my curves until they were around my knees.

"You're so sexy," he said, pulling them free. Unlike the dress, he tossed them to the floor, and he parted my knees and pulled me to the edge of the bed so he could stand between them.

I had never been with a man like him, or any man at all, at least in that capacity. There had been the awkward heavy petting and blow jobs in college but only to experiment and only ever with boys who didn't matter.

None were anything like Zane. Boys compared to his manhood. His size alone was what fantasies were made of. I braced myself for penetration, closing my eyes, but the next thing I felt as I lay there with my legs wide was his mouth, his tongue, warm and wet as he lapped at my sex.

I cried out at the surprise as he slipped a finger inside, and he quickly stopped. "Are you okay?"

"Yes, it's just amazing." I felt so stupid. Nothing had happened. My voice was small, and the anticipation of what he could give me was almost more than I could handle.

"Relax. Let me take care of you." He seemed as if it was his honor or something, and I wasn't used to anyone giving me this kind of attention. Sex had never been about me before. Or what little I'd had of it.

His fingers entered me again, and I relaxed as he instructed and let the pleasure take over.

It didn't seem fair that he was giving me so much attention, and I felt I needed to reciprocate. When he raised up, I pulled him down to kiss me and whispered in his ear. "Can I?" I licked my lips, and he smiled and took my hand to help me sit up.

"Please," he said.

I gripped his cock, looking him in the eyes as I moved forward to take him into my mouth. This was something I'd practiced, something I could show him that proved I knew what I was doing. I didn't want him to know I was not experienced.

His reaction, a little moan that escaped his lips, only made me eager to please him more, and minutes later, he was warning me, pulling me back. "Easy there," he said with a laugh. "You're going to make me finish before we start." He cupped my face. "You're really good at that."

He leaned down and kissed my mouth. Then he moved forward, placing his palm on my shoulder to ease me back. "I can't wait to be inside of you," he said, centering his cock at my entrance. He looked me in the eyes, smoldering as he rubbed his cock up and down, spreading my juices.

"Please," I whispered. "I want you." *To be the first.*

And just like that, the magic words were uttered, and he pushed forward, parting my folds with his thick head as he entered my slick channel.

As he met resistance, he met my eyes. "Are you okay? Relax for me." He never suspected I was a virgin, and I was prepared to keep that secret. I didn't want him to get weird about it, and it didn't have to be a big deal.

I relaxed, and he pushed deeper, taking my virginity and making it a memory. He thrust harder, working me nice and steady as he picked up the pace.

I felt my body tighten and my toes curled as the pleasure became the most intense feeling I'd ever felt. As I panted and moaned, he worked my sweet spot until I thought I'd come undone.

This was what I'd been missing? I'd waited my whole life for this moment, and I wondered if I should say something. But no, it didn't matter. It wasn't as if it meant anything special to him.

I moved my hips upward, showing my eagerness as he brushed my hair from my face and looked into my eyes. "You're so good. I'm so glad I met you."

He moved to kiss my neck, and I turned my face away to give him access as I thought about what he'd said. Then he pumped his cock in me a few more times and pulled out, shooting warm streams across my belly.

He collapsed beside me and got to his feet. "Shit, I'll get you something," he said. "I didn't know if you were on the pill or not."

"I'm sorry. I am. I should have said something."

"It's fine," he said. "That was amazing."

"Did you know this would happen?" I asked out of nowhere. But now that it was over, my brain was getting all sorts of screwed up.

He smiled from the bathroom door as he slipped on a pair of shorts. "I'd be lying if I said I didn't want it to, but no, I wasn't sure you'd go for it. If I thought you would have, I'd have been better prepared. I don't know what I was thinking. It's just been a while. And you surprised me." He turned to the sink and wet a washcloth.

It became clear that I was just a means to an end, a tool used for his release. And silly me, I already wanted it to be more.

He came back with the rag and handed it to me. "Here, I got it warm for you."

"Thanks." I sat up as he walked over to the bar and poured a drink.

"Do you want something now?" His words were as if we were back to business, and something about the finish had me second-guessing my feelings. Did I really want to be this into him when he was leaving soon?

I didn't answer, staring down at the tinge of red I had wiped. "I should go," I said, hiding the evidence as I moved to the edge of the bed. I wasn't sure he had noticed.

"What? No." He walked over, and I could see the confusion on his face. "Don't run off. We can take a shower and maybe go for round two. If you feel up to it." He pulled me close and kissed my shoulder, but I pulled away.

"I have an early morning, Zane. I should get home." I didn't even want to look him in the eye after the look of disappointment he gave me.

"Okay, that's fine." He shrugged like it wasn't a big deal, but I could tell he was bothered. "I'll call you a cab. I just thought you'd want to stay a while. Whatever."

"I have my car. It was fun, but let's not read anything more into this." I wasn't going to encourage him any longer. He was going to be leaving in a few days, and I was not ever getting out of Vegas.

I hurried to the bathroom and cleaned up before I got dressed. When I came out, Zane was standing by the bed with my shoes in his hand. "Here. I guess I'll see you tomorrow."

"Yeah," I said. "I'll see you." I was about to rush out, but he reached out to stop me.

"Hey," he said. "I had a good time, Tara."

I shrugged, trying to play it cool, but he smiled. Then he laid a kiss on me that had me rethinking my decision to leave.

A minute later, I ducked out to the elevator, hoping no one saw me leaving. As it closed me in alone, I giggled. "Wow."

Karen was never going to believe it.

CHAPTER 15

ZANE

There was a knock on my door first thing the next morning.
"Get up, motherfucker."

Clay's voice was enough to make me wish I had slept in.

"I'm awake," I said as I threw open the door, still in my shorts. "Do you have to wake up everyone in the hotel?"

"I wanted to go down and get something to eat, and I thought you might want to go and see your girlfriend."

"She's not my girlfriend," I said.

"Obviously." He looked at the bed. "Or else you'd still be in bed, dick deep in those sweet thighs. So, tell me, how was she?"

"Fuck off," I said.

"What? No inside scoop? We always used to compare notes before."

"Yeah? So what are you comparing?"

About that time, there was another knock on my door. "Is this our morning meeting?"

"I think it's sad how everyone assumes you're alone."

"Again, fuck you." I held up my middle finger at Clay as I opened the door to find Nick and Rylen. "She didn't stay the night, and it's not a big deal."

Rylen laughed as he walked in. "Oh? You're talking about the girl?"

"Yeah, the girl who bailed on him. She probably didn't like his little dick."

"Are you twelve?" I asked Clay. "Because you're acting like it."

Nick shook his head. "Yeah, and he wasn't any better last night. We all got kicked out of the club. We'll have to find another hot spot."

"It was ridiculous. I just wanted to play the piano."

"They didn't have a piano," said Nick. "And he argued with the bouncer about it until he finally tossed us all out."

"At least I didn't grind up on my cousin," Clay said, glaring back at him.

Nick's expression changed. "Hey, watch it. It's not like we've seen each other in years. And I didn't grind on her. I just flirted a little."

"You eye-fucked her," said Rylen, earning a hard look.

"Yeah," said Clay. "Thank goodness your natural instincts kicked in before you had a baby with flippers."

Nick balled his fist. "Can I hit him?"

"Be my guest," I said.

"Go for it," said Rylen at the very same time. "He deserves it for yesterday as well."

"Yesterday? You mean at dinner?" I was afraid to ask what happened when I left.

"Yeah. He made a pass and offended one of the girls, and they all left before dessert was served."

"It wasn't like we could touch them," said Clay. "Apparently, they have some rule against it."

"Yeah, it's called being respectful," said Nick, raising his voice. He probably had an entirely different outlook on that kind of display now that his cousin was the one participating, and I couldn't blame him. I wouldn't want my daughter to do something like that.

Clay got defensive. "I was respectful. I just asked for *her* to touch *me*. I swear, you guys have no sense of humor."

"You're not funny. But then, I guess nothing has changed since college."

"Ha, ha," he said. "Let's go get something to eat. I'm sick of you all being Debbie Downers."

"I'm not ready to go down," I said. "I just have to get dressed first."

"Fine," said Clay. "Come on, Rylen. Let's go down and get an eye-opener. I could use a drink."

"Whatever. Just try not to get us kicked out of this hotel. I really like my room."

"Funny," said Clay. He turned to me as they were leaving. "Try not to take too long. The girl has already seen you naked. No amount of flexing in the mirror is going to change her opinion now."

With that, he shut the door, and I turned to Nick, who stayed behind to wait on me. "I swear, I'm going to kill him before he leaves, and I'll spend the rest of my life in prison, knowing I somehow made the world a better place."

"Yeah, and I get to go home with him."

"So, since they aren't here, how'd it go last night?" I knew when Nick asked me, he wasn't asking to get the juicy, dirty details about sex with Tara. He was just a good friend making sure I was okay.

"It was hot, but then she left. It was kind of sudden and awkward honestly. She said we shouldn't make more of it than it was. That kind of threw me for a loop. I thought it was going well. She couldn't keep her hands off of me, and she instigated coming back here. She nearly fucked me in the cab and the elevator." I took a deep breath, thinking about it. It had been so intense. "Maybe she got what she wanted. But I can't help but think I was a little much for her."

"A little much?" he asked with a creasing brow. "What do you mean?"

"Like maybe I was too rough. I'm kind of big and bulky, and maybe I hurt her." I was sure I had torn her, but I didn't want to say so. She seemed to really like it at the time.

"Hurt? Did she tell you to stop?"

"No, it wasn't anything like that. Jesus, Nick, I'm not an animal. But there was blood on the sheets."

"Ah, you popped her cherry."

"Nah. No way. She definitely seemed experienced."

"It doesn't matter, my friend. Maybe she had regrets after. It was a big moment, and she barely knew you. Maybe like you said, it was too much." It was an interesting take on the way things had ended, and I felt horrible thinking she'd given me her virginity. "If she had told me, then I would have done things differently, you know? Like made it special or something."

This made it all even weirder, and now I knew I had to talk to her.

I got dressed, and we met the others down in the bar, where Clay was hitting on one of the waitresses. When I walked in, he whispered something in her ear, and she shook her head and walked away.

"Making friends, I see." I gave him a hard look. "The sad thing is, one of them is going to bite and get way more than they bargained for."

As the words escaped my lips, I hated to think that was what had happened with Tara. She had bitten off more than she could chew, and now she had regrets.

"Let's go," said Rylen. "I'm starving."

Before anyone could react, my phone rang. I glanced down and didn't recognize the number, but it was from North Dakota. "Hey, it's a call from home. I better take this."

My look of concern must have made them wonder. They stood there with me as if they were just as anxious to hear.

"Hello?"

"Hello, Zane."

The voice put me on alert, and I could tell the others caught my change in temper. "Heather. What the fuck are you doing calling me?" I hadn't gotten a call that she was being released, but I wondered what that bitch could want.

"Oh, I just thought you'd like to know that I'm out."

"You're out? Very funny."

Nick's hand fell on my shoulder, and the guys got serious, knowing how upset the woman made me.

"No, I'm not kidding. I'm out of prison on good behavior, and now, I want to see my daughter."

"You can't see her. That's never going to fucking happen, Heather. You might as well accept that you don't have a daughter anymore."

"That's a cute fairy tale, Zane, but you know there's nothing you can do to change her DNA. And she's mine. If you think I'm going to sit by and let you raise her without me, you're fucking mistaken."

"She doesn't know you anymore. You'd be doing her more harm than good, so if you care, if you love her, you'll just crawl the fuck back off to your gutter and leave her be. I'm not letting you see her. Deal with it."

"I guess we're going to have to play hardball, Zane. But you should know, I'm well rested and ready for a fight." With that, the bitch ended the call, and I clenched my jaw so hard I heard it crack.

"You okay, brother?" asked Nick.

"She's out."

"Fuck," said Clay. "How can they just let her go? Don't they have to tell you?"

"They are supposed to, but if they tried to call the house phone, I'm not there, and if they called the office, I'm not there. So who knows? She's going to try and take Mila."

"They won't give her to that junkie," said Clay. "We'll all speak up for you and what a good father you are. They'll never let that happen."

"Courts like to place children with their mothers," said Rylen, who was only trying to explain to Clay why I was worried at all.

"Fuck that."

"Yeah, fuck that. Before I let that happen, I swear to take her and run." I took a deep breath, trying to calm myself. Heather was good about doing that kind of shit. "She's just blowing smoke. I'm not worried about her." My parents were still away with Mila, so it wasn't like she could do anything anyway. Aside from that, I had security at my house. "Come on. Let's eat."

I knew seeing Tara would make me feel a whole lot better.

But when we got to the buffet, Tara wasn't there. Could the day get any worse?

CHAPTER 16

TARA

As it turned out, I had forgotten I was off the following day, and I felt terrible for lying to Zane about having an early morning.

Sleeping in was nice, and when I finally woke up, wishing I was still in Zane's arms, I knew I had no one to blame but myself for leaving.

Who knew what might have happened? What I thought was the best sex possible could have paled in comparison to round two.

When I rolled over in bed, my body ached in the most amazing ways, and I could have lain there forever, dreaming of him inside me until the knock at my door ruined my fantasy.

"Just a minute," I said, expecting it to be the woman from next door wanting to borrow my phone again.

"Hurry up, Tara," Karen said. "There's some weird guy down the hall looking for his peter. I don't want to be out here when he finds it."

I unlocked the five locks I had on my door and greeted her with a yawn. "That's Mr. Stan. He's looking for his dog, Peter." Despite my telling him that telling strangers he's lost his Peter and asking if they'd seen it was a bad idea. "He's harmless."

"Oh, well, that's a relief." She stopped and looked at me as if there was something on my face or in my hair.

"What?" I asked.

"You look different." She gave me the side-eye. "Did you do something to your hair?"

"No, I just rolled out of bed."

"You do look rather refreshed." She walked in, dropped her bag on the floor by my old green sofa, and plopped down. "Get dressed. We're going shopping."

"Shopping requires money," I said. "And I'm saving mine."

"Then go watch me. I've got to find something to wear. I have ruined two dresses this week."

"Do I even want to know how?" She had probably let some stranger rip it off of her while she was stealing his wallet.

She gave me a hard look as if she didn't like my tone. "I caught one on a nail sticking out of my shitty apartment's door trim, and another got torn by the cat's claw. Exciting enough for you?"

"Fine, I'll go. I might even splurge a little myself." It wouldn't be a bad idea to have a few nice things in case I had the chance to see Zane again.

"Splurging? Glowing face? Did I miss something."

I grinned and played aloof. "What? I don't know what you mean."

"Like hell, you don't. What is going on with you?"

"I went out last night."

"You went out?" Suddenly, her eyes widened. "With that guy?"

"His name is Zane." I walked into my bedroom to get ready for shopping, and she followed.

"And what exactly did you and Zane do?"

"What didn't we do, you mean?" I met her eyes in the reflection of my mirror and wagged my brows.

"You didn't."

"Oh, I surely did. I'm surprised you didn't notice that I'm walking funny."

"Was his cock as big as the rest of him? He's built like a fucking mountain, that one. Did you climb him like a tree?" She was practically bouncing on my bed.

"Settle down," I said with a laugh. "We went to Cirque du Soleil, and we left early and went back to his hotel room. I swear, just being around him made me so horny. I could barely wait until we got back to his room. I don't know what came over me."

"So, you lost the V-card to a tourist? I'm impressed. And he's a damned fine one. Tell me everything."

"Well, it was amazing, and I think my toes might have curled, but it got awkward after, and I bailed." I bit my lip and looked away, not wanting to see the look of disappointment on her face.

"So, he was one and done?" She shrugged. "It happens."

"No, he wanted me to stay, but I got a little freaked out. I didn't want him to know it was my first time."

"Guys eat that shit up, Tara. He would have loved it. They like to collect cherries. You didn't tell him at all? He wasn't suspicious?"

"No, I mean, maybe. I'm not sure."

I felt so nervous just talking about it. But we talked and talked through the rest of my getting ready, and I ended up having a million questions for my more experienced friend.

A few hours of shopping later, we were still talking about it. As we sat eating lunch salads at our favorite salad bar, she leaned in across the table. "Did you use protection?"

I glanced around and hoped no one was within earshot and, if so, that they weren't paying attention. "We didn't have any. But I trusted him. He said he was tested after his last relationship. And I'm on the pill."

"I'm going to pretend that's not completely hypocritical of you and just be supportive. But next time, you should bring some—at least three. Trust me. He's a nice guy, but even nice guy's lie now and then, especially when their cocks are swollen."

I nodded. "I was a little embarrassed at first, but then it just felt so good I didn't care, you know? It was just so hard not to want it to be more. I guess that's why I bailed. I don't want my heart to be broken. Zane is gorgeous and nice and even a gentleman, you know? I just don't know if he's looking for anything serious or more than what I've already given him." I picked at my lettuce, not able to eat. I had too much on my mind.

Karen reached for her napkin, wiping her mouth. "He'll let you know, but in the meantime, you have to ask yourself a question. What do you get from it? If the answer is amazing sex, then it's worth it. You don't have to put your heart out there."

"I told him that we didn't have to read anything into it. He just said okay without putting up any protest."

"Well, who says you can't use him the same way? Let's face it. If he's spending time with you, you're at least getting his company and your sexual needs met. It might even lead to more. It's been known to happen."

"I wouldn't want to think of him with anyone else," I said, feeling my stomach turn. "I really want to see him again." I wanted more, dammit.

"You have to start thinking in terms of being a hit-it-and-quit-it girl. You're too beautiful to be hung up on one man."

"I can't help it. He's the type who leaves you wanting more."

"What do you even know about him?"

"Lots. We talked a lot about his job and his friends. He works in the oil industry in North Dakota. He's a foreman, probably makes good money judging by the big tips he leaves me, and he said he owns his own home." I tried to think of the things we'd talked about before the show and before our hormones took over.

Karen took a sip of her drink and gave me a big grin. "How big is it?"

I winced, knowing she'd ask me sooner or later. "At least ten inches, two on the girth easily." Her eyes widened as I whispered across the table. "His body is amazing."

"Damn. That's enough to fall in love. I'm jealous." She gave me a pouty look. "Why can't I find someone who's nice and packing a snack like that? You're glowing just talking about him."

"I don't know what to do. He's leaving town soon, and I guess I'll never hear from him again."

"Tell him you'd like to stay in touch. You could maybe hook up now and then when he's in town. He's got a friend here, so who knows? It's a reason to come back."

"I don't know. What if he says no? What if he agrees with not taking things too far?"

Karen stabbed her salad and dunked it in ranch dressing. "At least keep him open as an option. It can't hurt anything. Maybe he'll have you come to his house and spend a sexy weekend in bed. You need a vacation."

"I don't know. It's all so fast. I guess I just got freaked out last night. I wish now that I had stayed. I think about him all the time, and I hated waking up alone this morning."

"That sucks. But just wait. You've awakened a monster, my friend, and now you're going to want it all the time. You'll be thinking about him in the shower and when you get all warm beneath the covers at night." She enjoyed teasing me. Always had.

I could feel the heat rising to my face as I looked around and spotted an old man sitting at the table next to us. It was unclear if he was listening, but I kicked her under the table anyway. "Shush."

"Are you going to eat that salad or not?"

"I can't. I can't stop thinking about it."

"You're hungry for more, aren't you?"

I shrugged and gave a little nod. "Maybe."

"Then nothing else is going to satisfy. You need to have more of that man. I'd make sure I did before he leaves."

"He's supposed to be around a few more days." I'd know how he felt if he stopped showing up at the buffet. If he didn't, I'd know he was avoiding me.

"So, seduce him. Make him want it again, just as much." She made it sound so easy. And I supposed things like that were easy for her. Her personality had always shined while I had always been way too cynical.

"How do I make him?" I asked. I had a feeling about what she was going to say, and I wasn't wrong.

"Jump his bones, honey. You can't go wrong with that."

She couldn't go wrong, maybe, but I was sure to screw it up somehow.

We finished what we could of lunch, and I forced myself to have a few more bites of the salad, which just didn't settle right.

After, we went to our favorite boutique, where I found a sexy blouse and a pair of designer jeans. "This is pretty," I said to Karen, who was in the dressing room next to me.

I turned in the mirror, looking at the way the material lay just right against my curves. There wasn't one seam digging in or pinching, and there wasn't a ton of loose fabric in odd places either, just smooth, form fitting, and flattering. It even showed off my breasts while not exposing too much of them, and I felt like a lady instead of a hooker.

"Come and show me," she said. "I need your help zipping anyway."

"Fine." I walked over and found her with her hair up.

I zipped her dress, and before she even looked in the mirror at it, her mouth fell open as she saw me. "Look at you, hot mama. That is spectacular and *so* your color."

"I feel good in it." I smoothed my hands down the jeans.

"It's the hormones. I swear, even your tits look bigger."

I panicked and turned to the mirror. I didn't want anything looking bigger. But I looked the same to me.

She giggled. "Maybe you're just sticking them out more."

"I feel good. Confident. Like I am wearing it, and it's not wearing me, if that makes sense."

"Oh, it does. Trust me. We all have those times when things don't fit, Tara. It took me a long time to figure out what worked and what didn't, so I just always stick with those lines."

"I guess I've finally found my lines," I said as I smiled at myself in the mirror and turned to look at the back again, checking the fit of the jeans, which was perfect.

"Well, you have to get it," she said. "And don't even say no because you already said you were going to splurge."

"Oh, I'm getting it, and with any luck, I'm going to get to wear it for Zane." I turned in the mirror, looking at the back and how it accentuated while flattering my curvy bottom. "I can't wait to see him again."

Karen laughed. "Well, then we should go to the intimates department because what you wear beneath those clothes is going to be equally as important when you have someone seeing them too."

My face turned red. I hadn't even thought of that. There was just so much to consider now.

By the time we were done, I had spent much more than I had set out to, but I was pleased with the things I'd gotten, including three beautiful bra and panty sets. It wasn't as if I didn't have pretty undergarments, but these were sexy but still tasteful, while making me feel a little naughty. Maybe it was just what I needed to take my confidence even higher.

I didn't know if Zane was ready to see me again, but I was ready for him.

CHAPTER 17

ZANE

As Clay and I walked down to meet up with Rylen and Nick, who had made an early morning run to the casino, I caught my friend giving me strange looks.

"What?" I said.

"You're too quiet. And frankly, you're scary when you're quiet. Always have been."

I didn't know whether to be insulted or not, but I took it in stride since it was coming from an overgrown child. He was probably smart to have a little fear in him. "I'm just thinking," I said. I didn't really want to talk about it.

"Did you confirm if she's really out?"

"She's really out. I'm not worried about her."

"I'm sure we'll have more fun tonight. We're going to the magic-show thing Nick was telling us about and then to the club after."

"I'm not worried about what we're doing, Clay. I'm not sure I can make it another day here."

"What happened to your girl? Did you see her at all yesterday?"

"No, she must have been off, and I haven't tried to call."

"You mean she's not blowing your phone up?"

I already felt like shit that she hadn't. "Look, I don't want to talk about it, okay?"

"Fine. I'm just your oldest and best friend who is trying to help bring you out of your funk. If you want to talk, I'm here."

"I appreciate it." A lot could be said about Clay, who wasn't always the most mature of us, but he was a good friend who cared when he wasn't a selfish fuck-up.

Nick and Rylen were standing in the lobby, talking on their cell phones, and both ended their calls when we walked up.

"Are you guys ready to get your grub on?" asked Nick.

"Yeah, but let me warn you. Someone's grumpy. And it's not me."

"Great," said Nick. "Who poked the bear? Was it the ex again?"

"No, it's just hard being away from home and my daughter, especially with this going on. And I have to tell my parents but I don't want to spoil their trip."

"I'd give them the heads-up," said Clay, and it was probably the most mature, sound advice he'd given me in some time.

"I will. For now, I just want to eat and forget my problems."

"Well, I don't know if it will make you feel any better, but your favorite waitress is working today." Nick pointed into the dining room where Tara stood at a table, smiling as she brought the couple their check.

I immediately felt a lot better, but now, I was nervous to see how this would go. For one, she had lied to me, unless she had called in, and I'd worried all night it was the latter and that I'd done something to hurt her.

The place was emptying out, and I watched Tara as she went to the back. She hadn't even noticed us yet.

"Man, she's looking good," said Clay. "Are you going to talk to her?"

"Mind your own business," I said. "She's working."

"I knew it! The sex was bad, wasn't it?" He gave a sly grin that I was quick to wipe off his face.

I turned and gave him a hard look. "Shut the fuck up before I feed you my fist."

Clay sank in his chair. "Sorry. I was just teasing. You're not fun anymore."

"And you don't know when to fucking stop. You're not a fucking kid, okay? So grow up."

Rylen and Nick didn't say a word, but I could tell they were glad someone had finally said it. Clay had been acting as if we were all still in college, and it was wearing thin on me, especially knowing what he was trying hard to forget back home.

I must have been a lot louder than I thought because when I turned around, Tara was standing beside me. "Is everything okay?"

"Yeah, sorry." I glanced at my friends and dared them to say anything. They didn't. "You look nice today."

"Thank you." She looked around the table. "Welcome to the Golden Flower. I'm Tara. I'll be taking care of you. What can I get you this morning?" She looked at me. "Would you like more dark roast?"

"Sure." She was cold, staying strictly to routine. It made me feel like a real asshole. I had obviously done something wrong.

"And for you other gentlemen?" She smiled at my friends and gave me a little glance out of the corner of her eye.

The guys all gave their orders, and as she walked away with a little extra wiggle in her walk, I noticed them staring. "Eyes front and center," I said. "Before I gouge them out."

"She's beautiful," said Nick. "You really like her, don't you?" He kept his voice low and respectful.

"I guess you can say she's made an impression." A big one. Bigger than I cared to admit to them. I watched as she came out with the coffee and served it.

"Here you go." She placed the cups on the table, and I couldn't take my eyes off of her. "Would you like to order at the table or eat the buffet?"

"Buffet all around," said Nick. "I'm buying, guys. No arguments."

I glanced down and noticed my coffee was as pale as her creamy skin. "Um, this isn't dark roast," I said, thinking she was fucking with me. Was this her way of getting back at me? I looked up and met her eyes, which seemed to have a nonchalant look about them.

She glanced up with piercing eyes. "Oh? I'm sorry you don't like my coffee." Her brow lifted as if she was challenging me. What had gotten into her?

I realized what she was doing. She really was fucking with me since I'd told her the last time that I didn't like the coffee. But that was okay. I could play along. "It's not dark, and I'm pretty sure it's not even coffee." It looked like creamer.

"Oh, well, if you don't like it, then maybe you'd like to come to the kitchen and teach me how to make it." She gave me a sultry look, and I got the invitation loud and clear.

I pushed my chair back and got up from the table. "Yeah, someone should show you how it's done. This is pathetic." I did my best to act as if I was upset, but I could see that Nick was onto us. Rylen and Clay kept their eyes averted, not saying a word.

"Fine then," she said. "Right this way." She turned and stormed to the kitchen, passing her friend on the way. "Cover me?" I heard her say, and the friend just smiled big.

"No problem," she said.

When we got to the kitchen, I chased after her past the cooks. "What's going on, Tara?" I thought she was just trying to get me alone so we could talk, but little did I know she had other plans.

She took my hand and led me to the back of the kitchen and into a storeroom, where she turned on the light and shut the door.

"Did I do something wrong? Because if I hurt you, and I mean in any way, I'm sorry." I wasn't going to fight with her. Especially not in the fucking pantry.

"You didn't hurt me," she said, coming closer with that sexy look of determination.

"Whoa, I know I was a little rough. I didn't mean to—" I didn't know how to say it, but before I could, she moved on me and kissed the words out of my mouth.

I cupped her face and kissed her back. This was what she was up to? It came as a surprise, and I had never been so happy to be taken off guard. If this was what she wanted, I was going to give it to her.

I turned her around and propped her up on top of a cart. It shifted and crashed into a shelf, making a terrible racket.

"Shh," she said with a giggle in her voice. "Someone might hear us."

I was so turned on that I could barely produce a clear thought. "What's gotten into you?" I whispered as I pushed her skirt up.

"You," she whispered in my ear as she tugged the front of my pants and began to undo my belt.

I pushed her skirt up even higher and slipped her panties down. "You are full of surprises," I whispered while I moved my hand between her legs. I cupped her sex and rubbed, applying pressure to her mound, which she ground against.

She met my eyes as she reached her hands in and pulled out my cock, wrapping her hands around it. My head was spinning, not sure if this was real or if I had never woken up. "I'm sorry I left the other night. I want to make it up to you."

She dropped to her knees and wasted no time sucking my cock. She nursed my dick in a way no one ever had, stroking me at the base as she worked the tip. But I didn't want an apology blow job. I wanted to be inside her.

"Stand up," I said, urging her to her feet. She wiped her mouth and smiled as I moved to kiss her. I rubbed her lips, parting them as I inserted a finger inside of her. I wanted her to be ready for what I was about to give her. She was so wet as I fingered her, working her into a frenzy. "You ready for it?"

She nodded. "Yes," she said in a breathless tone. "So ready."

Being in that storeroom, not knowing if someone would walk in on us, was such a turn on. I lifted her bottom back up to the cart. As I moved forward, she guided me in, and I wasted no time putting my head against her sex, nudging my fat head against her.

"I don't want to hurt you."

"Shh. You won't." She moved her hips forward, taking the head of my cock, and she winced. After another breath, she wrapped her legs around my ass and encouraged me deeper, taking the whole thing at once.

I waited for her to settle around it. Then I thrust harder, working myself up to a natural rhythm as I kissed her neck. It was a big shock that she'd even go for something like this, much less instigate it, but I wasn't about to miss out on the opportunity or to make the most of it.

CHAPTER 18

TARA

My clever way of getting Zane alone with me came as a surprise to me as well. At first, I had only intended to mess with him about the coffee, but the rest just unfolded, and I found myself in the storeroom, my back against the cool stainless-steel cart as he fucked me hard.

Having him inside me again was much better the second time around, and I was still kicking myself for not staying the night with him before.

He thrust hard into me, our bodies clapping, the motions shaking the shelf behind us. When the cart shifted, he held on to me and took me in his arms. After that, I wasn't touching anything but him, and he met my eyes with such an intense gaze, I could tell he was determined to give me as much pleasure as possible.

After a few minutes of that, he pulled out as he put me to my feet, and he spun me around, putting his hand on my back as he bent me over the cart. Before I could glance over my shoulder, he rubbed his thick head against my center, stroking it to spread my juices before gliding it back into my tight channel.

He brought his body down close, cupping my breast in the front as he kissed the back of my neck. "Does this feel good?" he asked.

"Amazing," I said. His cock worked a part of me that was so intensely sensitive, I couldn't keep it together.

As I orgasmed, he put his hand over my mouth, and it wasn't until then I realized I was making entirely too much noise.

"Shh," he said in my ear. "I know it's hard, but you're going to get us caught, and I don't want this to end right now." He planted another breathy kiss by my ear, sending chills all through my body and making me tingle in all the right places.

"I'm sorry," I whispered.

"You have nothing to apologize for. I just don't think I could stop now if someone did come in."

I giggled, and he laughed with me, his breath still warm on the back of my neck as he continued to thrust deeper. But something about the idea of how sneaky we were turned me on even more, and just thinking about someone seeing us like that brought me back over the edge.

"I'm going to come," he said. "Are you sure you're covered?" His voice was anxious, and I could tell he was close.

"Yes," I said. "Don't stop." I didn't want him to finish like before, leaving me feeling almost cheated from having him not finish inside of me. It was a strange thought but honest. And I had to be honest with myself about what I was feeling or else I'd get lost too deep too fast.

"I don't think I could if I wanted to," he said. "And I don't want to."

He pumped his hips several more times, and he stilled, his body tightening, his cock twitching inside of me as warmth spread through me. He kissed the back of my neck, then my shoulders as he slipped out of me, leaving me sated.

His next words came as a surprise. "You didn't have to lie to me the other night about working," he said. "I know I tore you, and I'm sorry I was that rough."

I realized he must have seen the tinge of red on the washcloth after all. "It wasn't that you were rough. I was just my first time." I figured it wouldn't hurt to tell him now. What was done was done.

His eyes nearly bugged out of his head. "What?"

"Yeah, I had never gone that far before." I pushed my skirt down and smoothed it with my hands. "But you could probably tell, right?"

"No, I didn't know. I mean, I wondered after, but damn. Why didn't you say something, Tara?" He put his hand on his head and then pulled up his pants. "Fuck."

I suddenly felt as if I'd done something wrong as he handed me my panties. "I'm sorry." I slipped them on beneath my skirt and smoothed it down again. "I didn't think you'd care, and I didn't want you judging me."

He let out a breath, and I couldn't tell what he was thinking, only that it probably wasn't good by the crease in his brow. "Stop apologizing. It's not that you did anything wrong, but damn, Tara. You could have told me. I'm not an uncaring asshole."

"I know you're not." I closed my eyes and shook my head. "Great, now I've offended you." That was the last thing I'd intended to do.

"No. I just don't want to come across as that guy, you know? I hate that you didn't think you could tell me that."

"Look, it's not a big deal, okay? I just don't want this to make things weird, and I just didn't want you to think I expected anything from you."

"I get it." He raked his hand through his hair. "Fuck. Your first time should be special, Tara. With someone who you know better, who you love."

"Okay, Dad. Well, it's a little late for that. I thought I'd settle for someone I thought was extremely sexy instead." I gave him a little smile and hoped he wasn't mad at me.

He smiled back and pulled me close, kissing my hair, which was still pulled back in a much messier bun than before. "I think you're extremely sexy too. But we need to talk about this. Can I see you later?"

"Are you asking me out on another date?"

He nodded. "Yeah, but if you're just going to pull me out of a show to fuck me, I'm not spending money on tickets." He laughed as I nudged him.

"It wasn't planned. It just happened. Like today. You make me want to do spontaneous things." He made me want to be adventurous, to take chances.

"That could get dangerous," he said with a laugh. "How about I take you out to dinner?"

"No." I shook my head, and he met my eyes with a look of disappointment.

"Okay, so where? I'll take you anywhere you want to go." It sounded as if he was willing to give me the world. I could only dream.

"I like the sound of that, but no. No more plans. We meet, and we wing it." That was more fun. Or at least, it had been.

"You know that's probably just going to land us in bed, right?"

"Come on. If the past twenty minutes prove anything, it's that we can be creative at the moment."

"You got me there. I'm game. So do I just pick you up at your place?" He took my hand and met my eyes.

"I'll meet you here again if that's okay." I still didn't want him to see my place. If he knew how little I had, he might think less of me, and I was having too much fun.

He nodded, and he kissed me hard as if he had to make it last all day.

That lingered on for a while, and it was like neither of us was ready to come out of the storage room anytime soon.

The kiss was interrupted by a knock on the door. "Hey, you two. I don't know what you're doing, although I can guess, so you might want to finish up and get your sweet butts back out here."

"That's Karen," I said as if he didn't know. "We better go. I don't want Ben to fire me."

Another knock and then Karen said, "Benny just got back from the bank. He's in the lobby with the hotel manager."

I straightened my clothes, and when we walked out, Karen was heading back out front.

Zane playfully slapped my backside as we walked down the back hall together, and I turned and gave him a grin. "I'm sorry, sir. I'm going to have to ask you to behave."

"Yes, ma'am. I'm sorry. And thank you for allowing me to show you how to make coffee. You're a wonderful student."

"You can give me lessons anytime."

He stole another kiss before he went through the kitchen and out to the dining room.

I looked around at the others who were all working. No one seemed suspicious, or at least not obviously suspicious.

When I went to the front, I found Karen waiting on my tables, and Ben was just entering the restaurant. He passed the men's table as Zane was approaching, and when he slid into his chair, Ben turned to greet them.

"Are you men enjoying the service here today?" he asked with a big cheesy grin, as if he really cared. He just wanted to see if we had been doing our jobs while he had been gone.

"Yes, sir," said Zane, who glanced up at me as I stepped within earshot. "Your waitresses have been very accommodating in making sure our needs were met."

His friends reacted, covering their mouths and my cheeks burned knowing they knew what we had been up to. Especially when the one with longish brown hair glanced up at me with a grin.

"That's good, gentlemen. Enjoy your time here at the Golden Flower."

I went back to stand with Karen, who nudged me. "So, did you get your second round after all?"

"I'm not going to talk about it with him sitting just feet away."

"Yes or no would do. You could blink once for yes, twice for no. I'm dying to know what I've waited all of these extra tables for."

"Stop complaining. You get the tips."

"The question is, did you get more than the tip?" she asked, wagging her brows.

"Stop it. Not here, not now. I'm about to have to go bring them more drinks and give them their check. I'm trying not to blush as it is." I wasn't giving her their table because I'd already started with them and I wouldn't miss the chance to talk to Zane again. "Besides, you owed me. I've been covering for your ass long enough, and I don't ask you what you've been up to."

"You should," she said with a wink. "You might learn something."

"I'm doing all right," I said proudly as I walked away.

I went to make sure the men had refills, bringing them another round. When I approached the table, Zane grinned, and while I stood beside him, pouring his friends more coffee, I felt his hand go up my skirt and brush against the back of my knee. "Thank you," he said.

The other men were making busy keeping their eyes elsewhere when I placed a cup of dark roast in front of him. "You're welcome."

He leaned in closer. "I'll see you later?"

"Can't wait." I turned my attention back to his table. "Is there anything else I can get you?"

Zane got up and stood with me. "I'm just going to get something to eat," he said. "Want to show me what's good?"

"I think she's already done that," mumbled Clay.

I could feel my face turn red as I heard something thump under the table. "I apologize for Clay's behavior," said the man who preferred newspapers. I couldn't remember his name.

Zane pegged the other man with a hard look, then gave a nod to his other friend. "You remember Nick?"

"Right, the newspaper guy. I remember." He was nice and had kind eyes.

Zane introduced his other friends. "This is Clay and Rylen."

"Oh, which one of you lives here?" I hoped the mouthy one wasn't the rich man, but it wouldn't surprise me.

"I'm from here," said Nick. "But you're probably thinking of Grady. He's supposed to be on his way."

"Well, it's nice to meet you all, and if you need anything else, just let me know."

"Thanks, Tara. It's good to meet you too."

As I followed Zane to the buffet, he stepped up beside me. "I'm sorry about that. Clay is reverting to childhood. I guess I'll see you later?"

"Yeah, for sure. I'll be here." I didn't want to be anywhere else but with him, and feeling that way had me worried.

Was I about to get a broken heart?

CHAPTER 19

ZANE

After our meal, we went to the casinos for more gambling, and I was on cloud nine the whole time, anticipating the night to come.

Tara still amazed me, and I hadn't felt that wild and adventurous in ages. It reminded me of the time before I'd become a father and my entire life had become about my daughter and fighting her mother's demons.

I slipped off to have a video call with my parents. Since they were still out of town too and having such a wonderful time, I just couldn't bring myself to tell them about Heather. So far, the house was safe, and as far as I knew, she hadn't tried to show up there.

"Did you like the safari drive?" I asked Mila when my mother put her on the phone.

"Yeah, it was fun," she said. "I liked the giraffes. They came right up to the car, and so did the ostriches. They are big birds, and Pop-pop said they bury their heads in the sand, but I didn't see them do that. Nana said he was just being silly."

"Yeah, they don't really do that, but some people think they do. I'm sure Pop-pop was just messing with you."

"We're going to go back to the amusement park again. It's my favorite. I drove a car, and Pop-pop ran into me."

"Bumper cars?"

"Yeah, Nana sat with me, but she let me steer."

It was good to hear how much she was getting to experience with my parents. I knew they all needed that time, a bit of a break in their day-to-day. And now that I'd met Tara, I was glad I'd come to Las Vegas, even if I was ready to see my daughter again.

Heather's threats had hit me hard. The only reason I wasn't on a plane back home already was because I knew my parents and daughter weren't there.

"Did you get any souvenirs?" I couldn't wait to see what she had to bring home. My parents had a long-standing habit of buying crazy knick-knacks and ridiculous things that they treasured as priceless memories.

"Nana bought me some dinosaur poop. It looks like a rock, but that's what the man said it was."

"Cool, I can't wait to see what that's like." I gave a little laugh, but Mila wasn't excited.

"It looks like a rock. You see one, and you've seen them all."

"That sounds like something you heard from Pop-pop."

"Yeah, he said it. He said we're still looking for the real prize, but I didn't know what that meant."

"You'll see." I'm sure he would find something to wow her with.

"Nana wants the phone, Daddy. I guess that means I have to go."

"I love you, Noodle." I missed my little Mila so much, and I felt a sting in my heart when she said it back.

"I love you, Daddy."

As she handed my mother the phone, I rubbed the tender spot on my chest and felt the ache in my soul. That little girl was my entire universe. She was what made it go round, my sun.

I didn't need anything else.

But I immediately thought about Tara. She could be my moon. If she would be?

Tara had made it all too clear that we shouldn't make a big deal out of whatever it was we were doing. And I guessed even though she hated her life in Vegas, she didn't feel like she had much more to offer.

My mother finally got on the phone. "Honey?"

"Yeah, I'm here, Mom."

"I was wondering how you're doing. Is the trip going well?"

"Yeah, it's good."

"Well, your father and I just want you to have a good time. But be safe, okay?"

"Yes, ma'am."

"How is Clay?"

"Acting like an asshole," I said, even though I rarely cursed in front of my mother.

"Hmm, that bad? Well, he's probably hurting, honey. He's fighting himself, so he's acting out. He did the same thing when he was a kid and his parents got divorced. He's going to be okay. He just needs a friend."

"I'm there for him if I don't kill him first."

She laughed. "Oh no. Don't do that. One parent locked up is enough."

I felt a sting in my chest. I hated to keep things from my mother, but I knew it was for the best—for now.

"Well, honey, you go and have fun. We're about to go and get something to eat."

"Love you, Mom."

"Love you too." She ended the call, and I closed my eyes, hoping that I was making the right decision.

"There you are," said a voice from behind me. "I thought you slipped off to bang a waitress."

I turned around to see Clay, who had a dumb grin on his face.

"Really? You're going to go there?" And after my mother had said I couldn't kill him.

"Look, I'm sorry, okay? I don't know what's happening with me. I guess I came here looking for fun like we had in the old days."

"We're not boys anymore. We're men, fathers. We have responsibilities. We just want to chill, and you're a bit much."

"Sorry. I'm just trying to have fun before I have to go back to it."

"It? You mean your kid?" I was already pissed at him, and this wasn't helping.

"No, my life. I love my son. Believe it or not, okay? I do. But what kind of father am I going to be? My old man bailed, and I've hated him since. I just want to be better, but I'm scared I don't know how or that I'll have all of these needs built up inside that are going to come out when he's old enough to resent me for wanting them."

"You're not your father. And you're not getting anything out of your system. You're just putting more garbage into it. Do you love Beth?" There was a time I didn't have to ask him that.

"Yeah, I mean, she's the mother of my son. I'll always love her, even if she doesn't want me."

"And why would she want you when you're not a good partner or father? You have to make yourself desirable. You're just a burden, and you can do better for her and your son."

"Like sneaking off to diddle waitresses? How come you get to have all the fun?"

"I'm not attached."

"I'm not attached either."

"That's where you're wrong, my friend. You are. Your heart is. And I think that's what your fucking problem is."

"Fuck it."

"Yeah, keep saying that. And eventually, *fuck it* will become *fuck it up*. And then you won't have your son. She will. You'll be the crazy ex in the scenario, calling and hoping to see him."

"I'm not your shitbag, ex."

"No, you just act like her. Maybe that's why it's making it hard to like you."

Clay's face fell, and I could tell that I'd hit a nerve. "Fuck you," he said.

At about that time, Nick came over. "Hey, I've been looking for you." He glanced at Clay, who looked like he wanted to put his fist through me. "Is everything okay?"

"Yeah," said Clay. "It's just fucking perfect. Where to? I'm ready to party."

"We're going to a private lounge. It's a friend of Grady's."

Without another word, we followed Nick back to the others and left in Grady's limo.

On the way, I got stared down by Clay, who was still licking his wounds from my harsh words. I knew the truth hurt, but he needed to hear it.

When we got to the lounge, which looked like it was at one time a speakeasy, we walked in and found our table.

Grady's friend, the owner, walked over to greet us. "Hello, gentlemen," he said in an effeminate voice. "Make yourself at home. Your first round is on me."

"These are my dearest friends," he said. "Zane, Nick, Rylen, and Clay."

"He saved the best for last," said Clay with a cocky tone.

"Oh, sugar, I'm sure he did."

"Everyone, this is Lex. Lex is a good friend of mine, and he'll treat us right."

"I hope you enjoy my little establishment. You all be sure and enjoy the entertainment." He stepped away.

Clay leaned into the table. "Did that man just call me sugar?" asked Clay.

"Well, you are the prettiest," said Nick.

Grady chuckled. "Yeah, you're his type. He's a good guy, though. He's been a good friend and is an old friend of my mother's."

Before I was even comfortable in my chair, a woman came over and took our drink order. She smiled, giving me a little wink, and while I was polite, I wasn't interested.

All I could think about was Tara and what had happened in that storage closet.

We chatted with a few other patrons, and Lex came back to check on us. Things were fine until Clay slapped one of the waitresses on the ass.

"Watch your hand, honey, before I break it."

"You don't want to do that," he said. "These things are gifted." He raised his hands and wiggled his fingers. "They can do magic."

The woman rolled her eyes.

"Want me to show you?" He jumped up from the table and ran over to the piano across the room, where the last act had just performed.

I was sure he was about to get us thrown out when the waitress told him to get down.

"No," he said, his fingers already gliding across the keys. "This one is for you, sweetheart." He broke out into song, playing and singing so that he had the attention of everyone in the room.

Before long, the waitress, who must have been won over by his talent, was smiling as he sang a song about Lydia, the tattooed lady.

"She's got eyes that folks adore so, and a torso even more so..." Clay wagged his brows and kept on playing, singing at the top of his lungs.

The crowd loved it, and I had to admit that for someone who had really grated on my nerves the past several days, it was hard to stay mad at him.

When he finished that song, Lex walked up to the table. "I had no idea you had such talented friends." He put his hand on his hip. "I should offer him a job. Is he from around here?"

"He's got a family back home," I said. The last thing Clay needed was an excuse to leave town. And life in Las Vegas would finish him off.

"That's too bad," said Lex. "He sure knows how to work a crowd."

When Clay was done, the waitress walked over, gave him another drink, and whispered something in his ear.

After that, he played another, and by the time he was done, the entire room was enthralled with him.

I sipped drinks and listened until it was time for me to go and get cleaned up to meet Tara. Then I slipped out while the others weren't paying attention.

CHAPTER 20

TARA

After my shift, I went home to shower away the smell of the kitchen and dressed in my new clothes. I wasn't sure where we were going to end up, but I was going to look good doing it.

I slipped on the jeans, still thankful they fit like a glove, and I put on the blouse I'd gotten to match and dug out the heels I already had in my closet.

I put them on, and they were a bit much, but I was going to take a risk. Besides, nothing else I had matched my top the way they did.

I went to the bathroom, where I stood and put on my makeup, and as I swiped on some lipstick, I glanced at myself and realized I might have overdone it.

"No, no, no," I said.

I blotted the lipstick, taking it down a tone, and found another one to put over it so it became more muted.

"That's much better." I took a deep breath and felt the butterflies in my stomach. "I'm ready."

There was nothing else to do but go. I grabbed my phone and put it in my handbag with my keys and wallet. I still had the fifty dollars from Zane's table, where they had all chipped in to leave me a nice tip, even though I'd neglected them while servicing their friend in private.

My face burned just remembering what I'd done. I had never been that bold, and I was lucky I didn't get caught. My body heated just thinking about it. I was practically vibrating with excitement by the time I got to my car.

I drove across town to the hotel and parked on the opposite of where I usually did for work. I still didn't want anyone to see me coming and going, especially management. If Ben knew I was sleeping with customers, he would tell me I was acting like Karen, and even though Ben was a pain in the ass, I didn't want him to get the wrong idea about me or to think that he had a chance. The man was bad enough.

I went into the hotel lobby on the opposite side of the dining hall, and I spotted Zane across the room, looking so handsome in casual jeans and a button-down shirt that wasn't tucked in.

I might have overdressed with the heels, but I didn't care. I felt good and pretty, and that was all that mattered.

He spotted me and grinned big. "You look gorgeous," he said as he leaned in to kiss my cheek. "I am running out of clothes on this trip. I hope I'm not underdressed, but I figured whatever we did, you'd just end up taking my clothes off anyway."

I giggled. "Oh? You're that sure of yourself?" I gave him a pointed look, and he pulled his lips in a tight line.

"Well, I mean, maybe. I guess I shouldn't take you for granted."

"That's right. You shouldn't." I had a pretty good idea where we'd end up too, but I thought it would be nice to at least try and play coy about it.

"So, where do you want to go?"

I took a deep breath and tried to rest my mind enough to think it over. I wanted to show him another side of Las Vegas, the lesser-seen side. "I have an idea, but it's a secret. If you're up for it."

He looked as if he was thinking it over and then nodded. "I like your ideas so far. Count me in. But do I get a clue?"

"We're going to take my car. And that's the only clue you get."

"Hmm, I'm intrigued." He offered me his hand. "Take me. I'm yours."

His? I liked the sound of it. In fact, I found myself liking it a lot more than I should. And I knew at that point, it was safe to say I was falling for him.

So much it made me second-guess my idea, but I decided to roll with it anyway.

I walked him to my car, and I laughed when he got in, his head nearly touching the ceiling. "I guess my car wasn't made for men as tall as you."

"It's fine. It's actually got a good amount of legroom." He had put the seat all the way back, and his knees were still bent.

"You're just being nice."

"It's fine really. I'm just enjoying the company."

I drove us out of town, away from the Strip and the neon that polluted the night sky.

"We're here," I said when I turned down a desert road.

"Did you bring me all the way out here to murder me?" he asked with a chuckle in his voice. "Should I be worried?"

"You're funny, but no, I just love it out here."

"I thought you wanted to be somewhere greener."

"It's not a place I come in the day."

"I'd hope you don't ever come out here by yourself."

"I'm a big girl, and I usually just sit in the car, but we can get out. I have a blanket in the back."

"Okay, sure."

The stars were out, and they looked like diamonds on black velvet, sparkling and twinkling above us. "Isn't it beautiful?"

"Yeah," he said. But he wasn't looking at the sky. He was looking at me.

I nudged him. "I mean the stars. Look up."

He looked up at the sky, and I watched as he reacted. "Wow, there are so many of them. I haven't seen a clear night like this in a long time."

"They are always there when it's clear. You just have to get away from all the light pollution. I love to take photos out here."

"You are a photographer?" He seemed surprised to hear it.

"I dabble. It's a hobby, but I don't get to do it often with work, especially how I'd like to. I paint mostly."

"What kind of paintings?"

"Landscapes," I said with a chuckle. "I use a lot of green. I give them a mystical flair, with little fairy rings and magic. I guess it's kind of girly."

"Well, you are a girl, and there's nothing wrong with being girly. I'd love to see some of them sometime."

"Do you want to spread the blanket and talk a while?"

"Yeah, I'd love to. It's very intimate here, as long as you don't think a coyote is going to drag us off for dinner."

"You could handle a coyote," I said. "It's the snakes you need to worry about."

"On second thought…" He chuckled.

"We don't have to if you think this is too romantic or something. I mean, I just thought you'd like to see something besides neon and poker chips."

"It's amazing, thanks. And no, I don't mind being out here with you. Even if it is a little on the romantic side of things. I mean, stargazing and all."

"It's not exciting, is it?"

"I'm very excited," he said with a chuckle. "Just being here with you is exciting."

My cheeks burned. "Thanks for entertaining me." I walked to the car, and he followed. When I popped the hatchback, he went for the blanket I kept folded up there, and he spread it out on the ground.

He took my hand, and I sat with him. "I want to lose these shoes," I said. "Do you mind?"

"Get comfortable." He sat beside me and lay back. His knees bent so they stayed on the blanket. "I know I am."

I slipped off the heels and joined him. But before I could say anything, he pointed up to the sky. "Do you see that? It was a shooting star."

"That's an airplane," I said with a laugh.

"No, it's not. Make a wish."

"You know it's a plane." I elbowed his side. "Stop teasing me."

"Look. There's another one."

"That's another plane."

"I don't believe it," he said. "It's a UFO. I'm sure of it."

"I think you're right."

He turned over on his side and faced me. "Why did you want me to be your first?" he asked. "Of everyone else in the world?"

"I like you. I think you're sexy and amazing. You're a nice guy. You're not like secretly married, are you?"

"No, I'm not secretly married."

"Do you have a girl back home?" I wondered about the tattoo and if he'd explain it now.

He smiled. "Not a girlfriend, no."

It didn't make any sense to me why someone hadn't snatched him up already. But then, maybe he was hard to hold. "Why? You're a catch."

"A catch? I guess they keep throwing me back."

"Is there something wrong with you that I'm missing? Because you seem pretty perfect to me." He was more than perfect. At least to my eyes and needs.

Zane made a sound of disagreement. "I'm not perfect. By far."

"You said you had gotten tested after your last relationship. Did something bad happen?"

"Yeah, it ended badly. She cheated on me and stole from me, and a whole lot of other shit I don't want to think about while lying under the stars with you. But I guess I've just been afraid to get back into anything. I put all of my time and energy into making a living and my home life."

"I can see that. It's why I've remained a virgin until now, I guess. I thought I'd lose my V-card a few times, but it didn't happen. I couldn't go that far."

"Well, if it matters, I'm honored to have been your first. I just wish you would have said something. I'm still mad at you for that." He cut me a look with his brows lowered, and it made him look almost pouty, which made my body tingle.

"Why be mad?"

"Because. Are you kidding? Aside from it being *your* special moment, I didn't even get to enjoy knowing I was banging a virgin." He cut me a look and grinned as I nudged him again. "Seriously, though, that's really hot. Not many people wait as long as you did. I'm glad it was me, although I think you deserve better."

It was sweet that he thought that way. "I think I had the best." I rolled over to face him, resting on my palm.

"I'm an ogre," he said. He reached up and tucked a strand of hair behind my ear.

"No, you're not." I nudged him again, and he laughed.

He leaned in and kissed me, and we lay there making out that way for what felt like hours. After, I rested in his arms as we watched the sky, and there really was a shooting star.

I made my wish. I didn't want him to ever leave. And if he did, I wished he'd take me with him.

After an hour passed, my stomach growled so loudly that it was embarrassing. I hoped he didn't hear it, but he turned his head and gave me a nudge. "Let's go back into town and grab something to eat." The suggestion couldn't be a coincidence.

"Okay," I said, sitting up. "I'm not going to complain."

"Well, if that tummy of yours growls any louder, I'm going to think there's a coyote in the shadows." He grinned and got to his feet. He took my hand and pulled me up.

"I'm so embarrassed," I said, rolling my eyes. "I didn't eat much at lunch."

"Do you know a place we can go to? I don't really want to eat buffet food again, no offense."

"None taken. I know just the place."

Zane grinned. "Then I'm game. You know this town better than me." He picked up the blanket and shook it out. Then he folded it and returned it to the back of the car while I got in behind the wheel and started the engine.

When he slid into the seat beside me, he shut the door and leaned over to kiss me.

When he pulled away, I sighed. "Does this mean you still like me?" I asked. "Even though I didn't take your clothes off?"

"The night's still young. But yeah, I like you even if you don't." He stole another kiss and pulled on his seatbelt.

The more I was with him, the more I was falling. *Heartbreak, here I come.*

CHAPTER 21

ZANE

I couldn't believe we'd laid on that blanket without getting naked, but it wasn't because that was all I cared about. After the fun romp in the storage closet, I thought that maybe she had a new scheme, but to my surprise, she didn't.

Her restraint was refreshing, though, and while I couldn't believe I felt that way about her, it was good just to spend some time talking. I wanted to learn more about her than what position she liked best, and even that surprised me.

Since Mila, I had changed. She made me want to be a better man, and in a way, I guessed Tara did too. I wanted to be good to her.

Then it hit me. *Am I falling for her?* I asked myself that as we drove out of the desert. *I think I am.*

"Don't get quiet on me," she said. "You're making me nervous."

"What? Nervous? I've seen you naked."

She grinned, and I loved the way her cheeks would blush anytime I said something naughty. "Do you like pizza?"

"Yeah, I love it." I wanted to tell her how it was one of Mila's favorites and how I liked to take her out to my favorite pizza place at least twice a month when I wasn't in the field, but then, I'd have had to tell her about Mila.

I wasn't sure she even liked kids or what she would think about me for having one and no wife. And of course, having to explain that was something I'd rather not do. I didn't want to spoil the night with Heather-drama. She'd taken enough from me.

We drove back into the city and made our way to the outskirts. She slowed the car and turned into the Cosmopolitan. "Are you taking me to another hotel buffet?"

"No, it's a little place I like to come to with Karen now and then."

"As long as it's not a buffet, I'm in."

"Hey, good things come from buffets, but don't worry. This is pizza, just like I promised, and it's the best."

"Why haven't I heard of it?"

"Because it's a secret." She giggled. "Seriously, it's word of mouth only."

"Okay, I don't know how a place does business like that around here."

She giggled. "They manage."

We entered the building and went to the elevators. "Are you sure you're not taking me to a room?" I asked as the elevator door closed us in alone.

She looked up at me and rolled her eyes. "You wish."

I belted out a laugh, but she captured my mouth, bringing her arms around my neck. We kissed until we reached the third floor.

"Come on," she said, taking my hand. "I'll show you my secret place."

"Mmm. This just keeps getting better." I was still not sure where she was taking me, but when we turned the corner down a long hallway covered with albums, I could tell that it was definitely not what I was expecting.

At the end of that hallway was Secret Pizza, and it wasn't much of a secret at all. The place was busy, and I could see why she liked it there.

"This is amazing," I said. She had really pulled off another surprise.

We found a private spot to sit, which was hard to do, but it was intimate enough that we could chat and hear each other.

"So, how are you not married?" I asked. She had asked me the same thing earlier in the night, and now it was my turn to direct the conversation back at her. "You're beautiful, smart, funny, and not afraid of hard work."

"Must be my coffee-making skills," she said, shaking her head.

"Well, maybe I'll have to give you another lesson." I gave her a wink as our order was brought to us. "I'm serious, though. Don't you want to get married and have a family?"

She blanched, cringing away as if that was the worst topic in the world. "I'd love to find that forever person, but I'm not sure about kids."

I slumped in my seat as she delivered that blow. "No kids ever? But you'd make a great mom."

She shook her head again. "I'm not sure about that, but I'm not saying never. I just don't want any now, and certainly not in this town or anytime soon."

"Oh, I can see that." As long it wasn't a *never* kind of situation. "What would you think about coming up to North Dakota sometime?" I threw it out there, hoping to get a good reaction. If she liked the idea, I was willing to make it happen.

Her brows lifted in surprise. "I'd like that. It would be nice to get away for a while."

A certain sense of satisfaction came over me. I'd love to have her at my house. "You could do some of your photography and painting and take a break from all of this."

"Yeah," she said. "It's just not that easy. I can't take off work for too long at a time. And my job comes first. I have to pay the rent."

I wondered if she lived paycheck to paycheck and struggled. I realized that I didn't know a whole lot about her personal life. "I understand that. But I like that you have responsibilities and make them your priority."

She giggled. "Thanks, but it's not like I have a choice."

"Oh, you'd be surprised. I've seen people let it all go just to get a quick fix of pleasure. It takes someone special who is willing to actually work for a living and keep going without letting it drag them down. I admire that a lot." Mostly because I had seen someone throw her entire life, freedom, and family away for drugs. And she had it all.

"Well, again, thanks. But I want to have a good life and eventually a home of my own someplace where it's quiet and peaceful. I want to hear nature. Not cars and noise pollution. Working and saving is the only way I'll ever have something like that."

I was all of sudden thinking about how I could give her all of those things.

"You'd like my house. I have a big porch on the back, and there are no other houses too close to mine, but I do have a neighbor across the street. It's really quiet." Other than when Mila was tromping through the house, but I wouldn't trade that noise for anything. Just thinking about her laughter made me miss her even more.

We enjoyed our food, both still talking about our lives and what we wanted from them. How work affected things, and how she didn't have a lot but was making it.

She was a strong woman. I loved that about her. She was just perfect for me, aside from the kid thing. Parenthood wasn't for everyone, though, and who was I to impose my life on hers? I couldn't have her resenting me for anything, and especially not Mila, when her life turned out different than she'd imagined.

Asking someone to take on the responsibility of helping you with your kids was a big deal. And if she had any qualms about kids, maybe she wasn't the woman for me after all. As much as it sucked, it was what it was, and Mila came first no matter what.

I'd just have to make the most of the next few days with her, and with any luck, we could keep in touch and see if life ever brought us both to the same path. But dammit, I just didn't want it to end.

"I've had fun tonight, Tara. The stars and the pizza were perfect." I took a drink of my soda and wiped my mouth. "That really was the best pizza I've had in a long time."

"Good, I'm glad you liked it. I felt a little pressure to please since I've been so spontaneous."

"Well, not getting me naked was a surprise."

"The night's still young," she said, wagging her brows as I had earlier.

"No, let's just enjoy each other's company. No more expectations." I was falling for her and was only going to make myself crazy when I had to go back home. "If it happens, it happens. No more plans, right? Does that include instigating?"

"Expectations aren't terrible," she said. "But if that's how you want it." She looked as if she was upset, and the silence stretched out a bit. "Did I say something wrong?"

The questions came from left field. "No, not at all. I guess I just don't want you to think that all I want from you is sex."

"It's not?"

"Damn. Really?" I thought she was past making me feel like a bad guy. "Still thinking the worst about me after all we've been through?"

She shook her head. "That came out wrong. I just mean you want more?" She looked a bit confused, and I could tell she was waiting for me to clarify.

"I meant it's not all I am interested in. I like you, Tara. I have fun with you. And I do hope we can see more of each other."

"You've already seen every part of me," she teased.

"You know what I mean. Would you like that? Maybe even after I've gone home? I thought you might like to keep in touch."

"Of course I'd like that. If you really mean it. I mean, you really want it too?"

"Yeah, is that so hard to believe?" Sometimes, I didn't think she realized how tempting she could be.

"And you're not mentioning me coming out to North Dakota just to be nice, are you? Don't get my hopes up."

"I'd never want to play with you like that, Tara. I don't like games. I don't want to be played with. I've been through that, so I'd never do it."

"Good," she said. "Because I really like you too."

CHAPTER 22

TARA

I had just finished getting ready for work the next morning when Karen showed up at my place. She pounded on the door as if someone was chasing her with an ax. "It's me," she called. "Let me in, Tara. I have to pee!"

I hurried over with my keys in hand and opened the door. "I was just about to leave for work."

She blazed past me and headed for the bathroom. "I know. I came to get a ride in."

"You live closer to work than I do." I didn't understand that logic. "Unless you didn't go home last night." Her hair was a mess.

"Yeah, I didn't. I stayed out all night and met the most amazing man. He was so generous, and well, I guess I was feeling a little generous too." She gave a little giggle.

"That's what you're calling them these days?" Generous? More like desperate and pervy.

"What about you?" she said, flushing the toilet. "Didn't you have a hot night out?" She opened the door and washed her hands.

"It was nice. We talked and made out a little." I had a wonderful time just getting to know Zane better, but I already knew that Karen would say it was boring.

"Made out? You mean you didn't sleep with him again? I figured by the way you two were going at it in the storeroom yesterday, you'd have been all over each other." She wagged her brows and gave me a devilish grin.

"It wasn't like that." I didn't know how to explain it to her without sounding too sappy. "It was just a nice time. We laid under the stars and kissed, and we talked over pizza."

"That sounds romantic." She gave me a glance sideways. "Interesting. Has it already moved to that level? You should be careful."

"It was kind of romantic, I suppose. But it was nice. Relationships are not always about sex, Karen. At least not the ones that are serious."

"Oh? Are you in a relationship with him now?"

"Well, no. But we like each other. He's expressed interest in more. He even invited me to his house sometime when I can manage to get away." I was still trying to figure out how I could manage that one.

I looked at the time on my phone as she swiped on some lipstick in my bathroom mirror. "We're both going to be late if you don't hurry. And I'm not getting in trouble for you today."

Karen rolled her eyes. "Take it easy. We'll be on time." She threw her lipstick in her purse and pulled out her brush.

"No way. I have a mirror in the car. You can brush your hair there." I headed to the door, and she pouted as she followed me out. I locked up, and we went to the parking lot, where I unlocked my car doors.

"So, you drove him out to the desert to your favorite place?"

"Yes."

"Did he call you to make sure you got home after?"

What kind of man did she think he was? "I texted him to let him know because he asked me to. He said he had a good time and sweet dreams."

"Did you at least talk dirty through the text?" she asked. Her game of twenty questions was exhausting. "Come on, Tara. Are you hiding something? It couldn't have been all romance and no passion."

"No, that's it. He knew I had to work. And some of us aren't that needy." My tone was a little harsher than it probably should have been, but I could already tell I was going to have a rough day.

"I'm just asking," she said. "No need to get snippy."

It was quiet the rest of the way in but only because she started texting the man from the night before. She giggled and played with her hair, snapping photos to send him.

I was surprised she'd pulled herself away from him at all to go to work. It wasn't often she found a man she wanted to talk to the next day. It wasn't love, but she was surely interested in his wallet, telling me all about his exciting life. He seemed too good to be true, but I didn't bother with the warnings. If she didn't know by then, she'd never learn.

When we finally arrived at the Golden Flower Buffet, I hurried to the office and clocked in. Then I went about my usual routine as Ben seemed to be amazed Karen was on time for once.

"Did you give her a lift or something?" he asked as he walked over to say good morning.

"Yes. She showed up at my house, so she should take some of the credit for getting here."

"Maybe she should do that every day," he said, straightening his collar.

I hefted up the pan of waffles and moved them to the cart. "Don't give her any ideas."

"Yeah," he said. "I guess the last thing I need is for both of you to be late."

Karen stuck her tongue out at him and kept on walking past him with a cart of plates and utensils. "Just be glad I showed up at all," she said. "After the night I had, I may never have to work again."

"Oh, no," I mumbled. "Karen, be careful. You don't even know him."

"Take it easy. I'm not running away with him or anything. Although it would be very tempting."

I pretended not to hear her as I continued setting up.

After I got things straightened up, I looked up to see that Ben had let in a few of our early patrons, and before I could look away, Zane appeared, shaking Ben's hand.

Beny sat him at my table, and as he breezed past me, he leaned in and winked. "You must have made an impression on him," he said. "He asked for you by name."

I smiled, and behind me, Karen giggled. "Boy, I'll say she's made an impression."

"Hush," I whispered as Ben continued to the kitchen. "I don't need to get him started."

She laughed even harder as I walked over to see Zane, sliding into the chair across from him. "Hello, and good morning. I'm Tara. How may I serve you this morning?"

"Yeah, I'm here for coffee lessons. I'm not sure you got the hang of it last time." He stroked his stubbly chin and gave me a narrowed look.

"Are you kidding? I'm a professional now. Want me to prove it?"

"Yeah, I'll take a cup, if you'll come out with me tonight."

"Hmm, I'm not sure." I shook my head. "I'll have to check my busy schedule."

"Oh? That's how it's going to be, is it? After I was such a gentleman last night? Remind me to misbehave next time."

I felt my cheeks warm with a smile, and I loved that we could joke around and play. "Given my record, *I'm* the one who behaved."

He chuckled. "I'll give you that one. Yes, you certainly and most regretfully kept your control."

Laughter bubbled from me. "Well, I guess I'll say yes then. I mean, since I don't have anything better to do."

"Good, but I'm breaking one of our rules."

"Which rule is that?" I asked.

"The no-plans rule. I already have our evening planned out. I have wanted to see the David Copperfield show, and I want to see it with you."

"Does that mean I can't encourage you to leave early to get you naked?" I didn't want to spoil his evening.

His face lit up with that remark. "You do the magic show with me, and I'll make my clothes disappear any time after."

"That sounds like a plan and a promise," I said.

He placed his hand on mine. "I had fun last night, and I want to spend the rest of my time with you as much as possible."

I couldn't believe he was going to devote the rest of his trip to being with me. He had come out to see his friends and spend time with them.

"What do your friends have to say about that?" I asked, knowing they were probably feeling slighted. He had gone out with me more than them.

He shrugged his shoulders like it wasn't a big deal. "They're fine with it. As long as I'm happy, they're happy for me."

"So, how much time do you have?" As soon as I asked, I regretted it, and by the time he responded, I put my hand up and said, "No, don't tell me. I don't want to know."

His mouth turned down in a disappointed frown. "Let's not think about it, okay?"

"I'm just going to miss you." I couldn't believe I'd said it. While it was true, I didn't want him to know how hard I had fallen for him in such a short amount of time. I wished he could stay or that I could go back with him. It just wasn't possible. Our lives were not prepared for a reset. At least mine wasn't.

He put my hand to his lips and then his heart. "I'll miss you too, and that's why I don't want to dwell on it too much."

I agreed. "Okay, so let's just make sure we spend all the time we can together."

"I like the idea of that. So, does that mean I get to keep you all night?" He gave me a big grin, showing his pearly teeth.

"We'll see." I figured making him wonder was best.

His eyes darkened with a warning stare. "I may have to put my foot down this time if you try to run."

"By the time the night is over, you'll probably be sick of me anyway." He would eventually be done with me and return to his life. Even if he was just taking a break from his friends, I doubted he'd devote the rest of his trip to me like he said he would. "You'll probably go back to your friends."

"Not a chance," he said. "They aren't as beautiful and interesting as you are."

Hearing him say those words made my heart flutter, and I could already tell he'd stolen a part of it that I might not ever get back.

As the crowd grew, I knew I had to get up and get to work. "I should get to it. The natives are getting restless. I'll bring you that coffee if you still want it."

"Hell yeah, I do. I'm going to sip it and stare at my favorite waitress while I think dirty thoughts about her in that storeroom in the back."

"She sounds like a very lucky lady." I gave him a chuckle and got to my feet, laughing when he didn't want to let go of my hand.

After I brought his coffee, he did just what he said he'd do, watching me work. His eyes only left to use his phone.

I brought him some pie when I brought a refill.

"What's this?" he asked. "I didn't order any pie, young lady. You've made a mistake."

I leaned over the table, sticking out my chest even though I wasn't showing any cleavage. "I thought if I kept you busy, you'd have to stick around a little longer."

"Clever girl. I'd love to eat your pie." He dug in the fork and took a bite to his mouth. "Delicious, thank you."

"You're welcome." I walked to another table and offered them a refill too as to not play favorites.

Finally, after stalling it as long as I could, Zane paid his check. "I'll see you later, Tara. Do you want me to pick you up at home?"

"No, it's okay to meet here again." I tried to play nonchalant and not make him suspicious.

"I don't mind."

He wasn't making it easy. "No, Zane. I'd rather meet here." I smiled and nodded to try and play it off.

He finally agreed without further argument, and just when I thought he would slip away without a scene, he leaned in and stole a quick kiss.

"Zane." I felt my cheeks blazing. I glanced around and made sure no one was looking.

"What? You could be my wife for all anyone knows. And I waited until your boss went to the back."

"Well, in that case." I stole another kiss on the cheek. "I'll see you soon."

I stepped away, watching him go and getting a great view of his ass. I was surprised when he glanced back at me and gave me a wink.

When he was finally out of sight, I went back to my tables and managed to keep them all happy somehow. Maybe it was my mood, my own happiness being contagious.

Karen breezed past me on the way to the buffet. "I see lover boy left."

"I think I've gone and done it now," I said with concern in my voice.

"Are you okay?" She put her hand on my shoulder. "Did he say something to you? It seemed like things were good."

"It just hit me. I've already fallen for him. He's going to leave soon, and I'm going to be devastated." My stomach twisted in knots.

"I'm sorry, kiddo, but that's just the way it goes with these Vegas love affairs. They never last. Just treasure what time you have left and get him to fuck you like there's no tomorrow."

"Without him, I'm not sure there is. I don't want to go back to the way it was before he came into my life. It really did suck being alone."

"You'll get back out there soon enough, and you'll find the right man eventually. Until then, have fun, and don't look back." She made it sound so easy, but I was sick inside.

I didn't want anyone else. I wanted Zane Ballard.

No one else would do.

CHAPTER 23

ZANE

After meeting in the hotel lobby, we went down the Strip to the show. As we walked into the theater, I couldn't help but notice she seemed a bit nervous.

"Isn't this exciting?" I asked, wondering if she'd tell me what she felt.

"It is. I still can't believe that you got away from your friends again. They must be pretty sore."

"No. They are too busy trying to get drunk, get laid, and win at gambling to worry about me."

"Oh, I see. Have they met anyone? Even for a night?"

I thought of Clay and how he was determined to fuck up his life. "I don't know. Nick just lost his wife not long ago, so he's taking it easy. We haven't really talked with him about it, but we're all just trying to be sensitive." It was a hard time, and while he was going to get back out there eventually, he was enjoying his trip.

"Oh, that's terrible."

"Yeah, it's pretty sad. They were so in love. It really made me think of how short life is. We really should make the most of things while we can." And that was why I was going to enjoy Tara as much as I could until it was time to leave. Hopefully, if things went well, she would want to stay in touch.

"Yeah, and that's with everything. Not just love."

"Right. Especially who you spend that time with." I could see the two of us spending a lot of time together and her fitting into my life nicely. But as much as she was ready to leave Las Vegas and escape, I knew it wouldn't be that easy. She had put down roots there. And that wasn't something that was solved on a whim. Not when you had responsibilities.

We found our seats, and when I sat, I put my arm around her. "I've wanted to see him since I was a kid," I said. "I even had my parents buy me a magic kit when I was younger, and I learned as much as I could. I would do performances once a night in the living room, and my mother made me a top hat and cape. I called myself the Great Zane-O, and my mom would act as my assistant. It was all fun and games until I wanted a pet rabbit, and they started to encourage me less."

She laughed. "We had a magician come into the Golden Flower once, and he did this trick with water, but what he didn't know was he'd set the trick up wrong, so he ended up spilling water all over the table and the woman he was performing the trick for. She was livid. After that, Ben won't let performers do their tricks."

I thought about Clay's impromptu performances. At least the Golden Flower didn't have a piano lying around.

When David Copperfield took the stage, he hyped up the crowd with an electrifying trick. He elevated a woman in a chair and tilted it to the side. She was screaming and freaking out but managed to keep her seat. The crowd loved it, and so did Tara.

He continued to wow the audience, and I was so wrapped up in the show, I didn't realize it was time for the big finale until he asked for another assistant.

Even though Tara didn't raise her hand, he pointed down to her where we were in the third row. "Could you come and give me a hand, miss?"

"Go on up," I said, encouraging her when she began to blush. "You'll be awesome."

He got her up on the stage before he announced the next trick. "Isn't she lovely, ladies and gentlemen?" The crowd went wild as he led her to a small block that had been put in the middle of the stage. "But I'm afraid I'm going to have to make her disappear."

The crowd booed, and I felt a sting in my chest as I thought about what he was saying. He was going to make her disappear. A world without Tara would be a tragedy indeed, and I didn't like the idea of it.

I shifted in my chair as he had her step into a ring. The ring was surrounded by silk, and when he pulled it up, he gave it a shake. The silk billowed as it covered her, and when he pulled it away, she was gone.

I swallowed hard, and I moved to the edge of my seat. Then I felt a hand on my knee.

Tara appeared beside me, and the spotlight shone on her. The audience went wild. She was grinning ear to ear and a little winded.

"How did you do that?"

"I didn't," she said. "It was Copperfield."

As the master of magic ended his show, I took her hand, and we filed out. "How did he do it?" I asked. "And don't tell me that they had you sign a disclaimer because you didn't have time."

"A magician never reveals his secrets, and neither does his faithful assistant."

"You weren't his assistant. You were from the audience. Now tell me. It was a trap door, right? Did you fall down into the floor and land on a pile of pillows?"

"In this skirt?" she asked, rolling her eyes. "No way. Although I do think the man at the bottom of the steps had a good peek up my skirt."

I frowned. "That's not funny. Do I need to go and defend your honor? Because I've suddenly got an itch to punch someone."

"Oh, come on. You're teasing me."

"Am not. I don't want anyone else seeing you."

She turned her face down and turned her eyes up at me. "What does that mean exactly?"

I hadn't really thought it out, but I knew I didn't want her to be with anyone else. I also didn't want her being gawked at or pawed at. The more I thought about it, the angrier I got. I pulled her into my arms and kissed her, causing her to stumble. She caught herself against me, though I would have never let her fall.

"Right now, all I want to think about is you and me."

"I like the sound of that," she said, trying to catch her breath. While anyone else might have pressed me for more answers, Tara was content to just let the topic go for the time being.

But I had something to say. "I didn't like the idea of you disappearing," I admitted.

"Well, don't worry. I won't disappear on you tonight." She took my hand as we left the building, stepping out into the night air.

She looked beautiful. "Good, because I'm not letting you go. Did you want to go get something to eat before we go up to my room?"

"You really don't plan on taking no for an answer."

"Not tonight," I said, pulling her closer. "But only because I don't think you want to leave."

"I don't." She looked deep into my eyes. "I don't have anywhere else I'd rather be."

We took a cab back to the Golden Flower. Neither of us were able to keep our hands off of one another on the way. I slipped my hand up her skirt and got a feel of how wet she was for me.

"You are eager tonight, aren't you?" I whispered in her ear.

Her hand moved over the front of my pants, causing my cock to grow even harder, pushing at the seams. By the time we got into the elevator, I was so worked up, I didn't know if I was going to make it all the way up to my room. But I managed somehow.

As soon as we hit the hall, I hurried her down to my suite, and when we went inside, I put out the do not disturb sign and locked the door.

"No getting away from me now," I teased.

"You say that like I'd try." She rolled her eyes and put her arms around my neck. "Now, where were we?"

"Right about here," I said, reaching for my buttons. "Take your clothes off."

"Wasting no time, I see."

"I want to watch, and I want you to stay naked."

"The whole time?" she asked, her eyes lit with surprise. "What if I get cold?"

I laughed. "You won't. I'm going to keep you warm. And we have blankets." I finished with the last button and peeled my shirt off, throwing it to the chair beside us.

Tara turned reached for her hip and unzipped her skirt. She slowly slipped it down to reveal the pretty pink panties she wore beneath it. As she worked on her shirt, which had a few more buttons than I'd realized, she stepped out of it.

I reached down and picked it up, placing it in the chair with my clothes. She took off her shirt, revealing her matching bra. Her body was amazing. Every peak and valley was mine to explore, and my body was still responding. My cock begged to be free.

I didn't move to take my pants off, though. I was too wrapped up in watching her remove her bra.

As her thumbs hitched into the elastic of her panties, I shook my head. "No, leave those on."

"Hmm, that's going to make things interesting," Tara said with a giggle. "But what about you? You're not even naked yet. You're being very unfair to me and my eyes."

"Take it," I said, glancing down at my big bulge with a challenging tone.

She licked her lips and stepped closer, reaching for my belt. "If I have to be naked, then so do you." She undid my belt and stripped it off in one quick pull before tossing it to the floor. She undid the button and the fly, and my cock was already forcing its way out.

I helped her get my pants down, but she surprised me by dropping to her knees. She looked up at me and smiled. "You said to take it. That means it's mine now."

I loved the way she tried to take charge—and even more so when she began sucking my dick. She took it deeper than usual, relaxing her throat as if she was going to try something new.

As her body responded, gagging a little on the fleshy shaft, she pulled out and looked up at me with watery eyes.

She began to stroke me and took it back into her mouth, making love to it, worshiping it. As my head began to spin, I doubted I could ever get enough of her.

I was falling for her way harder than I'd expected.

CHAPTER 24

TARA

Zane was in a rare mood, and I was going to take advantage of it. I could tell he was surprised when I did exactly what he'd said and took his cock in my mouth.

Even though I was sure he had just wanted me to undress him, I was going to take the opportunity to make sure the tables were turned. He had insisted that he wasn't going to let me go, but we'd see how things went in the morning. Until then, I wasn't going to get my hopes up. Or at least, I was going to try not to.

Each time I was with him, I was only hurting myself more and more by falling harder, but the pain was something that was put aside while I was in the moment with him. Eventually, it was going to come crashing down, and when that happened, I wasn't sure my heart would survive it.

I focused on my actions, trying to push the thoughts from my mind, and apparently, I was doing a good job because Zane had really gotten into it. He moaned and rocked his hips, and his hand rested on my head.

"That's so good," he said, taking my arm. "Come up here." He encouraged me to my feet. "I need to be inside of you." He stepped closer, kissing me full on the mouth, and removed my panties before he lifted me up against him, scooping me up from where I stood.

He carried me to the bed, and after he planted me on my back, he quickly dropped his pants and kicked off his shoes, leaving them at the end of the bed. "Scoot to me," he said. "I want you right here." He pointed to the bed in front of him.

I moved closer, letting my ass touch the edge of the bed. My feet landed on the floor, or at least, my toes did. But they didn't stay on the floor long. Zane lifted my legs by the ankles and parted them wide, stepping between them and rubbing his cock up my middle.

The anticipation of him sliding inside of me was enough to nearly push me over the edge, and he hadn't even put it inside me.

Zane's eyes burned into mine, and it was as if he had something to say, but instead, he said it with his actions. He pushed the tip inside, and while it wasn't the widest part of him, it made me whimper.

All was well when he pushed farther, burying his cock deep inside of me, so deep his heavy sac pressed against my ass.

"Does it feel okay?"

"No." I shook my head, wrapping my legs around him to keep him close. "It feels wonderful."

He chuckled. "Good. I want to make you feel wonderful. Always."

I relaxed and let him thrust into me, pounding me harder, his hips working like a machine, hammering away at my core. He had me filled so full that I thought I'd come apart at the seams, and when I found my release, it was after such a buildup that I lost all inhibitions.

I raised up on my elbow and turned on my side, bringing one leg forward. Zane growled out in pleasure, gripping my hips. He spanked my ass, giving it a little slap, and the heat sent a lick of sweet pleasure through me as he rubbed it.

"What was that for?" I asked, wondering if he wanted to get kinky.

But he smiled. "Did it feel good?"

"Yes," I said.

"That's why. You've got the sexiest ass. I couldn't help myself."

As if he was dropping hints, I moved again, rolling from my side to my stomach, and he moved forward as I got on my knees and backed into him.

"Mmm," he said. "You are going to spoil me when you start giving me what I want, Tara. I didn't mean you had to turn over for me."

"It feels good like this." He hit my most sensitive spot, and that only made my pleasure more intense.

"Even better," he said, leaning over me to cup my breasts, which were slapping together from the motion.

"I get a better view of your ass, but I have to say, I miss your eyes." He whispered in my ear. "Look back at me, Tara."

I turned my head and met his eyes, and his look was intense, like he could reach his climax at any moment.

I wanted it too. I wanted him to give it all to me, as if by doing so, I'd keep a part of him with me. *Careful, a voice told me. You don't want to end up with a kid.*

Thank goodness I was on birth control. I pushed the voice from my head and tried to throw caution to the wind. I was more concerned with my heart getting broken.

As he worked me steadily, the pressure got more and more intense, and it wasn't but a minute later that I orgasmed. Zane kept riding me. "Fuck," he said. "You're milking my cock. Don't stop."

His breath hit my ear, and I rode the wave of pleasure until I found myself falling into the pillow, but Zane didn't stop. He kept pounding and pounding as if he were punishing my little pussy. It was bliss.

"I'm going to come, Tara."

"Don't stop, Zane. Come inside of me." I closed my eyes, and he quickened his pace even more. And as my next orgasm found me, he gave me one more hard thrust and stilled, holding me against him, pumping his sweet nectar inside of me as I milked him for every drop.

He leaned forward and kissed my shoulder as he slipped out of me. "That was amazing, Tara. And the next round is going to be even better."

I was spent, or so I thought. I rolled over to my back and saw him pumping his cock in his fist. I saw how he was still hard and ready to go, and I was instantly turned on, my need for pleasure amped up even more than before.

"Do you need a moment?" he asked.

I couldn't believe he didn't need a moment. "Nothing but you inside of me again."

"I'm going to have that little pussy sore by the time we're done. If you want a rest, it's fine. I understand. I'll be okay."

"I'm serious," I said. "I'm ready for more." I wanted him to stop treating me like I was so delicate. "Do your best to break me. Just not my heart." I gave a little giggle to play it off.

Zane chuckled as he moved between my legs, centering his cock. "We have all night, remember?" His warning glace was giving me the chance to back out and take a break. "Because I'm not letting you go. And once this gets started, it's going to go on for a while, and I'm primed for round two, baby. Are you sure?"

"Are you trying to talk me out of it?" I asked, not at all missing the fact that he'd called me baby.

"No, but just giving you a chance now. Once I'm back inside of you, I'm not leaving there for hours."

"Promise?" I moved my hips, rubbing against his thick head.

He chuckled. "I guarantee it."

I met his eyes. "Good, because I don't ever want it to end, Zane." I wondered if he could catch what that meant.

When he met my eyes and gave a little nod, I knew he did. It was his next words that had my heart burning inside my chest. "I don't want it to end either, baby."

With that, he slowly entered me, and I felt all of the feelings I had been too afraid to feel. Not only was it pure ecstasy, but there was no doubt in my heart that I was in love with him.

I felt as though I had a dangerous secret, something that I couldn't ever speak of for fear it would all go away.

But then, it *was* going away. He'd leave, like it or not, back to his life in North Dakota.

As I shuddered, he slowed his thrusts and looked at me. "Are you okay? I can stop if you need me to."

"No. I'm good. It feels so good, I'm drifting."

He chuckled. "Stay here with me." He pointed to his eyes. "Look at us, Tara." He turned his eyes down to get a look at us, at what we were doing. He slowed his hips. "Does that feel good?"

I nodded quickly in response. "Yes," I said breathlessly. "You're amazing."

"No, we are. We're amazing together."

Us? Together? Those words could sure fool a girl into thinking this was more, but I couldn't let that happen.

It was hours and multiple orgasms later, and we were both worn out, having slowed down to rest and kiss after many positions.

He laced his fingers into mine up over my head and whispered in my ear. "Are you ready for this?"

I felt his cock twitch as if it were waiting for my go ahead.

I nodded, and he worked his hips steadily, clapping against my body until he found his release, and as he pumped inside of me, he leaned down and kissed me hard.

After, he gathered me close, planting kisses all over me. "You were amazing," he said. "I didn't want to stop, but you look like you're about to pass out."

He rolled over onto his back, and I made a move to get up and go to the bathroom, but he caught my hand. "Where are you going?"

"To the bathroom," I said, giving him a smile as he seemed to relax. "I'll stay if you really want me to."

"I don't say things I don't mean, Tara."

"Good to know," I said. "I'll be right back." I headed into the bathroom, and when I came back, he had straightened the covers and was lying in bed with his arms up over his head.

"Come here." He curled his finger at me, and I went over to get under the covers.

He pulled me closer and snuggled me up against his body. I felt so safe in his strong arms, secure in his warmth.

It was nice for a change, and I fell asleep, hoping that he wouldn't put me out early in the morning. There was always that chance.

Things had a way of coming to light the morning after.

CHAPTER 25

ZANE

The morning light shone in from the balcony window, casting its glow across the angel in my arms. I kissed her forehead and held her closer. I didn't want to disturb her, and yet, I couldn't wait for her to wake up in my arms and kiss me good morning.

The night before had been so good, I was still basking in the afterglow. It had been so long since I'd gone for hours like that, and I was impressed I still had it in me. But then she made it easy and brought it out of me. I wanted to please her, and I hadn't wanted to please anyone that way in a long time. Hell, not even Heather, back when it was still good.

Tara made a little moan, and I smiled, thinking of how she'd panted the night before. I'd had her squealing at one point, wiggling on my cock like she didn't know which end was up. It was hot as fuck, and my cock was getting hard just remembering.

She was special. That was for sure. I wasn't going to leave Las Vegas without telling her how I felt about her. It had happened all of a sudden. One minute, I was just seeking some company, and the other, I couldn't imagine my life without her in it.

I only hoped that she was willing to work something out.

She stirred beside me and opened her eyes. She blinked a few times at the ceiling, so I leaned in and kissed her neck. "Good morning, sexy."

She rolled over and snuggled closer, pulling the covers over her head. "I look horrible."

"Are you kidding? You could never look horrible." She was not only the sexiest woman I'd ever laid eyes on but the prettiest. "I like you with sleepy eyes."

"Ugh, I don't have a toothbrush," she said.

"I do. There's an extra one in the bathroom."

She made a move to escape, but I put my leg across her hips. "Not so fast, sweetheart," I said, keeping her with me.

Tara giggled. "Stop it. I have morning breath."

"So what? We both do. I want to hold you."

That seemed to get her attention. "I figured you'd be ready to get rid of me," she said.

"Oh no, you don't get away that easily. We're going to go and have breakfast together today. Anywhere you want."

"No buffet. I'm not going there on my day off."

I could relate to that. I didn't want to go anywhere near the man camps when I was on furlough. "I don't blame you. We could go anywhere you want."

"I'm starving."

"Me too." I could use a bite, considering we'd gone straight back to the hotel room instead of having dinner.

"There's a little grill up on the other side of town, and they have the best steak and eggs you'd ever have anywhere in your life. If you want, we can go there. My car is here."

"Okay." I kissed her shoulder and let out a sigh. "But I wanted to stay like this."

She giggled and pushed my leg off of her.

"Run while you can," I said as she got up from the bed and walked naked across the room. "Fuck, she's hot."

I had a lot on my mind, and getting back inside of her was part of it. I tried to refrain from being a Neanderthal and settled for breakfast instead of sex.

A half an hour later, we were sitting at a small table in the little grille, holding hands and laughing like a couple.

"This is fun. I'm usually just sitting at home and listening to the radio at this point on my usual days off."

"Well, I'm glad that you had some time off. I haven't spent this much time with anyone in a long time, and it's kind of nice." It was amazingly nice, but I was trying to keep my excitement to a minimum.

She shifted in her chair as she giggled. "I've never done this morning after before, so it's all new to me."

"And I like that too. I am glad you haven't been with anyone but me. You're a good girl, Tara. I'm used to the bad ones. So, it's really inspiring."

She glanced around the room as if everyone had heard me. "It doesn't bother you? That I don't have the kind of experience some women do?"

How could she think there was anything wrong with being a little inexperienced? "No, I want all of your experiences to be with me," I said. "Look, Tara. It's been a great week with you. And I'm enjoying this so much that I don't want it to end. But I want to talk to you about something really important. I haven't exactly told you everything about me." I had been contemplating how to bring up my daughter, but it always seemed like a terrible time.

Her face fell. "You're married." She held her stomach and backed up her chair.

"No, I'm not. I haven't lied to you. Look. Let's just finish eating, and we'll talk."

She agreed, but I could tell she was nervous. Maybe I shouldn't have brought it up at breakfast. I was about to go ahead and tell her when my phone rang.

"Hey, it's my parents. I really should take this." I got up and stepped away from the table before she had time to protest.

I stepped around the corner near the men's room and answered. "Hey," I said.

"Zane, darling, it's Mom. I'm sorry to call you so early, but you should know that the Jenkinses called us. They said that there was someone at your house and that they were pretty sure it was Heather. Sarah Beth couldn't find your number, but she said that she and her husband both heard things being broken, so they called the cops."

"Jesus," I said under my breath.

"We're on our way home now, and—"

"You're what?"

"Well, we had already left, and we didn't want to upset you or make you feel like you had to leave your trip early, but Mila was ready to get back home, and your father has never liked traveling away for more than a few days."

"Do not go home, Mom! She might be there, and I don't think you or Dad could stop her if she wanted to take Mila from you. She's dangerous." I couldn't believe this was happening. "I only stayed here because I thought you were out of town too!"

I looked up to find Tara standing just feet away. I wasn't sure what she'd heard, but she could tell I was upset. "I have to go. Go to Elaine and Mark's house. I'm on my way. First flight out."

"Oh, honey. Be safe. I didn't want you to cut anything short."

"I have to go." I hung up the phone, and Tara walked over.

"I paid the tab," she said.

"What? No, I have it."

"It's done. Don't worry about it."

"I'll give you the money back," I said, taking out my wallet. I pulled out a couple of twenties and offered them.

"No, thanks. I'm going to go."

"Tara, wait. I want to talk to you."

She seemed really upset. "Look. It's been a lot of fun, Zane, but you're going home now, and I don't know what you have to rush home to, and frankly, I don't really care. I had a blast, but I think we should just leave things on a good note and say our goodbyes here."

"What? Why?"

"Look, I don't want to get hurt, okay? You have your life, and I have mine. And I just think that you and I want different things. That's all. You're a good guy from what I know of you, and last night, well, it was amazing, but I'm afraid that's all I can take."

She sounded so final, and all I could think about was my psychopath ex trashing my house and coming after my child. And that stupid security system that was supposed to alert me. I went into the app and found where it had cut itself off pending an update as she stood there ending things.

"I still think we should talk, Tara. There are a lot of things that I need to say, and it's just a bad time."

"I think parting ways here is best."

She couldn't mean it. Things were going so well. "I'll call you," I said.

She shook her head. "No, you don't have to do that. Let's just leave things as they are."

She turned and walked away from me, leaving me standing in the middle of the diner.

So that was it? She just dumped me and walked out on me. And I was so wrapped up in my ex's bullshit that I couldn't deal with it. I wanted to punch a fucking wall. I swore to myself that Heather would never lay eyes on my girl, and here she was, trying to steal her.

And as if it wasn't bad enough, she had ruined things with Tara and me as well. I wasn't sure I could repair them.

I hurried back to my hotel room and packed my shit, throwing it in the suitcase as if there wasn't a moment to spare. I called the airport, and after a thirty-minute game of phone tag, I had booked my flight.

I had to call the guys, but when I walked to their rooms, they were not around. I decided that while waiting on my flight, I should reset that fucking camera app.

I got it up and running, and the first thing I got was an alert. I watched the stored footage of the bitch doing her damage. She not only broke her way into the house through the side window, but she had gone all through the house, including my daughter's room.

Thank God she wasn't home. I still couldn't believe my parents had headed back without telling me. But I should have warned them about Heather being out. I had made the decision not to, and if I had, then maybe they wouldn't be on their way back. It was too dangerous for my daughter, and I could only hope that my father wouldn't think he could handle her on his own.

As I finished with the app, I heard a commotion outside. Was it the guys returning? I hurried out to find Nick and Rylen, but Clay wasn't anywhere to be found.

"Hey, I'm going home," I said.

Nick froze in his tracks. "What happened? Is it your parents? Mila?"

"No, it's Heather. She trashed my fucking house last night looking for her. The neighbors called my parents, who are on their way back home already."

Nick's eyes widened. "Shit, you don't think Heather would hurt them, do you?"

"To get to Mila, anything is possible. I just can't believe I didn't notice my fucking house alarm app needed updating or else I'd have seen this last night." I took the phone and held it up to show them the footage.

"Damn," said Rylen. "That's fucking bad."

"Where's Clay? I wanted to tell him that I'm going home. He's expecting us to fly back together in a couple of days."

"We'll tell him if you leave before he gets back, but honestly, I'm not sure where he is."

"I'll call him," I said, dialing his number.

Nick frowned. "Man, I'm sorry about all of this. And just when you and Tara were hitting it off. That went well, didn't it?"

"Yeah, it was perfect until my parents called. Look, man. I have to leave in less than an hour. I should get my shit together and go see Grady on my way to the airport."

"I'll ride along," said Nick.

"Me too," said Rylen. "We'll see you off."

"Thanks." It was nice to know I could depend on my friends, even if I couldn't depend on Tara.

I felt horrible that I had kept Mila from her, and from then on, I vowed to never hold back from her again, if I could ever get her back.

First things first, I had to make sure Heather didn't get away with what she'd done.

CHAPTER 26

TARA

I hurried from the restaurant and back to my house, where I turned up the music and went on a cleaning spree that would make a germaphobe proud.

I had to get him out of my head, and the only way to do that was to work through everything that had happened between Zane and me. Then I could accept that it wasn't going to happen again.

Not only had he broken my heart, but he had lied to me. There had been some secret he'd been holding on to, and just when he was getting the balls to tell me, he had to take off? I wasn't buying it. I had a feeling he'd had one of his stupid friends call and try to make something up so he could bail on me.

I should have known from the start that he was too much for me, too good to be with me, and out of my league.

I wiped away my tears and kept dusting, taking aside each and every little item in my house, which surprisingly was much more than I'd realized, and wiping them clean.

With each new item, I thought of the ways I liked him, and I dissected them, picking apart what must have been the truth all along.

He had to be in a relationship.

What else could have him rushing back home in such an angered state? All of those precious, sweet things he'd said to me were just to get into my panties.

And I had fallen for it. I was so stupid to think it could have been real. Las Vegas romances rarely were.

Just as I was about to kick the walls down and live in the back alley, I decided I needed to get out of there. I grabbed my bathing suit and sunscreen and hurried out to the car. I was going to get in some fun if it killed me.

I drove the short distance to the Golden Flower and went directly to the pool. I found my favorite spot and tried to think of anything but Zane as the sun beat down on me.

I put on some sunscreen, and it was a good thing. I ended up falling asleep, and it wasn't until I heard Karen's voice that I roused.

"What the fuck are you doing here?" she asked, taking to her chair. "I came here to sulk, and I didn't think I'd find you here. Where's Zane?"

I made a face, and her eyes lit as if she understood. "What did he do? Do you want me to go kick his ass? Because I will."

"He's gone." I waved my hand dismissively as if it wasn't a big deal.

"Gone? Oh, he had to leave today, or did something else happen?"

I debated playing it off as if nothing was wrong, and he hadn't broken my heart. "Both," I said, not sure if I could talk about him without crying.

Karen sighed. "You're going to have to explain. What happened, Tara? Did he hurt you?"

"Just my heart," I said. "He wasn't who I thought he was. It turns out he had some secret he needed to tell me. And he got this call from his parents, and he took off. I'm so stupid. The way he talked to me last night—calling me baby and telling me how pretty I was and how he didn't want it to end—it was all a lie."

"What a dick," she said. "So what was the big secret?"

"I don't know, and I don't care. He got a call and had to take it privately. He said it was his parents, but who knows?"

Karen grumbled. "Why do men do shit like tell lies, knowing we're going to learn the truth sooner or later?"

"Why do they wait until we love them to spring the truth on us? Why not let me down days ago?"

"I'm so sorry," she said. "You love him?"

"Sadly, I do. It's okay. I'll be fine. I just have to get him out of my system."

"The best way to do that is to start dating someone else. Fall off one horse, and you get back on another. Which is why I'm going to go out tonight and find me another man."

"I'm pretty sure that's not how that saying goes, and I thought you were happy with the latest tourist?"

She rolled her eyes. "He was a liar too. Turns out, he's not rich, he's married, and he has kids."

"Poor kids. They'll be the ones to suffer." I hated to see kids dragged into the middle of adult problems. I'd lived my entire childhood that way.

"Poor kids? Poor me." She flagged the waiter and ordered herself a drink. "Do you want anything? It's on me."

"No, thanks. I seriously can't think about food or eating or anything. I just miss him already."

"You miss the idea of him, that fake idea you had of who he was. He's not that person and never was."

No, he hadn't been. Was any part of what he told me true? "Then I'll be mad at myself for falling for a fake person."

"Hell no, you be angry with him today. But you go out with me *tonight*. We'll find you another man." She patted me on the leg like it was all set, and that was how it should be. Like I was just supposed to move onto another man like I hadn't ever met Zane.

But Karen didn't get it. "I don't want another man. I want Zane. He said he'd call me, and I told him he didn't have to. I'll probably never hear from him again, and if so, it's my own fault."

"Longing for him isn't healthy. You just determined he's a liar, a bad guy, and yet, you miss him."

I knew she wouldn't get it. She moved from man to man as often as she shaved her legs. "Leave me alone. I'm not used to this." He had really made me fall for him.

"Fine," she said, closing her eyes. "I'm going to soak up some sun. You sit there and cry, and it will all be a memory soon enough."

We stayed in the sun for a while longer in silence as I thought of how final things were. Over and done, just like that.

My phone rang, catching my attention. I held my breath as I glanced at it, and I nearly tossed it in the pool when I saw Ben's name across the screen. "Dammit."

I didn't know whether to ignore him or not. If he wanted me to work, I could use the distraction and the money.

"Who is it?" asked Karen. "Is it him?"

"No, it's Ben. He's probably calling me into work, and I just don't know if I want to."

"Tell him no." She made a face and adjusted her sunglasses to stare at a man across the pool. He was older and balding but had a nice body.

"I don't know. I may just go in and get the extra money. I could use it for rent."

"No," said Karen. "Take the day to heal. Besides, you don't want to run into Zane while he's leaving."

"He's probably already gone." My phone stopped ringing, and I let out a breath, realizing I'd just missed the opportunity to earn money. Zane really had messed me up.

"Let's find out if he's left," she said. "What name is his room under?"

"Zane Ballard, maybe? I not sure. It was one of the special suites, and his friend paid for it." Unless that too was a lie. Who knew what Zane had lied about? If that was, in fact, his real name. Maybe it was something else, and his friends had all used aliases.

Karen called the front desk anyway. We knew the lady who worked it, and Karen came right out and asked her about it. "Did a man from the special suites check out this morning?" She went quiet, waiting on the woman's response. "I see, thanks."

She ended the call and gave me an apologetic look. "She said he checked out about twenty minutes ago. I'm sorry, Tara. I know you really liked him."

"It's okay. I just gave him my virginity and my heart. It's not like I married him."

"It's bullshit. He stole them both with his lies. You deserve better."

My phone began to ring again. "It's Ben. He's not giving up. I should just answer it. What's the worst it could be? Do I have to go to work? It isn't as painful as losing Zane."

Karen shook her head. "You didn't lose him. He missed out. *You* dodged a bullet. Think of it as a good thing. You know better now. And if he does call you, you can tell him off."

I gave her a hard look and answered the call. "Hey, Ben. What's going on?"

"I need you to come up here this evening for the dinner crew," he said in a demanding voice. "Melinda is sick, and you're the only one I know who can hustle the way she can."

"Okay, fine." I needed the money too badly to turn down the chance. As tired as I was, I had no choice but to work when called. "But I am not staying after closing. The others can clean up. I want to be home in bed early for my shift tomorrow."

"It's a deal. I'll see you later. Be here at five."

"Okay, fine." I hung up the phone, and Karen shook her head, giving me a look that said how unimpressed she was.

"I can't believe you caved in and are going in to work. You are overly emotional right now, and then you're going to pack on a load of work on what's the first day off you'll have for days?"

"Look, some of us have to pay our own bills. I'm not going to scam every tourist in town to do it. So, give me a break, okay?"

"Fine." She turned her eyes to meet mine. "More for me."

"You can have them all, thank you. I don't ever want to fall in love again." I got up from the lounger and grabbed my bag. "I'm going to go. I need to shower off this lotion and do my laundry before my shift."

"I'm really sorry about what happened. I hope you know that you can always talk to me when you need to. It hurts now, but it won't hurt for long."

I knew she meant well. She was trying hard to be a good friend and was saying all the things a good friend should. "Thanks, I'll see you later."

She smiled and got to her feet. "Wish me luck. I think I just found my next meal ticket."

I glanced across the pool where the older man was smiling at Karen. I shook my head and walked away.

After walking to my car and looking for Zane along the way, hoping he'd stuck around to see me, to talk things over, I gave into reality and headed home.

As I walked into my shitty apartment, I realized that maybe I hadn't been honest either. I hadn't let Zane see the real me, and maybe all he had to tell me was something simple?

"Nah, it couldn't be." And even so, if that were the case, he would have called me by now if he really cared. I glanced at my phone, still finding no new messages.

CHAPTER 27

ZANE

While waiting on my plane, Rylen, Nick, and I went to Grady's house for a quick goodbye. Even though I wasn't ready to leave, I couldn't wait to get home and give Heather what she had coming.

When we arrived at Grady's house, we were relieved to find that Clay had crashed there.

"What happened to you last night?" I asked as he came out to the kitchen from his shower.

They had all gathered there for a bite of breakfast, and even I was up for the fancy omelets Grady was whipping up.

"I had a blast, but I also had too much to drink. I ended up passing out in the car, so Grady just brought me here. I slept on that lumpy sofa, and I'm pretty sure my back will never be the same."

"It was as far as I could carry you," said Grady, who plated an omelet with onions for Nick. "Be lucky I didn't leave your ass in the car or on the floor."

"Thanks," mumbled Clay. He turned his attention back to me. "What's up with you?"

"I'm going home."

"Oh man, did your night with Tara suck that bad? Did she make fun of your tiny dick?"

I saw his eyes move to Nick, who was standing behind me. When I glanced over my shoulder, he was shaking his head and giving Clay a warning glance.

"It's Heather. But yeah, I'm pretty sure shit is all fucked up with Tara too now. I hadn't told her about Mila. Not because I was ashamed to be a father or anything, but she was a stranger, and I didn't realize I'd fall for her. When I was going to tell her, my mother called about Heather's latest stunt."

"What did she do now?" asked Clay

"She trashed my house."

"I thought you have security?"

"No, I have cameras, but they were updating, so I missed it. I was with Tara, and let's just say my phone was the last thing on my mind. I knew Mila was safe with my parents, who, by the way, are already on their way home and will probably be there before me. And who will most likely not take my advice to stay away from their house."

"Shit," said Clay. "I'll come with you, man. You shouldn't see Heather all alone. You'll kill her."

"No, I'm going alone. I'll be fine. You just stay and enjoy yourself." I was liable to kill him on the way if he kept up his shenanigans. "I'm not going to kill her. I'd never hurt her, though God knows I've thought about it. She's Mila's mother. Besides, I can't hurt her any more than she's already hurt herself."

"That's the truth," said Grady. "She's going to keep fucking up until they lock her away for good." He flipped another omelet off the griddle and onto Rylen's plate.

"She's done it. Trashing my house, disobeying a restraining order, on top of other things. She's going back in for a long time. I'm making sure of it. I bet she's already high." It made me sick that she had her freedom. She didn't deserve to be out.

"Man, I'm sorry," said Nick. "I don't know why people can't just do right for their kids."

I glanced at Clay.

"I hear you, man." Clay hadn't been there for his own kid. "I'm going to try to do better for mine."

"That's good to hear," I said. I was afraid he was really going to screw things up and lose his rights. Beth wasn't the type of woman who played around.

Grady pushed a plate in front of me, and soon, there was no talking, only lips smacking.

"That was so good," said Nick, breaking the silence. He had gobbled his up in a matter of bites.

"Yeah, thanks, Grady." I took another bite of mine.

Rylen finished his next and got to his feet. "Come on, Nick. Let's play a game of nine-ball. I've got five bucks that say I'll beat you my first round."

"You're on," he said. "I'll break."

They left, and Grady finished making his own omelet and joined Clay and me at the table. "So, did your girl end it?"

"She just came up while I was on the phone with my mom, and I told her there was something I had to tell her. I don't know what she heard of my conversation, but I was talking about Heather and Mila, so I know she's probably putting shit together in her head. Add that to the tattoo on my chest, and I'm pretty sure she thinks Mila is my wife or girlfriend. She didn't even give me time to explain, and she told me not to call her. I was so dumbstruck with everything going on that I didn't try to stop her."

"Damn, you should have gone after her," said Clay. "I mean, you do seem to care about her."

"Yeah, but at that moment, all I could think about was my house and Heather trying to take my kid. I didn't have time to worry about anything else."

"Shit," said Grady. "That's understandable. I mean, she could have waited around to see. Maybe she isn't worth it."

"Maybe I think I'm in love with her." I knew I was. Pretending I wasn't sure was a way to make it not hurt so badly.

"Seriously?" asked Clay. "You just met her. You don't even know her."

That didn't make any sense to me. No one knew anyone until they did. What difference did it make how long it took to fall in love with her? It only took a moment to realize it, and after that, it just was.

But I couldn't explain that to Clay. "It doesn't matter, man. I've gotten to know her, and I love everything about her. She is a good woman. And I need a good woman in my life. In Mila's life."

"You think she would want to be in Mila's life? Like a mother? She doesn't even know about her. So, you're just guessing. What if she hates kids?" Clay had brought up a few of my worst fears.

I wasn't going to let that get me down. "How could anyone hate Mila?" My daughter was perfect and good. She was sweet and smart and funny. Just like Tara. "They'd get along great. She'd be a better mother than Heather."

"No matter how wonderful Mila is, being a mother is a big deal."

Says the man who is fucking up his own family. I wasn't going to throw that in his face.

"If you really feel that way, then you should try and call her before you leave. Talk it out."

I shook my head. "There's no time. I came here to say goodbye and check on Clay. I guess I need time to sort it all out. I can't bring her into this shit show." I glanced at my watch. "Shit, I've got to go. I have to catch my plane in twenty minutes. By the time I get to the airport, I'll have no time." I got up from the table and carried my plate to the sink.

"Come on," said Grady, abandoning his plate. He grabbed his phone. "I'll have you there in no time." He made a call and went to get his wallet. "The car will be ready when you are."

"I want to ride," said Clay, scraping the last bit of his eggs into his mouth. "I want to see what the bitch did to your house. You still have the footage, don't you?"

A few minutes later, we said goodbye to Nick and Rylen, who stayed behind, still playing their game for money. Then we got in Grady's limo, and his driver set out to take me to the airport.

Clay sat across from me, looking at the footage of Heather destroying my house. The only room she hadn't destroyed was Mila's.

"Man, she's really breaking your shit," said Clay. "Oh, was that your collector cars?"

I gave him a hard look. "I'm glad it amuses you. And yes, it was my fucking collector cars. The ones my dad and I built together." I had to remind myself that it was all just things. As long as Mila was safe, she was the only thing that mattered.

"So, what's Tara's last name?" asked Grady. He was typing on his phone.

"Wright, why?" I didn't like the sound of the question. It made me wonder what he was up to.

"No reason," he said. "I just have a friend who is a PI, if you want me to have them check her out. He's the best in the area, and he owes me a favor."

I wondered how a PI could owe him a favor. I probably didn't want to know, but it seemed that Clay had met a vast array of colorful people in his life.

"What? No way. Thanks anyway, but it's not like that. I just need time to deal with this shit at home, and then I'll reach out to her and straighten it out. If it's meant to be, she'll be there. It'll give me the time I need to think, and with any luck, it will all work out. If not, then I guess I will just stay single forever."

"You won't be single forever. It just means she's not the one, man. It happens. You have a crush."

"Crushes are for children, and I'm a man. I know what I want. And I want Tara. I just hate that my life is so fucked up right now. It's embarrassing to have to deal with it and especially with someone new in my life. Maybe it's best she's not around to deal with it. Heather would flip out if she knew she was being replaced. Hell, she'd probably hurt Tara or try to. I can't do that to her."

"Are you sure she's the one? Like the one. Would you marry her?" Grady gave me a look as if to tell me to make absolutely sure.

"I would. Not right away, of course. I'd want her to meet Mila and make sure they fit, but yes, I could see myself marrying her. Does that sound crazy?"

"Yes," said Clay, earning a hard look from me and an eye roll from Grady.

Grady patted my shoulder. "I can keep my eye on her if you want."

If there was anyone I could trust around my girl, it was Grady. "Just keep an eye on her if you happen to see her around. But don't stalk her. I don't want to upset her."

"I'll check in at the buffet and make sure she's not talking to other men." Clay meant well too, but I wasn't sure I wanted him spying on her.

My pulse quickened as I thought of other men trying to get to her. It sucked I had to leave her behind. "Look, could you just give her a message for me?"

Grady nodded, putting away his phone. "Yeah, man, anything. You know I'll always have your back." He had always had it, even in college when his head was in the clouds most days. If it came to a friend needing him, he was there. It was the only time he put the game controllers away.

"As long as she's worthy," said Clay, as if he had any say. "Then you're better off without her. And so is Mila."

I wondered how he was planning on determining her worthiness. "No, I need you to do this for me," I said. "Please?"

"You asking me please has me worried. But yeah, I'll do it." I knew I could count on Grady, but Clay? He was a toss-up.

As the car pulled into the airport, I gave them the message to relay.

CHAPTER 28

TARA

I had gotten out of work early enough the night before that I should have had plenty of sleep, but once I got home and found myself alone with nothing else to do, the thoughts of Zane being gone crept in.

I had tossed and turned for hours, got up, and fixed myself a grilled cheese sandwich. Then I had a good cry until I couldn't keep my eyes open any longer.

And that was why, during my early morning shift, my eyes were puffy and I was dragging ass.

Karen walked past me and leaned in, "Hey," she said. "If you need to go home, I'll cover for you. You look like you didn't sleep at all."

"I'm fine."

"Did he call you or something?" She looked as if she was trying to understand.

"No, I didn't hear from him. But I'm good. I'm moving on."

"Let's spread out and get some work done," said Ben, who came by and stuck his head in our conversation. "And next time I ask you to work, you stay and clean up. You were supposed to go home and rest, and you're dead on your feet."

"See? Even Benny Vinnie can tell."

"Yeah," said Ben. "And I can tell you have tables to attend," he said to Karen. "Get moving."

"On it, Boss," she said, rolling her eyes.

Ben turned to me. "And you have people at your table. Go get their drink orders. They asked for you by name again."

For a brief moment, I thought Zane was back, and my heart went into a flutter. But when I looked over, it wasn't Zane but his friend, Nick, and the other one with the shaggy hair, Clay.

I wondered what they were up to. Had he sent them to see if they could get lucky too? I walked over and greeted them with a forced smile. "Hello, gentlemen. Can I get you something to drink?"

The shaggy-haired one gave me a sly grin. "You sure can, sweetheart. How about you sit on my lap and tell me what's special?"

His friend looked just as surprised as I was.

"I beg your pardon? You're Zane's friend. Is this some kind of joke? Some way of getting me to be a bad person so he can feel better about dumping me."

His friend looked as if he was eager to hear Clay's response too.

"Um, I was just kidding around."

"Well, it's not funny. What do you want to drink?"

"I'll have lemon tea. Half and half for an AP."

"One Arnold Palmer coming up." I rolled my eyes and turned my attention to Nick. "And for you?" I tried to be sensitive, knowing the man had lost his wife.

"Just water, please."

I walked away, and when I came back to the table, the two were arguing. I was within earshot when I heard Nick's voice raise.

"Yeah, well, if she tells Zane, he's going to beat your ass. Just watch it."

I walked up slowly, giving them time to finish their talk before approaching. "Here you go."

"Wait," said Clay as I was walking away. "I'm sorry about getting flirty. I was really just fucking around and thought I'd see if you were really that into our boy or if you showed interest in all of your male customers."

"You wanted to see if I'm a slut? Thanks a lot. That's so flattering." I shook my head.

"Hey, Tara. Ignore him and listen to me. Zane really likes you. He's just had something come up in his life that he had to go home and take care of."

"I'm sorry," said Clay. "Look. I just needed to know if you were worthy of our friend's love. He's crazy about you."

"But he's a liar, and he's hiding things." I shrugged. "So that's that." I didn't understand the point of them defending him.

"Do you always dismiss men you care about so easily?" asked Nick. "Because I'm pretty sure you're upset about what happened. Even I can tell your eyes are puffy from crying."

I put my head down and took a deep breath, not sure how I wanted to deal with this situation.

Clay shook his head. "He was about to tell you everything when you tripped out on him, and I don't know what kind of ideas you have in your head about what it was about, but it's not what you think."

"And how do you know what I think?" I asked Clay in a snippy tone.

"I'm not going to sit here and fight with you about Zane. He cares about you, and that's all I wanted you to know. You're not giving him a chance, and I think it sucks."

"What do you mean? I'm not doing anything."

"You are, though. You're the one who called everything off because you jumped to conclusions." Clay seemed really angry with me, and all I could think about was that Zane liked me.

Had I jumped to conclusions? "I was protecting my heart."

"Yeah? So what then? Fuck his heart? His feelings don't matter?" For a minute, it seemed as though the man was projecting.

Nick leaned into the table toward his friend. "Hey, Clay. Chill out, man. She's upset. It's a mess, but she hasn't done anything wrong."

"Sorry," he said. "I think you should just hear him out. And I guess I came here to see if you're even willing."

"He hasn't called me. If he cares so much, why not pick up the phone?"

"Because his life has taken a turn. He's busy with that, and well, you made him feel like he needed some time. Besides, I believe you told him not to bother."

"But he left something for you. I can bring it to you later if you want it. If not, I'll tell him you never want to see him again."

"I want it." If Zane really had something for me, it was the right thing to hear him out. "I work in the morning."

"I'll drop it by. I just had to be sure you're worth it. He's a good guy and my best friend."

"So what's his big secret?"

"Nah, I'll let him tell you."

I stormed away and went to the back, where I breezed past Karen. I had tears in my eyes, and I couldn't help it, but I guessed I'd made a mess out of everything. Why had I been so quick to dismiss Zane? I should have at least given him a chance to explain.

Karen stormed into the kitchen and pulled me aside. "What did they say to you?"

"Zane likes me, and I'm the one who blew it."

"What? I'll go kick their asses out if you want. They can't come in here and make you cry."

"No, they're right. I apparently should have waited for Zane to talk to me. And now, I'm not sure he'll forgive me for screwing everything up. But he's sending a message to me through Clay tomorrow."

"Why doesn't he just call you? This is bullshit. I bet they're just fucking with you, and I, for one, am not going to stand for it." She turned and stormed for the door, but I grabbed her hand and tugged her to stay with me.

"No, don't make it worse. I'll see if he shows up with something, and if he doesn't, I'll know it was all just bullshit. I don't know what his big secret is, but it looks like I'll at least find out. He's probably so upset with me. He's having troubles at home, and here I've gone and made them worse."

"Don't think that way. Did one of those assholes say that?" She looked back at the door as if she could see through it. I knew if I let her go, she'd be out there in Clay's face in a heartbeat.

"In so many words." I had never wanted to be a burden on Zane, and now it looked like I had.

My stomach twisted in knots, and I felt as if I needed to lie down. "I am going to give them their check, and I'm going to take a break."

"I'll give it to them," she said.

"Karen, please don't do or say anything. I don't want it to get any worse."

She let out a deep breath. "Fine. I'll just drop the ticket, and then I'll step away. But if one of them talks to me, I'm going to let them have it."

Now I had one more thing to worry about.

About that time, Ben came through the doors and spotted us there.

"What the hell is this?" he asked. "Get back out there and wait on the customers. You both have full sections right now."

"I'm going," I said, wiping my eyes.

"What the fuck is wrong with you?" he asked. "You look like shit. You'd have done better to go home last night instead of fucking off work early without cleaning up so you could go out with your little friend here." He was making some huge assumptions.

"No, that's not it at all," I said in a harsh tone. "And for your information, I went home last night just as I said I would, and even if I hadn't, it's not your business what I do in my free time. As it happens, I just don't feel well."

"Be sick on your own time," he said. "We've got customers out there waiting to be served. Your little petty problems can wait."

Petty problems? That had me steaming. I'd never had any problems interfere with work. "I give all of my time to you and this restaurant, Ben. I don't have any of my own time to be sick on, and unfortunately for you, it doesn't work that way." It wasn't like I could pick and choose when it happened.

"Yeah, and you call her every single time your ass is in a sling," added Karen. "She barely gets any time off as it is."

"Says the girl who puts my ass in the sling," he said. "Get to work, Karen!" He got in her face, and she turned and went back to the floor. Then he spun around. "Take a minute to clear your head, take something for your cramps or headache or whatever the fuck it is, and then get out there. That bimbo friend of yours can't handle this all alone."

I nodded, knowing I'd never bend over backward to help him again, money or not. I'd work two jobs before I let him own me. But for now, I had to play my part.

"Yes sir," I said, knowing it wouldn't do me any good to argue with him. He had my future in his hands, and if he fired me, I'd be screwed. Being poor meant swallowing my pride, even when the lumps were bigger than my throat.

I hated having to be in that situation, but such was life. I had to suck it up and get back out there.

I went to the bathroom and washed my face, and while I was prepared to get back to work, I wasn't prepared to wait all night to hear from Zane. I took out my phone and texted him.

Call me?

I wasn't going to call him. If he really did have a lot on his plate, I wasn't going to bother him. I had to be patient while I wondered what kind of secret he had.

Was it that he had been married before? And the woman was trying to get him back? That Mila tattoo that I'd tried to ignore, was it something to do with her? And if so, was I up for the competition?

All I could do was wait and hope it wouldn't take too long.

CHAPTER 29

ZANE

The entire flight back, I couldn't help but worry about my parents, Mila, and Heather being in the same town, but thankfully, they had followed my advice and detoured to my aunt's house along the way.

As it turned out, I was home alone long before I expected them. While I sorted through the last of the mess, wondering how I was going to explain to Mila what happened, I heard a noise outside.

I had a feeling I already knew who it was, and I wasn't going to make a big deal out of her being there. That was exactly what she wanted.

"Looks like you had a wild party," said Heather. "Too bad for you. Looks like they really trashed the place. I bet the lawyers would love to know about it."

"As much as they'd get a kick out of the security footage I have of you destroying your daughter's home."

I pulled out my phone, and my heart skipped a beat as I saw a message from Tara, asking me to call her. Instead, I hit the alert button for the security app. The cops would be on their way soon enough, and all I had to do was keep her talking.

That wouldn't be a problem. She liked to talk, especially if she thought she was being clever.

She was quiet a minute. Then she sighed, walking over the trash I'd swept into a pile and dragging her foot through it. "Do you think I believe that? You're bluffing."

"Think what you want, Heather. I really don't give a fuck." It was going to be wonderful to see her go back in lockup for good.

She gave a little giggle. "Speaking of fucking. There's no one here but us. Maybe you'd like to scratch an itch with me? We always were good together."

"I'm pretty sure fucking you would give me an itch, and I'm just not that desperate." I wouldn't touch her with a ten-foot pole, much less my ten-inch dick.

"Come on, Zane." She stepped closer and put her hand on my arm. "You know you miss me, babe. I know you do. I know you want us to be a sweet little family. I'd be willing to try." Her other hand slipped down to my crotch, where she cupped my balls through my pants. "Let's fuck and make up."

As angry and frustrated as I was, I couldn't help but feel sorry for her. She was so delusional, so fucked up. Her glassy eyes showed me she had gone out and gotten her latest fix.

"You're high as a kite," I said. "You don't even know what you're saying."

"I'm hot for you, Zane. Still."

"Well, I'm not hot for you. At all. As a matter of fact, you make me sick, and I hope I never have to look at you again." My words were harsh, but they were the truth she needed to hear.

"Give me my daughter, and you don't have to see either of us again."

"That's never going to happen. You're pathetic, Heather. You're a horrible mother, a selfish, inhuman piece of shit."

She kept that smug look on her face until the sound of sirens could be heard. Before she could run away, I caught her arm. "I don't think so."

"Let me go, Zane. Don't do this to me. Don't let them lock me up again, Zane. I'm going to do better." She struggled to get away from me, but I held on to her arm, not letting it go until it was to be put in handcuffs. "I hate you for doing this to me."

"You did this to yourself, Heather. You don't love me, and you don't even love Mila more than your next fix. You're unfit, and now you're not free anymore. You're going back where you belong."

The cops came in, and I turned her loose.

"I want my baby," she cried to them. "Please, I want my baby. He's got my baby."

It wasn't going to do her any good to carry on with her lies. The cops, who we'd gone to school with, knew the truth. As much as I was glad to see her go, it was a heartbreaking display, but only because it should have never come to that.

Heather had had it all and threw it away.

As the cops took her away, I breathed a sigh of relief. I called my mother's phone, and she answered anxiously. "Zane? Is it good news? Can we come home?"

"Yes, ma'am," I said, watching them put Heather in the car. "She's back in custody, and I should have the house in order before you get home."

"Oh, good. Thank the heavens. I was so worried about you. We're on our way. Give us half an hour."

We ended the call, and I glanced down to see the message from Tara.

Should I, or shouldn't I?

I was still hurt by her decision to end things, but I had a feeling that Clay and Grady had given her the note I'd left already.

As much as I wanted to call her, it just seemed like I needed to see my little girl for the moment and have things ready for her when she got back. The house still needed vacuuming, and there were still broken dishes in the kitchen that needed to be swept.

I decided to bide my time. First things first, and then I'd tell her everything. If she wanted me, she could follow the instructions given. It was what I'd planned and the best way to do things.

If she truly wanted me, she'd make the next move. She was the one who'd ended it, after all.

Before I knew it, the time had passed, and my parents were in the drive. The house was clean, but it wasn't the way it had been before. All I could think to tell my daughter was a lie. The truth would be too damaging.

I went out to greet her, and when she saw me, she ran toward me. "Daddy!"

I dropped to my knees, and she ran into my arms, throwing her little arms around me. "God, I've missed you, Noodle!"

I picked her up and carried her over to get her things out of the car. My father was already a step ahead of me, and he had a concerned look on his face that was very similar to my mother's. Neither would say a word, but I'd catch them up later.

"How was your trip?" I asked her as we walked into the house.

"It was fun. Daddy, why did you take everything away?" She glanced at the wall where one of my favorite paintings used to hang. Then she pointed to the area where my cars had been destroyed. "You got rid of the cars?"

"Yeah, well, it was time for a change. I thought you and Nana might want to see what you could find next time you go out to the store, and we'll put up whatever you like."

"Okay," she said. "But I hope you like unicorns, Daddy. That's just what this place needs."

"Wonderful," I said, trying my best not to sound too sarcastic.

My mother looked around and covered her mouth. I could tell she wanted to cry. The loss in the home was much more than she expected, and I was glad she couldn't see the inside of the cupboards. They were practically bare from Heather pulling everything out onto the floor.

As I put Mila down, she ran to her room, and I walked over to see if my mother was okay. "It's just stuff, Mom. She didn't get Mila, and that's all that matters to me."

"Anything you need, just tell us. We'll help."

"I appreciate it, Mom, but we're good."

My father went over and opened the cabinet, and my mother looked up and began to cry. "She got to the plates?" I'd had custom dishes made with my monogram. My mother's friend, who had passed away months ago, had been the potter I'd used.

"I know. I know she went for that on purpose. It's going to be fine. I'll have more made somehow."

"She's evil, that one."

About that time, Mila came out of her room, a confused look on her face. "Daddy?"

"What's up, Noodle?"

"Where are my clothes?" She looked as if she was going to cry.

I glanced at my mother. "Um, let's go take a look." I had been so focused on the things in her room that I hadn't thought to look in the closet. When I opened the door, the rack was empty except for one little outfit I'd saved from when she was a baby. It was the outfit we'd brought her home in.

"I wanted to change."

"I'm sorry, sweetheart. I thought you and Nana could get you some new ones. You've gotten so tall that those wouldn't fit you anymore."

How did a mother take her child's things? And worst of all, I had to take the rap.

"Yes, honey. I told your father that we needed to get you all set up with a new wardrobe. It's going to be so pretty. You'll love it."

Mila's eyes lit up. "At least I still have these," she said, pinching her leggings and pulling them away from her skinny little legs. "I love my pink sparkles."

Those were getting a bit short too. "Why don't you see if you can get a new pair of those in her size?" I said to my mother. "Unless you want me to take her?"

My mother shook her head. "No, we'll be fine. I know just where to go. And besides, you intimidate the salesclerks."

"That's not intimidation, honey," said my father, wagging his brows.

My mother rolled her eyes at him and scooped Mila up into her arms. "Come on, honey. Let's go see if we have some money in my purse, and maybe we'll all go out for ice cream."

"Yay!" Mila cheered as she followed my mother out.

My dad looked at me. "Son, I'm sorry we headed back without telling you."

"It's okay. I should have told you I knew Heather was out. I just didn't want to ruin your trip."

"It's understandable. You don't think they'd let her out again, do you?"

"Not after all of this. And now I get to tell them about the closet. I hadn't noticed she'd wiped out her things like that." I wondered if she had taken them with her. There was no telling. I hadn't noticed the trashcans were full when I threw the other stuff away.

"I never want Mila to know anything about her. She doesn't deserve this."

"No, she sure doesn't. And I just hope the next time you find someone, you know what the hell you're getting into. I know your mother encourages dating. Make sure whoever she is, she's worth all of this. Heather wasn't."

"I know." I gave a nod. "I actually did meet someone in Las Vegas."

"She isn't some drugged-up stripper, is she? You need to find a mature woman. Someone who could be a mother to my granddaughter."

"She is. Her name is Tara. We're talking, but I'm not sure it's going to work out."

"Well, I know you are aware my stance is a little different than your mom's, but I think it won't hurt to just be you and Mila for a little while longer."

Dad walked out, leaving me there. He had a good point. While I wasn't going to pursue anyone else, I still wanted to give Tara another chance. If she was even interested.

I joined them in the other room, and Mom and Mila decided that we should go out to grab some ice cream.

It was good to be with my little girl, to see her smile and hear her laughter. She was all that mattered in my life, and I wasn't going to lose focus of that again, not for anyone. Whatever happened with Tara happened.

I loved her, but the ball was in her court, and a text message for me to call her wasn't going to cut it. Maybe I was just stubborn, but all I wanted to do was spend time with Mila for the evening.

CHAPTER 30

TARA

Even though I'd barely had a wink of sleep in two nights, I was at work with a smile for my customers.

"Thank you, honey," said one of the older women who had come in with her husband at least three other times that week. "I'll just have a coffee. Make it that dark roast you brought me yesterday."

"Yes, ma'am," I said, swallowing hard the same way I had every single time someone ordered the dark roast, which happened way more times than I remembered.

Usually, everyone wanted the house blend, but it seemed like there was an influx of dark roast drinkers, or maybe it was just me being overly sensitive.

I hurried to the back, got her and her husband's drinks, and brought them back to the table. They thanked me, and I left, glancing over at the table that Clay and Nick had sat at the day before. It was open, and I was still waiting like a fool on whatever he was supposed to be bringing me from Zane.

Karen breezed past me. "Don't look so anxious. It could have been bullshit."

"Thanks for making me feel better," I said. "It's not like I can help how I feel. I want to hear from him. I haven't even gotten a text back."

"That's because you need to move on. He's over it. He's back home with whatever girl he dates there, and he's moved on with his life. You should take the hint and do the same."

I stirred the gravy and made sure the items in the back of the buffet were brought up to the front. "That's real nice of you to be so blunt. Thanks for the words of encouragement."

"You should have gone out with me last night. I met a couple of guys, and they were so hot. You'd have liked the one. You know you should really get back out there. It's going to hit you sooner or later, and all of the batteries in the world won't save you."

"What the hell are you talking about?" I regretted asking the minute the words left my lips.

Karen looked at me like I was so naïve. "You're heightened libido," she said with a giggle. "You'll be buying toys to save you when it gets to be too much. It's common knowledge. You're going to want it even more now that you lost it. You may as well face it."

"I'm good, okay?" I glanced around to see if anyone was paying attention, but luckily, there wasn't anyone within earshot. "I don't need toys and batteries. I need Zane. I need Clay to show up." I dropped the tongs and went to the back, trying to get away from her.

She meant well, or at least that was what I told myself, but I knew she thought I was a fool. A fool in love. That wasn't the worst thing to be, was it?

I hid in the back for as long as I could, peeking out now and then to make sure my tables were okay and to see if Clay and Nick had shown up.

Then I spotted another handsome man sitting at my last table. He was alone and dressed to the nines in a fancy suit. He had that devil-may-care smile that reminded me of Zane's a whole lot, and I took a deep breath knowing I had to go and talk to him.

But before I could make it to the table, he was joined by Clay, and the two men shook hands across the table.

I strolled up, prepared to play aloof. "Welcome to the Golden Flower Buffet. I'll be your server today. My name is Tara. How may I help you?"

"Wow, that's quite the spiel. You didn't have to say all that for us." Clay grinned.

I took a deep breath, trying really hard not to tell him off. "Well good. Then this should be easy. Tell me what you want to drink."

"Juice with gin."

"You can go to the bar for the gin, but I can bring you the juice."

"He'll have juice and so will I," said the other man. "I'm Grady, by the way. Zane's best right- hand man."

"You are the one he was here to see."

"That's me, the one and only. He told me a lot about you. Said he was crazy for you, and now I get it. You're gorgeous."

"And you're a flirt."

"I would never," he said with a hearty chuckle that made his hazel eyes sparkle. "Zane would murder me. He doesn't share. Never has."

"Not even when I offered him one of the Babin twins," said Clay.

"Yeah, our boy doesn't give himself away that easy. He's a gentleman, a protector."

"You sound as if you're in love with him." I had never heard a man say so many sweet things about another with such a twinkle in his eye.

"He's like a brother to me. We've known each other since we were kids. And that means something. Like when he is in love with someone, that's—"

"Enough with the games. Did you have something to give me from him or not?" I put my hand on my hip, and it was all I could do not to tap my foot.

Clay shook his head. "Now I see the appeal," he said. "She's just as tough as he is."

"If not tougher." Grady leaned onto the table and pulled something from his coat pocket. "Here. It's the letter your man sent to you. He was hoping you'd understand everything once you read it."

He passed me a small envelope, and inside, there was a folded piece of paper and an airline ticket. I read the letter and hoped it would explain more than just why he hadn't texted me back.

Tara, I don't know what I did to upset you, but I had wanted to explain something. While I wanted to share my life with you, there was a part of it that I just couldn't share. That is, until I found myself in love with you.

Knowing you don't want kids has made things tough, and that's because I have a five-year-old daughter. Mila is the world to me, and she has to come first, but if you want, I'd love to keep in touch and see where things could go.

I understand if you don't want to be a part of our lives, but I'm afraid we're a package deal if things are to go any further. Enclosed are some tickets to my hometown, as well as a voucher for an all-expense-paid stay at the Heights in Williston.

I hope you come and see me sometime and take a break from your life to be a part of mine. If only for a while.

I miss you already, Zane.

"I don't understand. His big secret was that he had a kid?" That wasn't the worst news in the world. I loved kids. I just hated seeing them in horrible situations. And I wouldn't raise one in Las Vegas like my mother did me.

"He's very protective of her. He wasn't hiding her for any other reason but to make sure you were decent before bringing his kid into it."

I could understand that. "So, this is for me to go and see him?"

Clay nodded. "Yeah, he's hoping you'll make the next move. And honestly, I think you owe him that much." He gave me a look as if I'd done his friend dirty, and perhaps I had when I hadn't let him explain.

But how was I to know the other woman in his life was a five-year-old daughter? "I would have understood."

"He's got some other issues with her mother. But he should be the one to explain all of that."

"Oh, great. Let me guess. She's still hooked on him."

"No," said Clay. "The only way she'd get hooked on him is if he was made of cocaine."

Grady pegged his friend with a hard stare. "Again, it's probably best that he tells you."

"I don't want any drama." I shook my head.

"She's in prison," said Clay, earning another look. He gave it right back to his friend. "What? She's going to find out sooner or later."

"Later would be better. It's not our place."

"No, I appreciate it, really. It's hard wondering."

"Yeah, I was thinking the same thing. So, tell me. Are you going to go and see him?"

I smiled. "I think I am. I just don't know when I could."

Grady smiled as he got up from the table.

"I could go and get that juice," I said.

"No, thanks," he said. "I think we'll just head to the bar after all." He laid down a hundred-dollar bill and turned to walk away.

"Oh, you don't have to do that," I said. "I didn't even wait on you."

Clay smiled. "Let him. He doesn't have enough to do with it as it is."

"For your trip," he said. "I hope you don't change your mind." He turned and left, taking Clay with him, the man glancing back once as they headed for the lobby.

I stared down at the tip and the airline ticket. I still couldn't believe he had sent it. I wanted to go so badly. I missed him so much.

I ran to the back, where I found Karen and Ben arguing. Once he walked away, she turned to me and smiled. "I'd like to wipe the smug smile off his greasy face."

"Yeah, me too. Maybe you can tell me how to tell him I'm going to North Dakota without getting fired."

"What? North Dakota? To see Zane Ballard?" She had it right. Ding, Ding.

"Look at this," I said as she grew concerned, her brow creasing to show how much. "It wasn't bullshit. He likes me, and I nearly blew it."

"These are round trip, and it says your hotel is paid. And your food? I'm so jealous."

"I'm going."

"Really? You're sure?"

"Yes, I'm in love with him, Karen. And knowing I nearly blew it, I can't just sit here and let the tickets go to waste. I have to go and make this right."

"But what about the buffet, your bills?"

"I've been socking away some money for an emergency. I think this counts."

"Fuck it. You're not leaving me here. I'm going too. Besides, you need a chaperone."

"But there's only one ticket." I wanted her to go, but she was going to have to pay her own way.

"I've got some of my fun money saved up, and I can't let you go alone. What's that you always tell me? I have to be careful. Unless you don't want me to go." She searched my eyes.

"No, of course, I want you to go. I'm just not sure how we're going to both get away from here with Ben in a shit mood. I want to leave first thing in the morning."

"Count me in."

I took a deep breath. "I have a few days of sick time and vacation."

"I'll figure something out," she said with a grin. "Then it doesn't matter what that lump says. We're going to North Dakota."

CHAPTER 31

ZANE

Waking up in my own bed was nice for a change, and to my surprise, I wasn't alone. I looked down at the end of the bed and found Mila curled up in the corner of the mattress as if she had barely made it to the bed before falling asleep again.

I didn't scold her about it. It wasn't often she did that, and I knew she had missed me as much as I'd missed her. Instead, I went to the kitchen to fix us breakfast and plan our day.

She finally came into the kitchen, her bare feet padding across the floor as she marched to the nearest bar stool. "I want cereal," she said.

"We don't have any cereal," I said. *Or any bowls.*

I had to pull out paper plates for us to eat on, but Mila didn't notice. I had stopped at the market on the way home from ice cream to get eggs and bacon, knowing I'd want to do something special for our first morning home.

"What are you cooking?"

"Eggs and bacon. You like that. I've made it before."

"Yeah, I like bacon. Only Nana says it's the Devil's candy."

"That's only because she doesn't want Pop-pop eating so much of it. It's not good to overindulge the way Pop-pop sometimes can."

"What's indulge?" she asked, tilting her head to the side.

"It's like when you take more for your enjoyment." I thought of Tara at that moment. Man, had I indulged in her.

I felt a bit hollow inside, still wondering if she was going to call or be as stubborn as me. Maybe my uncertainty was a sign. Was I ready for a relationship? Was Mila ready for me to be in one?

Mila leaned on the bar, resting her chin. "Like when you eat out of the ice-cream carton?" she asked, knowing my mother had gotten on to me about that.

"Sort of like that, yes."

"And when I eat too many cookies because they're my favorite?"

"That's right. We all do it. Especially when we really like something." I put a plate of eggs and bacon on the bar and sat beside her. We usually had our breakfast at the bar together, sharing a big platter. She'd take what she could eat, and I'd have the rest. It was nice to be back at home with her and our usual routine.

As we both dug in, me going for the eggs while she took a strip of bacon, it went quiet for a moment. Then she said something that surprised me. "Did you go on a date while you were in Las Vegas, Daddy?"

"What, Noodle?" I wasn't sure I'd heard her right.

"Did you go on a date? Like with a lady."

"What do you know about dates?" I didn't want her to have that word in her vocabulary until she was thirty.

"It's when you go out with a lady and kiss." She took a bite of eggs.

"That's not *only* what a date is. You don't always kiss. Sometimes, you just talk and look at shooting stars." I left out the part where we'd made out hot and heavy on the blanket. I didn't want to think of her ever doing the things I'd done in my life on dates.

Mila looked at me, her little lashes fluttering as she blinked. "You didn't answer my question." She pointed a piece of bacon at me as if it were a weapon.

"Why did you ask?" I had a feeling who had planted the idea in her head.

"I overheard Nana ask Pop-pop if you went on any dates. He said he didn't know."

"And what would you think about that? About me going on dates?"

"If she's a nice lady, I'm happy. But if she's mean, I don't like her. And if she could tie my hair in a ponytail without making my ears turn red, you should keep her around."

I laughed, nearly choking on my last bite of eggs. "They don't turn red. And that was only one time."

Mila giggled. "It hurt, and Nana said you did it wrong."

"I'm a man, and men don't know how to do those things sometimes. So what do you think? Should I go on more dates?"

"Only if you want to." She took another bite of eggs and bit into her bacon.

"But would it bother you?" I didn't want to do anything that could upset her life. Her happiness was what really mattered to me.

Mila shrugged. "Would you still be my dad?" The question came with her puppy dog eyes, and that melted my heart.

"Of course, Mila. I'll always be your dad. That's not ever going to change, okay? Ever. You're stuck with me, kid." She didn't have a mom who had stuck around, and I wondered if she felt like all parents felt that their role was optional. I couldn't explain that her mother was selfish. "For your whole life."

She smiled. "Then I'm okay with it. Would they be my new mom?"

"Only if you liked them and wanted them to be." I wasn't going to push someone, even Tara, on her if she didn't like them. "But I'm not rushing into anything like that." At least it didn't seem likely.

"So? Did you?" She giggled.

I realized it was probably best to be vague. "You're the only girl in my life, Mila. You're all I need. It's me and you against the world."

After breakfast, I cleaned up the kitchen, and Mila and I put on a show that she liked to watch. I was just about to doze off when my parents showed up at the house.

"Knock knock," said my mother as she stuck her head in the front door.

"Hey, there's our favorite Nana," I said, sitting up on the couch. "You caught us being lazy."

"I'll say," she said, pointing down at Mila, who was stretched out on the floor sound asleep. "It's been a long time since you two took a mid-morning nap. It's nearly lunchtime."

"We just ate," I said. Or so it seemed.

"Well, we came to see if you wanted to go horseback riding. We could pack a picnic lunch and go out to our favorite spot by the stream."

"Yeah, sure."

My father nudged Mila. "Wake up, little one. Pop-pop is here. We're going to the stream."

As if someone flipped a switch, she sat up, bright eyed, and smiled. Then she hugged my father, who scooped her up.

"What do you want to take on our picnic?" he asked.

"Chicken nuggets!" she said.

"How about cold sandwiches?" asked my mother, knowing Mila wasn't going to like that idea as much.

"If it's all you got," she said with a shrug.

"I'll bring you some chicken nuggets for dinner. How about that?"

Mila smiled. "Do I get to get a toy?"

"Don't you always get a toy?" he asked with a chuckle.

My father was determined to spoil her rotten.

We changed into some clothes suitable for riding, and thankfully, Mila had a pair of jeans packed for her trip.

"I'm all set," she said. "I've even got my horse." She held up her stuffed unicorn, and my parents chuckled.

"Honey, you're not bringing that this time," said my mom. "There won't be any room."

Mila's bottom lip poked out. "But I wanted my own horse." She was going to ride with one of us, and she always complained about not having a horse.

"Go ahead, Noodle. This once. But you can't hold it the whole time, and it will have to ride in my pack."

"Okay, Daddy."

My mother gave me a hard look. "You're going to spoil her if you're not careful," she said. "It's not going to hurt to tell her no once in a while."

"I tell her no all the time. I don't see the harm in it."

Mom shook her head, and when my father and Mila went out to the car, she leaned in closer. "Your father said you met someone?"

"It's nothing, Mom. I did, but I'm not sure it's going to work out."

"Is she a nice girl?"

My mother was going to grill me about it until she knew everything. "She's nice. Her name is Tara, but we've parted ways, and I'm not sure it's going to lead to anything. So could we just please drop it? And please don't let Mila hear you talking about it. She's already asked me if I was dating. She's turning into your clone."

"That's not a bad thing," said Mom. "It could be worse."

She turned and went to the car, leaving me to lock up. I had boarded up the window and was pretty sure that no one could get in. The only crazy person who'd want to was locked up, and thankfully, she wouldn't be a bother to me anymore.

My mother had been right. It could be worse than Mila being like her. She could end up like her own mother. Not that I'd ever let that happen, but I knew it was what my mother was implying.

But being like Heather wasn't all bad. Mila had some of her mother's good qualities, and those were the things I'd loved Heather for back when I did.

It hadn't been all bad in the beginning, but the end had obliterated my memories of her, and only now and then through Mila did I get a glimpse.

We arrived at the trailhead just before one in the afternoon and rode out to the stream where Mila had caught her first fish. She had let it go, of course, but only after she'd named it. It had been such a wonderful day that we had continued to go there as a family over the past year.

It was a quiet place, with only the sounds of nature. The colors made a beautiful picture, and I couldn't help but think of what Tara had said about finding a place that was green. It was green here, green and lush, and a perfect vision of inspiration.

She didn't know what she was missing, and I sure hoped she'd use the tickets, if not to come and see me, then to see this place or something like it.

We ate our lunch as the horses grazed and drank from the stream, and after, we lay in the field while Mila and her Pop-pop picked wildflowers and chased bugs.

My mom searched for rocks in the stream, and I looked up to the sky. The clouds were puffy and white, and when Mila came over, she lay down next to me.

"Look, Daddy!" She pointed to the clouds. "It's a face in the clouds."

"Yeah, and that one looks like a bear. See it?" I had forgotten how she liked to find shapes in the clouds. "And that over there looks like a marshmallow."

"They all look like marshmallows," she said with a giggle. "You're silly, Daddy."

If I couldn't be with Tara under the stars, then at least I could be under the clouds with my little angel. One day soon, she would be too old for this sort of thing. I was missing way too much of her childhood being away at work.

She got up and scampered off with my dad, and I sat up, no longer in the mood to daydream.

"You miss her, don't you?" said my mother.

I thought she was talking about Mila. "Yeah, I've missed her so much. I almost came with you guys. I probably should have."

"No, I meant the girl you met. You had a look in your eyes before Mila came to join you. It was a look of longing. And I don't think you regret that trip to Las Vegas as much as you'd like to convince yourself you do."

I did miss Tara. "I've been trying to give myself some time to settle back with Mila," I said, glancing up at my mother. "Tara wanted me to call her. But I didn't want to drag her into all of this."

"What? Your beautiful life? Look around you, son. This is something to share with someone you love, and if you love her, and I'm not saying you do, but maybe put in some effort to see where it goes. Your whole life can't be about Mila's happiness. She's going to grow up, and you need to make sure when she does, you aren't left all alone."

I took her words to heart. Was Tara someone I could spend the rest of my life with? Maybe it was time to make some effort.

I found my phone and walked out along the stream until I had service, but when I called, there was no answer.

I sighed and hung up without leaving a message.

CHAPTER 32

TARA

As I went through the security checkpoint at the airport, I had to drag Karen along with me. "Stop being difficult," I said. "You're the one who jumped up and wanted to come along."

"I'm coming, and I just forgot how much I hate to fly."

"It's going to be fine. When we get there, you can soak in the jacuzzi and order room service."

"What if it's not the big place it promises to be? Isn't it like crazy in the mountains with bears and bugs? What if their idea of fancy is like an army cot and a mosquito net?"

"It's not like that," I said, not really knowing if I was right or not. "Zane said it's beautiful, and I doubt he'd send me anywhere tacky."

We made it through the security and gathered our things in time to board.

"Hold my hand," she said as we handed off our boarding passes. The attendant smiled, but I could tell she thought we were both crazy.

We found our seats, and I felt butterflies in my stomach as I prepared for my first plane ride.

"You're going to have to tell me what to expect," said Karen, who didn't want to sit by the window. "I've never flown before."

"Wait, I thought you had. *I* haven't flown before. I depended on you to be my rock. I wish I'd known this sooner."

I had to remind myself that I was going to see Zane at the end of the trip, and by the time we took off, I was ready for the adventure.

"That wasn't so bad," I said once we were off the ground.

"Yeah, it's not terrible," she said, popping her gum. "I can't wait until we get there. How long is this flight?"

"It's almost three hours, but that will go by in no time."

Karen, though scared, still managed to drift off to sleep, but I read my book and got to the ending just as the plane was coming in for a landing. I couldn't believe I had finished the whole thing.

Now I was ready to go see the room. "Wake up," I said, nudging Karen. "We're here."

"I slept through the landing?" She had kept her seatbelt on the entire time, so I didn't think it was important to wake her.

"Yeah, I figured ignorance was bliss."

"I had a good dream." She glanced out the window. "Wow, look at this place!" She grinned ear to ear. "Oh, I'm going to like it here."

"Me too. I hope I didn't come all this way for nothing."

"Do you have the address Clay gave you?"

"Yeah, and he said he should be there. That I should just show up. It would be fine. I just don't know. He's spontaneous, but I'm not."

"Do it. He knows his friend."

"Yeah, maybe it will be a nice surprise. Besides, I want him to know I made an effort. I messed things up. I should fix them."

"Don't be so hard on yourself. You didn't know what his big secret was, and anyone could have reacted the same way."

She was right, and not only that, but I'd done my best to take steps to fix it. I had told Ben he'd be without me for a few days, and while he hadn't made a fuss when Karen said the same, he was not happy to lose me.

Good thing he couldn't do without me. Unlike Karen, I knew I'd have a job waiting for me when I got back. She couldn't say the same, and yet, she still came along.

We called for a car, and it wasn't long before we were on our way to the hotel.

"So, do you think Zane has any other friends he could introduce me to if things go well?" She glanced out the window and back down to her phone.

"Other than Clay? I'm not sure." How many hot single friends could a hot and single man have? Judging by the crew back home, I'd say Zane had more than his fair share.

Karen wagged her brows. "Hey, I can get down with him. He's hot." The last thing I needed was for her to get a crush on Zane's friend. It wasn't that I didn't want her to be happy, but I also didn't want their drama to be our drama. We had enough of our own.

"He's having some problems from what Zane said. This isn't Vegas, Karen. You're not going to have as many men to take your pick of."

"Well, I can wade in shallow waters. Besides, there aren't as many sharks there." She sighed. "I wonder where the men are around here."

"The man camps," I said, teasing. I was sure that was what Zane had called them.

Karen's eyes lit up at the mention. "Man camps? That sounds like my kind of place. Maybe Zane will give me the address."

She'd have more than she could bargain for out there. "That's what they call the units the men stay in at the oil fields. You're not going there."

"You're absolutely no fun." She gave me a hard look, took out her compact, and began patting her face.

"I'm pretty sure it's a no-girls-allowed kind of thing."

Karen shrugged. "Their loss."

All of a sudden, my eyes caught the amazing view of the mountains. "Oh man, will you look at that?" As far as the eye could see, it was the most amazing scene. My fingers itched to paint it, and there I was with no canvas or paints. "I hope that's our view from the hotel room."

Once we got to the Heights, I realized my view was going to be even better. "Can you believe this?"

It must have cost him a fortune, and when we checked in, we were led to our room. The young man was handsome, and he wore a big sappy smile as he caught Karen winking at him in the elevator. "You're cute. What's your name?"

"Finn," he said, checking her out.

"Well, Finn, do you have a girlfriend?"

Finn laughed. "Actually, no."

"What do people like to do around here?"

"Lots of things," he said.

"Well, that's kind of vague," said Karen. "Maybe you could show me around later when you get off of work?"

I couldn't believe her. She was the tourist, and she was still playing her game. At least I didn't have to worry about her being bored.

Finn looked like he was mulling it over and nodded. "Sure, if you want."

"That sounds fun." She walked him to the door and gave him a big tip, flashing enough cleavage at him to make him grin again.

She shut the door and joined me at the sofa, where I placed my things. She plopped down as if she was glad to be on solid ground. "Isn't he cute?"

"He's at least six years younger than you are. If not more."

"I'm okay with being the older woman in the relationship. We can't all find perfect men like you. But Finn's a start. Someone to keep me company my first night in town."

I walked to the bedroom and checked out the bathroom with the big tub, just like the brochure had promised. "This place looks new, doesn't it?"

"Newer than the Golden Flower," she said. Our hotel was a lot newer than most in Vegas, or at least newly renovated.

"Zane called this place a boomtown. The oil industry is really popping around here."

"Lucky you. You said he's a foreman, right? Maybe he's earning a good living. You need a rich man."

"I'm not with him for his money. I'd like him regardless of what he made or has." I took out my phone and turned it on. I had turned it off at the airport, knowing no one was going to be able to reach me on the plane.

My heart sank as I realized he had called me. "Oh no. I missed him!" I tried to call him back, but there was no answer. "Shit. Shit." I raked my hand through my hair as I felt like crap.

"It's okay. Calm down."

"What if he thinks I didn't answer on purpose? What if he thinks I don't want him?"

"You're here. I'm pretty sure as soon as he sees you, he's going to get it."

"I need to go and see him. I can't put it off any longer. I'll just go to his place. It can't be far."

"You can't go looking like that," she said, looking me up and down. I had traveled for three hours in a plane and read a book, not rolled around in the mud. "Change and freshen up. He's probably going to fuck you stupid as soon as he sees you."

"I'm sure he won't do that. Besides, if he has a kid like he says, then she will probably be there."

"Oh yeah. I forgot about her. Are you sure you want to share Zane with another person? He's always going to want her around, and she's going to be in the middle. You know how it was when your mom dated. You hated the men like I did my mom's boyfriends. What do you think will happen? She's going to be a little stink, just watch. You need to tell her that you have her number right away."

"She's a child, and that attitude is precisely why I hated my mother's boyfriends. They were always quick to tell me who was boss and try to put me in my place. I don't have to be that person, and I'm pretty sure Zane wouldn't want me to be that way to his daughter."

"Well, it's inevitable. There will be problems."

"That's not true. It's all how we make it, and it's going to be wonderful." I was trying to psych myself up, and all the while, I remembered hating my mother's last boyfriend so badly that I still got angry every time I thought about him.

"Great. Now I'm afraid to go."

Karen made a face as if she realized her mistake. "Sorry. I guess I was projecting. Just because I was a little shit to my mom's boyfriends doesn't mean this little girl will hate you. I'm sure she's cute. And sweet."

I let out a long breath. "What if she hates me?"

"She won't. You'll be the coolest woman her dad has brought home. I'm sure you'll be best of friends." It was amazing how her tune had changed, all because she was trying to cheer me up.

I went to the bathroom and brushed my teeth. Then I swiped on a little more lip gloss and brushed out my hair, which fell in waves to my shoulders. When I looked for something to wear, I went for something simple, jeans and a shirt. Nothing fancy, just casual comfort.

I had no idea how long I would be there or if I'd sleep over. I decided to pack my toothbrush just in case. It was a bold move, and maybe it was a bit too much.

I decided it was better to be optimistic. After a quick goodbye to Karen, who wished me luck, I headed out to catch my ride. Next stop, Zane's house, and then I'd know whether or not I'd just made the biggest mistake of my life.

CHAPTER 33

ZANE

After figuring out I'd lost my phone, I searched the house high and low and decided I must have left it at the stream.

By the time I got Mila loaded into the car to go and look for it, my father drove up in the drive, blocking my exit.

"Looking for this?" he asked, getting out of the car. "I heard it ring and thought I'd drive it out."

"Thanks, Dad."

"Yeah, I think it's your girl from Vegas," he said with a wink. "You might want to check your messages."

I glanced down and realized she hadn't left one. "Thanks. Sorry you had to drive back over."

"Can you stay and play a while, Pop-pop?"

Dad shook his head. "I wish I could pumpkin, but Pop-pop has to get back home. Nana is cooking me dinner."

"Okay." She hung her little head in disappointment as she stepped back from his truck.

Dad shut the door and drove away.

"Come on," I said. "Let's get our own dinner. We can order out if you want."

"Chicken nuggets?" she asked as we went into the house.

"I think we can do better than that." I wasn't driving into town for fast food when I could order something in. "What about that pasta place you like?"

"Yes," she said.

She ran ahead of me to the kitchen and found our menus we kept in a basket. "Here it is," she said, pulling out the right one. "I want this." She pointed to the picture of her favorite baked macaroni and cheese with chicken.

"How about a salad on the side? That's what I want with my spaghetti."

"Okay, but I'm not eating those sprouts. You can pick them out."

"We'll make it a house salad. That one doesn't have sprouts. But you have to eat it."

There was a knock at the door.

Mila's eyes widened. "Pop-pop came back!" She ran to the door, and I couldn't get around the counter fast enough to stop her.

"Honey, wait!" I called.

She threw open the door, and I heard her little voice say, "You're not Pop-pop."

Before I could see who was there, I heard Tara's voice. "Hello, honey, is your daddy home?"

When I rounded the corner, she was standing at my door. "Mila, go play in your room. I need to talk to my friend."

"Okay." Mila smiled and waved at Tara. Then she ran to her room, and I heard the door slam.

"What are you doing here?" I wanted to hear what was on her mind.

She got a look of surprise on her face. "Um, I got your letter with the tickets."

"I guess I just didn't think you'd use them to come and see me."

"Oh, I thought that was the point. Was I mistaken?" She had a look of disappointment in her eyes. "I could leave."

"No!" I stepped back and tried to blink away all of the thoughts in my head. "Sorry, come in. I'm just a little shocked you actually came."

"Me too," she said, walking into my house. She looked around, and

I could tell it was more than she expected. "But I knew I had to say I was sorry for what happened. I should have heard you out. I made things worse by jumping the gun."

"When my mom called, I wasn't trying to hide anything. It's just my life, my problems? They were personal, you know? And I didn't know if we were at that level yet. Or if you wanted to be."

"So it was your mother who called?"

"Yeah. My ex, who is Mila's mom, was causing a bit of trouble here. I had to come and deal with it." I gestured for her to have a seat on the couch, and I took the chair beside it, not sure how close she wanted me. I knew how close I wanted to get, but pulling her to my lap at this point seemed a little too bold.

"And I just made it all better, didn't I? I'm so sorry, Zane. I was just so scared of getting my heart broken that I didn't want to hear any big secrets. I had no idea you had a daughter. That wasn't even on the list of horrible things you could have been going to tell me."

Her comment sent a charge through me that sat me up about five inches taller. "Well, I don't think having a child is a horrible thing."

Her eyes widened. "Oh, I didn't mean it like that. I meant it's not horrible. I *like* children."

"But you don't want any?" She didn't have to spell it out.

"No, I'd love to have some of my own one day. But I guess I just can't see raising them in Sin City."

"Oh," I said, realizing I might have misjudged her as well. "I was trying to protect my girl. And that's the only reason I didn't bring her up. I love Mila, and she's the most important thing in my life."

"I get it. I just don't really see why you didn't tell me sooner."

I moved to the couch with her. "I didn't realize at first that I wanted to let you into that part of my life. But now that I know, I wanted you to know all of me. Even the baggage that comes with me. I figured if you knew and still stuck around, you might really want to make this work."

"I do, Zane. I wouldn't have come here to work things out if I didn't."

I moved to kiss her so quickly that I was sure I'd taken her breath away. She moaned a little, accepting my tongue, and I moved her back against the cushions before realizing my five-year-old was just down the hall.

"I'm so glad you showed up."

"Well?" she asked. "Can I meet her?"

I grinned ear to ear and stole another kiss before getting to my feet. "Come on. You can see her room."

I took her hand, pulled her to her feet, and walked her down to Mila's room, where I knocked on the door. "Noodle?"

"Daddy?"

I opened the door. "Hey, Noodle. I have someone I'd like you to meet."

Mila peeked up from the coloring book and smiled. "Is she your date?" she asked.

Tara's smile faded. "You had a date?"

"No." I shook my head and hoped she'd give me time to explain. "She means you. She overheard my parents talking."

Tara nodded. "Hi, you must be Mila," she said. "I'm your daddy's friend, Tara."

"Are you his girlfriend?"

Tara was clearly put on the spot.

I folded my arms and gave her a hard look. "Well? Answer her."

Tara let out a deep breath. "Well, I'm a girl, obviously, and I'm your father's friend, so sure. Don't you have friends who are boys?"

"Yeah, but I don't want to kiss them." She gave Tara a matter-of-fact look.

"She's got you there," I said.

"Daddy, can we go fishing again before it gets dark?" The days were a bit longer, but I knew Tara was tired from her long trip.

"Maybe another time when we don't have company." We had just gotten back from the long day of riding, and I had figured she'd be exhausted. "How about tomorrow?"

She sighed and gave that pouty look, but Tara smiled. "I'd like to go fishing in the morning," she said. "I haven't been since I was about your age. Do you think you could show me?"

"Yeah," she said. "We go to our special pond. It's right through the woods." She gave me another pleading look.

"Tomorrow, okay?"

"Yes," said Tara. "I'm a little tired from my flight, but if you'd go in the morning, I'd love to see a special pond."

"You can show her your tackle box," I said to Mila.

Tara's eyes widened with excitement. "You have your own tackle box? That's so cool. I wanted one when I was young, but I was told no because of all of the hooks."

"Hooks are sharp," said Mila. "I can't play with those."

I chuckled. "She has one that doesn't have any hooks in it. I keep all of the hooks in mine."

"I think it's great that you fish together."

"Well, we have tea parties, too. She's got to even things up a bit."

"Tea parties? Now I have to see that."

"I have a tea set!" Mila ran to the other room to get it.

"You don't have to agree to fish just to please her," I said.

"I know, but I'm ready to see some of this beautiful state you've offered to show me. And thank you by the way. I needed a getaway."

"Well, I'm glad you were able to get off work."

"Ben is pissed off. Karen came with me, so I'm sure he's feeling abandoned."

"She came too?" I was shocked they had both gotten off work at the same time. Ben didn't seem like the kind of boss to let that happen without consequence, and I hoped I didn't make problems for her at work.

"Yeah, she did. And if I know her, she's already entertaining the bellboy at the hotel."

I laughed but wasn't sure I liked her having men over to the hotel room. Hopefully, the woman would have better judgment when Tara was around. From what I could tell, she was about as wild as Clay, and I didn't want Tara involved in anything like that. But I couldn't exactly say it. She was her friend, and I was glad Tara hadn't had to travel alone.

Mila finally came out of the back with the tea set. "I can make you some tea if you want. Or coffee. I can make coffee too." She placed the little set on the little table in her room. "How do you like it?"

"Hmm," said Tara, giving me a glance. "Dark roast is my favorite."

"Okay, I'll make us some for tomorrow too. Daddy likes to drink coffee before he goes fishing."

Tara smiled. "Are you going to catch lots of fish?"

Mile smiled and nodded. "Yeah, you can even use my pole if you want. Its name is Lucky."

Tara laughed. "Well, that's the perfect name for a fishing pole."

"Do you want to go out and sit on the porch for a while? We could see the sunset from there."

"I'd like that," said Tara. "I've never seen a North Dakota sunset before."

"First time for everything," I said.

"I like sharing my first times with you." She met my eyes, and I wanted so badly to hold her and kiss her. We had so much to discuss, and the little remarks were only reminders of that.

We headed out to the porch, and the girls managed to talk more than I thought they would.

Tara walked over to the railing and looked out across the field and past the old barn I'd meant to tear down when I bought the place. "This is so beautiful," she said. "It's just so lovely. And colorful in a natural way."

"Who needs neon, right?"

"I want to paint it," she said, wrapping her arms around her middle.

"You should."

"I didn't bring any paints with me."

"Daddy won't let me have any paints, so you are out of luck."

Tara met my eyes. "You should get her a paint set."

I hung my head as if I got the point. "I've been looking for one. I thought watercolors would be nice."

"Watercolors are fun."

"They have pencils, and all of the reviews said they were less messy. Mila hasn't had the best luck with paints." I glanced at my daughter, who walked over and hopped up in the swing as if she didn't hear me.

"The pencils are great for detailed work, but let's face it. She needs to have freedom with her expression."

"She's wearing the same sparkle tights she's had on for three months. I think I'm allowing room for expression."

Tara giggled. "That's not what I mean. I just mean that the paints are more fun."

"See, Daddy? I told you I need to paint."

"She painted all over her headboard and walls the last time she had paint. I'm not sure she's ready."

"Daddy, I was four then. I'm five whole years now. I know how to use paint. I'm not a baby."

Tara winced. "Sorry, I didn't mean to start World War Three. I just know how much being able to paint has helped me."

"Fine, I'll get a simple paint set, and if you can manage it like a big girl, then we'll add to your colors."

"Thanks, Daddy. I can do it. I promise I'll be good." Mila got up and went further into the yard, where she tried to catch a cricket.

I took a deep breath and let it out. "Can you help me get the right paints? Maybe we'll find you a set too. You can paint the North Dakota sky."

"I'll just snap a photo and do it when I get back home." She took out her phone and captured a few different shots. "You weren't kidding. This place is incredible."

"You should see my stream," said Mila, who I wasn't aware was listening. "We were there today. You missed it."

"We can take her again sometime if she is interested."

"Could we, Daddy?" Mila got excited. "Can we take the horses again?"

"We'll see." I glanced up at Tara, who looked a bit nervous. "Would you even want to get on a horse?"

"I'd try it," she said. "If you'd show me how."

"I'll have to teach you," I said. "There's nothing to it. And you can ride my mother's horse. It's really docile."

"I'd love to meet your parents."

"Oh, and I'm sure they'd love to meet you too." They were both going to have a lot to say about her just showing up, but I needed to let them know it was all my doing. I'd sent her the ticket and asked her to come. They didn't need to know the rest.

Mom would be happy for me, but my father? I wasn't sure he was ready for me to move on with my life. He was always afraid that something was going to happen like it had with Heather. As if I only attracted bad girls. Tara was nothing like that.

We sat on the back porch until after dark and went back inside.

After a few minutes on the couch, Mila fell asleep next to me while I showed Tara some of Mila's photos that her mother hadn't found to destroy.

"She's worn out," said Tara. "She's amazing."

"Yeah, she's everything. Now you see why I'm so protective?"

"Oh yeah, you're just being a good father, Zane. I don't hold that against you. I just hope you won't hold what I did against me. I didn't know what you had in mind. I was just being protective too. Of my heart."

I held her hand. "I should drive you back to the hotel for tonight. Not that I don't want you to stay, but—"

"Oh, yeah, I get it."

"Well, it's just if my parents knew you were here, they could watch her and we could go out if you want to. We could spend the whole night together, but I can't just spring it on them after the long day they had. But no pressure. Don't feel like you have to use your off time here."

She smiled at me. "Of course, I'd like to go out and be here. I came here for you, Zane. I took a chance hoping you'd still want me."

How could she think I'd ever stopped wanting her? "We have a lot to talk about then, don't we?" I said. More than we had time for with my little girl around.

"Yeah, I guess we do."

"Let me just get her to the truck. I'll drive you back."

"No, I'll call a car."

"She's fine. She's slept in the truck a lot, and I want a little more time with you."

After carrying Mila to the truck, I drove Tara into town and pulled up at the hotel. "I can wake her, and we can walk you up if you want."

"No, don't wake her. Call me later?" she asked with hopeful eyes.

"Of course, I will." She was about to leave, but I caught her arm and leaned in for a kiss. "Goodnight," I whispered against her mouth before kissing her again.

"Fishing in the morning?" she asked.

"Yeah, if that's what you want."

"I'd love it." She gave me another kiss and hurried out, shutting the door just hard enough to get the job done but not enough to wake Mila.

Watching her walk away was harder than I thought. I wanted her to stay the night with me. But first, we had to talk about things we'd left undone from Las Vegas.

I wasn't going to pin her down to my life, especially if she wanted a different one.

CHAPTER 34

TARA

I couldn't believe how adorable Mila had turned out. Not only was she an absolute doll, with curly brown hair and a cute dimply smile, but she wasn't bratty at all. Not even when she could have been, asking about paints and fishing.

And Zane? Oh, man, did I miss that man? I couldn't stop thinking about him the night before, and we texted until I fell asleep. I woke up to another one wishing me a good morning. He'd also reminded me to be ready for some serious fishing.

"You're going *where?*" asked Karen.

"Fishing. You know, you bait a hook and throw it in the water and then wait for a fish to bite? Then you reel it in and—"

"I know what fishing is, smart ass. I just can't believe you're going to do it. It's your vacation. Shouldn't you be sipping cocktails at the pool? Have you seen that thing? It's all indoors, and it's gorgeous. The fountain is bigger than ours."

"And I sit by a pool every single day at home. I came to see Zane, and besides, Mila wants to go."

"Oh, I see. So it was the kid's idea. I thought Mila was a girl." She made a face. "That's a funny name for a boy."

"She is a girl, and I used to want to go fishing when I was younger. I think I got to cast once and I've wanted to since. It will be fun."

Karen made a face. She was never the type to play in the dirt or to do anything a boy would do. "I thought you'd want to go down to the spa with me. There are some big strong men in this town. You could upgrade."

"No thanks, I'm totally in with Zane. What happened to Finn?"

"He was a nice young man but too nice for me. I think he was falling in love. So I sent him away early. I just hope he got the hint, or this trip is going to be miserable."

"I think you reap what you sow." I went to see if I had a pair of shoes fitting a trip to the water. I had packed two pairs of jeans and a pair of comfortable sneakers. I decided that would have to do. I would have to ask Zane if he had an old T-shirt I could wear. Maybe he wouldn't mind. I texted him to ask if he could bring one.

Before I knew it, he and Mila were at the door. Karen answered before I could get to it. "Come right in," she said. "Well, aren't you a pretty little girl?" she said to Mila. "My, I can see a resemblance."

"Mila, this is Karen. She's friends with Tara." Karen smiled at the little girl, who smiled up at her with a big grin.

"Hi," said Mila. "Do you want to come fishing too? We can share a fishing pole if you want?"

I glanced at Karen, but she was already shaking her head. "Um, no thanks, sweetie. I've got pressing business to take care of." And by pressing, I assumed she meant her body against some stranger.

Zane handed me the T-shirt, and I was anxious to see what it looked like. It was grey and had a Clover Oil logo on the front. "It's perfect, thanks."

I went to put it on, and when I came out, Zane smiled. It was big on me, but I'd managed to tie it at the hip to make it work. "I'm ready when you are," I said, grabbing my handbag. "I'll see you later, Karen. Enjoy your day."

"You too," she said. "Try not to fall in."

Zane gave me a strange look, and I shrugged. Karen was strange, and while I loved her company, she could be a handful.

We left the hotel and drove out to the stream. Mila had wanted to take the horses, but Zane said no. He had too much stuff to carry and didn't want to deal with the horses. I was relieved. Fishing was going to be enough of an adventure, and since I wasn't too comfortable around horses, having never ridden one, I was glad to ride in the truck, even if some of it was bumpy.

"Sorry," said Zane, going over another bump.

"This isn't the same stream," said Mila.

"Yes, it is, Noodle. We're just driving in instead of taking the horse path."

"You will like it here," said Mila. "There are pretty rocks in the water, and my Nana always takes some home. You should see the box she keeps them in. It's so heavy. She'll have enough to make a stream of her own someday."

I glanced at Zane to find him smiling at Mila, and I didn't think he'd ever looked quite as handsome. It was as if he hung on her every word, and she had him wrapped around her little finger.

When we got to the stream, I had to take more photographs. I had remembered to bring my camera and was excited to get such a beautiful day for photography.

I snapped a few, getting every angle, and Zane unloaded the fishing gear. "Do you need a hand?" I asked, putting the camera down to go and offer a hand.

"No, I've got it," he said. "Go ahead and take more. I'll get your pole ready."

"Thanks." I looked over to see Mila playing in the stream, and she was like a little pixie dancing in a magical fountain. "May I take some of Mila?"

"If she wants. I'd love a copy."

"May I?" I asked Mila.

"Sure," said Mila. She didn't look up or pose or anything, and in fact, she kept on doing what she had been doing, which was searching for rocks. "I'm looking for something to bring my Nana."

"If you want to find her a pretty one, one that's nice and flat, I could make her a pendant out of it. Then you could give her a necklace."

"You know how to do that?" asked Mila, looking surprised.

"Yeah, it's not too hard. I bet I could show you."

"Will you help me look for rocks?"

"Okay, we'll see what we can find before we start fishing." I went to join her, slipping off my shoes and rolling up my pant legs.

"Oh, here's a nice one," I said. "See how it's flat on one side? That will lay against her like this." I held the rock to my breastbone.

"Oh, that's going to be pretty. Can I have one too?"

"If you find another rock like this one, I can make you one." I'd have to go and get some wire and cord, but I figured I could find it at the nearest discount store. Mila was having so much fun with the idea, and I wanted to make her happy.

After our rock hunt, we cast our lines, fishing and enjoying the beautiful sunshine. Zane applied sunscreen to Mila and offered me some, helping me to smear it on. Mila helped too, rubbing it on my arms.

We still managed to get sun-kissed but thankfully not too badly.

"Could you show me how to bait the hook?" I asked Mila, impressed that each time she needed more bait, she carefully did it all by herself.

"Sure," she said. "The best way to do it is like this." She positioned her tongue in the corner of her mouth and carefully held the hook. "Then you put it on like this, but watch that barb. You have to be really careful, or it will go through your finger, and you will cry."

"Oh, okay, I think I can try it," I said.

Zane handed me the end of my line, where he'd tied on my hook. "Take it slow," he said, giving me a big smile as I did exactly like Mila had. "There you go. You're a natural."

I cast my line, and it wasn't a minute later I was reeling in my first catch. "I've got one!" I screamed, and Zane laughed, quickly reeling in his own to help me.

"That's a baby," said Mila.

The thing felt a whole lot bigger than it was.

"You got a perch," said Zane. "It's a hefty one, though."

"What are you going to name it?" asked Mila.

"Name it?"

Zane nodded. "Mila names the fish before she throws them back."

"Oh, I see. Well then, in that case, maybe we should call him—"

"It's a girl," said Mila. "Can't you tell?"

I gave Zane a strange look. "What do I do? Look under the tail?"

He belted a laugh. "It could be a boy, Mila."

"I want it to be a girl."

"That's fine with me," I said. "How about we name her Pearl? She has pearly scales."

Mila giggled. "Pearl is a good name. Goodbye, Pearl. Don't forget to write." She looked up at me as if I was supposed to give a farewell wish also.

"Um, Pearl, be a good fish and live long and prosper."

With that, Zane tossed it back in the water. "Born free," he mumbled.

When Mila went back to fishing, I stepped over with Zane, who was getting a new hook by the truck. "Do you ever keep any?"

"When she's not with me," he said with a wink. "Maybe someday I'll get to fry some up for you."

"I'd love that."

"Are you going to come and see me tomorrow?"

I smiled. "I told you. I'm here for you."

"Good," he said. "I like this." He looked around us.

"Me too." It was the kind of life I could get used to.

CHAPTER 35

ZANE

After another long day of fishing and another drive back into town to leave Tara at the hotel, I went home and crashed. And when I rolled over the next morning to find Mila had made it as far as my bedside, I got up and scooped her up from the floor, blanket, unicorn, and all.

I carried her to her own bed, where I found she had piled every one of her stuffed animals in her bed with her the night before.

I held her close as I pushed them to the floor. Then I tucked her in.

"Daddy?" she said, stirring.

"Yeah. You don't have to get up right now."

"Is Tara coming over again today?"

I sat on her bedside, kicking one of the stuffed animals that had gotten underfoot. "Would you like that?"

"Yes, Daddy. I like having her around. She likes the same things I do, and she's really nice."

"She is, isn't she?" She was amazing in many ways.

"Yes, and she's pretty. And she likes you." She giggled.

"I like her too."

"Is she your girlfriend yet?"

"Are you sure you'd want that? I mean, having your old dad get a new girlfriend. It might mean that we have to share all of our time with her."

"She's fun. I don't mind."

"Well, that's good because I really like her, Noodle."

Now there were just two more people to talk to, and as if they read my mind, my phone rang. I went to my bedroom and got it off of the bedside table. "Hey, Mom."

"Honey, I'm making pancakes, and you know I can never make just enough for two."

"We'll be right over. I'm sure we can help you with that problem. And if you're not too busy, I'd like to talk to you about something."

"Sure, honey. See you soon. I better get back to the griddle." She ended the call, and I went to get dressed before going back to the living room to holler at Mila. "Get up and get ready, Noodle. We're going to have pancakes at Nana's house."

"I'm ready," she said, coming out of her room with a pair of blue pants and a striped shirt. It was the first time I'd seen her without her sparkle pants in a while.

"I like that on you," I said, hoping to encourage her to wear something different. The only time she didn't wear the sparkle pants, she had on a nightgown, and that was to wash them. Unless something had changed while I had been gone?

"I'm expressing myself," she said. I liked Tara's influence on her already. They had been good together, and I couldn't wait to spend more time with her. "Are we going to Nana's house now?"

"Yes. She's making pancakes."

"Good, I like Nana's pancakes. Is Tara coming?"

"No, honey, and let's not mention her at first. I want to talk to Nana and Pop-pop about her and make it a surprise." I didn't want them reacting in front of Mila. Hopefully, it would go well.

We loaded up in the truck and drove the short distance to my parents' house. Dad greeted us at the door. "You're just in time for yours, Ladybug." My father picked her up and carried her into the kitchen as I followed. "Look at the strawberries. I know you're going to love those."

"Is there whipped cream too?" asked Mila.

"All you want," he said.

"Not too much," said Nana. She turned and looked at me. "Hey, sweetheart. How are you enjoying your time off?"

"So far, so good."

"Did you ever hear from that girl you met? What was her name again?" She flipped over a pancake and poured another one.

"Tara. And yes, as a matter of fact, I have. That's what I wanted to talk to you about later." I glanced at Mila.

My father looked up from the table. He had placed Mila in her chair and sat beside her. "Did she call you?"

"She went fishing with us yesterday," said Mila. "I like her."

My mom smiled, and my dad looked a bit surprised. "You mean she came here," he said. "That's pretty serious, son."

"It's just to see what we can make work. So far, it's going well. She and Mila really like each other."

"You mean you've already brought her to your home? To your child's home?" Dad didn't seem to like it, and I knew he worried that Tara might turn into Heather.

His temper got Mila's attention. "She's a nice lady, Pop-pop. She went fishing with me, and we looked for rocks. She's making me a necklace." She leaned up and whispered in his ear.

His eyes softened a bit, and I was sure she had said that Tara was making one for Mom. "Well, I'd like to meet her," he said.

"We both would," said Mom. "Why don't you ask her to come over later? Your father was going to ask if you wanted to have a barbeque, and well, now we have a good reason."

"I'm sure she'd like that. I'll give her a call."

"Where is she staying?" asked my father. I wanted to tease him and say in my bed, but I wouldn't do it with Mila's little ears, or my mother's, around.

"The Heights," I said.

"Hmm, well, at least she has good taste."

"I'm sure she's wonderful." My mom smiled, and I noticed a little bit of a spring in her step as she finished the food.

We all had a wonderful meal, and my mom was particularly interested in our fishing trip the day before. "I had wondered why she looked a little pink," she said.

"Yeah, I couldn't keep her out of the water," I said. "She had a lot of fun with Tara. They both like to paint, hunt rocks, and Mila even taught Tara how to bait a hook."

"That's my girl," said Pop-pop. "Teaching that city girl how it's done."

"She's a hard worker. She works as a waitress. I met her at the hotel I stayed in." I gave a little smile, remembering the fun we'd had in that storeroom.

"A waitress?"

"Yes, Dad, a waitress. You know, an honest wage-earning job. Besides, if I have my way, she will never have to work again."

The comment took my father by surprise. "It's that serious?"

"I think so. As I said, that's what we're trying to figure out. She's incredible, smart, funny, beautiful inside and out. It didn't take me long to fall for her."

"She sounds almost too good to be true," said my father, giving me a hard look.

My mom stared him down. "I'm sure she's everything he says and more."

"It's the *and more* part I worry about," he mumbled.

I looked over at Mila, who had gotten syrup on her shirt. "Honey, why don't you go and wipe that off with a warm rag before it gets too sticky?"

She got down from her chair and hurried to the bathroom.

While she was gone, I looked at my father. "Tara isn't Heather. And while I know you blame me for that, you did get an amazing granddaughter out of it. So stop worrying."

It was worry that had him acting as if everyone was going to turn out bad. He had cared about Heather, and she had won his heart, only to turn against his family and hurt his son and granddaughter.

"Well, I'll give her a chance. If she's everything you say, which is a little hard to believe about a girl from Vegas, then I will give you the benefit of the doubt."

"She isn't from there. She was brought there as a kid and never moved away. She's self-sufficient in a thankless industry, with little pay, and she manages, from what I've seen, to keep her head above water. I think she's amazing and admirable."

My father grinned. "Oh no, you really are in love." I had come to her defense, and he had recognized it for what it was.

But it was too soon for that. "There's still a whole lot to work out. I don't want to scare her off. I didn't tell her about Mila right at first. Now that I have, I'm easing into things. I know it doesn't seem like it, but I am."

"Well, if it makes you feel better, I do trust you. You'll do what's right and best for Mila."

"Always," I said. My word was a vow. Mila would always come before everyone, including myself.

CHAPTER 36

TARA

I was surprised when Zane had called about dinner with his parents and even more surprised when they wanted Karen to come along as well. I thought it was a nice gesture to include her, but when I asked if she wanted to come, she had made a face and said no thanks.

"Are you sure you don't want to go?" I asked, giving her enough time to change her mind. "You had an invite."

"No, thanks. It's sweet they offered, but I've got a date." She gave a sly smile and went back to filing her nails.

"Really? A date? Like a real date, or a date like you're conning some fool into buying you a meal? Because the Ballards are cooking, and you don't have to sell your soul to eat with us."

She gave me a funny look. "No, it's a date. Like I really like this man. He asked me out, and who knows? Maybe you aren't the only one who will get a North Dakota love connection."

I really wanted the best for her, but I thought she moved too fast, and that was saying a lot, considering my relationship with Zane. "Well, be safe, and call me if you need to."

"I'll be fine. Have fun at your dinner, and good luck. You just might need it."

"I'm sure they are nice people," I said. "They raised Zane and did okay with him, and the little girl is well mannered."

She looked up at me as she shook the bottle of nail polish. "Well, I know I give you a hard time, but it's only because I want you to be sure. I care about you, and you're my best friend. I want you to have a happy life."

"I think I can have one with Zane," I said, feeling sure of my words. I smiled, thinking of how magical the past few days had been. I was living a dream and never wanted it to end. "Well, I'm going to meet them downstairs. I'll see you later."

Zane was supposed to call and tell me when they were there, but I had wanted to see a bit more of the hotel and maybe take a peek of the pool that Karen had said so much about. If I found time for a soak, I might just have to give it a try.

As I walked through the lobby, Finn spotted me. "Hey," he called out. I couldn't avoid him, so I waved.

As he ran over to see me, I said, "Hey, Finn."

"Is Karen upstairs?" He looked really anxious to see her again.

"She's getting ready to go out. She's really busy these days." I wasn't sure what story she had given him for being in town, if she'd given him any.

His shoulders fell. "Oh, well, could you tell her I said hi? And to give me a call?"

"Sure," I said. "I'm sure she wishes she could see you too." I hated to break his heart. I'd leave that to her.

It was then that I glanced up to see Zane walking toward us. "Are you ready?" he asked. He gave the young man a dismissive look as he walked away, and he turned his attention back to me. "Mila's already at my parents' house."

"I'm ready." Ready to be alone with him. It felt like forever since we'd really kissed, and not just some quick peck but the deep and passionate kisses I'd gotten used to from him.

He must have missed them too. Before we could get in the truck, he opened my door and kissed me before I could even get in.

"I've missed you," he said, pinning me there.

"It's only been since yesterday." He couldn't possibly miss me as much as I had missed him.

"Exactly. That's twenty-four hours."

"It hasn't been that many," I said. I giggled at how serious he was being.

"Okay fine. I don't want to do the math, but one hour is too many."

"Now that, I can agree on, Mr. Ballard." I searched his eyes and wondered if he was going to let me stand there all day being lost in them.

"You keep calling me that, and we'll never make it to that barbeque." He waited until I climbed in and shut the door for me before he walked around.

I nudged him when he slid in beside me. "Don't tell me things like that. I might just have to turn into a bad girl for you."

He laughed. "Just don't do that before meeting my parents. My father has reservations about how fast things are moving. I told him you're a good girl."

"Oh? He doesn't think you should be dating?" I really wanted his parents to like me, and hearing this was a disappointment. It also made me worry. "How long has it been?"

"Almost four years. But don't let it get to you. He's a big teddy bear, and you'll win him over in no time." He started the truck, and we were on our way.

"Wow, it's been that long?" I couldn't believe he had not been with anyone in that time. There had to have been some non-romantic hookups? Maybe?

"Yeah, well, I tried to fix things with Heather. Probably held on for Mila's sake a little longer than I should have. But I just wanted what was best, and then I realized that her mom isn't ever going to be good for her. Some mothers just aren't cut out for the job."

"It's good that you care enough about her to try, though. Some men wouldn't even bother. My mother never cared that much to sacrifice for me. She knew we were better off with my grandfather, but she left anyway."

"I'm sure your mother loved you. I know that in some twisted way,

Heather loves Mila. I just can't have her in Mila's life. It's not healthy for Mila."

It was sad, and before it could make him upset, I let the subject drop.

"I had a lot of fun yesterday with you and Mila," I said, hoping to lift the mood.

"I'd sure like to know what you think of her. She's great, isn't she?" He glanced my way as he slowed the truck to take the next exit.

"Yes. Oh, and I have those necklaces. I went to the hobby store, and I picked up some things. I thought I'd run this by you before I just gave it to her. And if you don't want her to have it, I'll understand." I took a small pack of paints out of my purse. "I didn't wrap it so I could show you."

"That's sweet. You didn't have to do that." He seemed to really like it.

I breathed a sigh of relief that he hadn't gotten upset I'd bought it without asking first.

"I wanted to get the string for the pendants." I had used a method of tying knots to encase the stones in the string like a net. "I could have used wire wrapping, but with Mila's age, I thought the string method was best. Wires can be a bit sharp."

"That's beautiful, Tara. They'll love those."

I smiled, feeling a certain sense of pride. "My art teacher showed us how to make these. She was the one who encouraged me to paint. I've always wanted to be like her, and I guess that's why I wanted to give Mila the paints. It's something Mrs. Cooper would have done for me."

"If you could, have a little talk with her about taking care of them. I don't want to end up repainting her room again."

I agreed. "Oh, I'll let her know. She's capable of being responsible, and I know she can handle it. Besides, she's not to use them on a whim. She should ask you first."

"Oh, they will definitely be put up. She can only use them at the table. Although I'm sure she'll still make a mess. She's good but messy."

"All great artists are," I said.

"She really is talented for her age. I was blown away. I thought my mom helped her. They'll be excited she is getting her paint set. My father has been on me about it."

"I like your father already. I just hope he likes me." I wanted to win them both over and felt as if I was going to an audition of sorts, to see if I could have the part as Zane's girlfriend.

When we arrived at their house, they both welcomed me with open arms, and Mila ran over to give me a hug. I wanted to save the surprise of the paints for later, but I went ahead and gave Mila the rock necklaces.

"Give this one to your Nana," I said. "I hope she likes it."

"She will, and thank you! These are so pretty." She put hers around her neck. "Nana!" She ran over to Zane's mother, tugging her apron. "Look at what Tara made for you. I found the rock, and she wrapped it up. You can wear it." She showed the woman her own, and she seemed really impressed.

"This is beautiful," she said. "How did you learn to tie such intricate designs?"

"It's just something I learned in art class years ago. My teacher encouraged us to do all sorts of different crafts as well as fine art. It was a lot of fun."

"Are you an artist?"

Zane chimed in. "She likes to do landscapes. It's one of the reasons I thought she'd like to come out to North Dakota."

"I'm only self-taught," I said, feeling the heat rise to my cheeks. "I'd like to do more with it and my photography."

"It sounds like you are very creative. Mila has a bit of that creative gene as well."

"Oh, I've heard. As a matter of fact, I brought Mila something. But perhaps it should wait until after dinner?" I glanced at Zane, who nodded to give me the go-ahead.

"I think it's okay now. Unless you want to wait?" He walked over and put his arm around me.

"Now is good." I reached into my bag as Zane called Mila over. "I remembered you wanted these. But I hope you know that this is a very special set."

Her eyes widened, and she put her hand over her heart. "For me? Those are real artists' paints!"

"Yes, but only if you promise to mind the artists' code."

"Artists' code?" she asked, hanging on every word.

"Yes. It means you have to take special care with your tools and supplies and use them responsibly." It was something my art teacher had taught us. "That means washing your brushes and cleaning up after yourself each time, and making sure to keep the paint on your canvas."

"I will," she said. "I'm not a little kid anymore. I'm going to be a great painter."

I held out my hand and had her shake on it. "I know you will, Mila. I can't wait to see what you create."

"It's going to be a masterpiece," she said. "Look, Daddy." She held them up for him to see.

Zane smiled. "Those are really nice, Noodle."

His father smiled too. "Good job," he said. "I've been trying to get him to do this for months." He looked at his son. "I like her already. You should keep her around." He winked and gave him an elbow.

"I'm working on it," said Zane, making my heart flutter.

We had a wonderful dinner after that, and I helped clean up after, which seemed to impress his mother even more.

"You know, you're the first woman he's brought home like this," she told me. "The last was Mila's mother, but she was already pregnant."

"Oh, I'm not—"

His mother laughed. "Oh, honey, that's not what I meant. I only meant to say that you're special."

"Thank you," I said. "I think Zane is pretty special. And Mila too."

As I dried and put away the final dish, Zane came into the kitchen from being with his father and Mila in the living room. "Are you two done?"

"Yes, this is the last dish," I said, glancing at the microwave clock. "Oh, wow. I didn't realize how late it was getting."

About that time, his father walked into the room, holding Mila. "Tell him what we decided," he said to her.

Mila shook her head as Zane reached to take her. "Nope," she said. "I'm staying with Pop-pop and Nana."

"You are?" Zane looked at his father.

"Yeah, I thought it might be a nice night for us to stay up and watch that monster movie I promised her."

"The Mummy?" asked Zane as if he was making sure his father wasn't showing her anything too scary.

"Yes," said his father. "She'll be fine. Nana can pop us some popcorn."

His mom nodded. "I can do that. You two should go and spend some time together. We'll be fine."

"Thank you," said Zane. "I'll pick her up tomorrow morning."

"No rush," said his father, giving him a wink.

Not long after that, Zane and I left. My body was already yearning for his touch by the time we got to the truck.

It was going to be a good night.

CHAPTER 37

ZANE

I was so glad my father had liked Tara enough to keep Mila for me. Having time alone meant everything, and I couldn't wait to spend the night with her.

"Your father is really sweet to suggest keeping Mila."

"Yeah, he likes you. You made an impression with the paints. He's been trying to get me to buy her some real paints for a month now. He's bad at spoiling her. Worse than me, even."

"That's great. You can tell that she really loves him."

"Oh yeah, those two are partners in crime for sure. My mother has her hands full between them."

"Your mom is so nice. She would have been a fun teacher to have."

"Yeah, well, I think she was impressed by that whole artists' code angle. That's the kind of thing she would think of."

"I learned it from my art teacher actually. The same one who taught me to make the necklaces. She seemed to like hers."

"She did. She'll wear it. She likes things that are natural like that, and she loves rocks. She's pretty special."

"I can tell you've had a great relationship with both of them."

"Well, they're my parents." I didn't understand how it could be any different.

"Yeah, but some people don't have good relationships with their parents. Not the friendly type of relationships anyway. I know my mom and I were never like that."

I hated to think that she had ever had a bad life. All I wanted to do was make her life better. "That's sad. I guess I never really realized it was not the normal way of things. I mean, I had my days of making them worry, but when Mila came along, I grew up fast. I guess I had to, with Heather being such a screwup."

"It's a good thing you're her father then."

"I didn't want you to know what she had done. My parents called in Vegas to tell me she'd trashed my house, and I came home to a real wreck. It was bad, and she was already high. I knew it was going to be bad. She's a junkie, Tara. She used to take Mila with her when she ran drugs and slept with her dealer. I have no idea what my little girl was exposed to before I realized what was happening."

"Oh, wow. I'm so sorry, Zane. But Mila seems really healthy. And like she doesn't remember."

"I wish I didn't remember. The thought of her using my child as a drug mule? Well, let's just say it doesn't make me think pleasant thoughts. And I didn't want that shit to scare you away."

"You couldn't scare me away, Zane. I care about you, and I'd never judge you for your past. Or hers. You're a good man."

"I don't know what I'd have done without my parents helping me out. They've done everything. Taken Mila when I needed them to and gone to court with me countless times. I owe them everything."

"Well, you're very lucky to have them. And for the record, I like them a lot. I really like Mila a lot too. You're all stronger for what you went through. And Mila? She's incredible. She's so fun to be around."

I laughed. It was good to know she felt that way. That she got it and didn't mind the drama of my past. "I like to watch her grow and experience new things. She's funny. And the things she comes up with? She's going to be a genius and rule the world someday. I don't know how I got so lucky."

"Well, she must get that from you."

"You're just saying that," I said, giving her a teasing look. "You're just trying to butter me up now that we're alone."

"Please," she said, teasing me back. "I'm surprised you haven't pulled this truck over and taken advantage of me yet."

"It's really hard. I promise you. I've wanted to get you alone since you came back. I thought I'd never get to see you again. It really messed with my head."

"Me too," she said.

The good thing about my parents' house was it wasn't far from my own. "We're home," I said, turning into my drive. It was a long path to the house still, and she undid her belt and moved closer.

"See?" I asked. "Already trying to take advantage of me. Can't even wait until we get inside to jump my bones."

"Jump your bones?" she said with a laugh. "You sounded like Karen."

I chuckled. "Oh no." I parked and turned the truck off. "I bet Karen doesn't do this." I leaned over and kissed her.

"Nope, can't say she does." She giggled. "Would probably turn you on if she did, though."

I moved back to look in her eyes as I shook my head. "No, it wouldn't. I don't share. Not even for kink. I'm very greedy like that."

"I like that," she said. "You can be greedy with me."

I kissed her again, taking exactly what I wanted. "Careful. I might just have to show you how greedy I can be."

"Do your worst," she said, rubbing my thigh. Her hand moved up and rubbed my cock through my jeans. It bulged against the fabric, pinching against the seams. The sense of longing grew worse as I craved her.

"Let's go inside. I want to show you my bedroom." I was glad Heather hadn't destroyed my bed. If she'd had an inkling I was with another woman, she would have.

When we got out of the truck, I met Tara at the front and kissed her again, then patted her ass as we walked to the door. I unlocked it and flipped on the lights as we went inside.

I locked it behind us, all the while her hands still roaming my body, and I turned and scooped her up in my arms to carry her.

She put her arms around my neck to hold on and kissed me as I made my way down the hall. When I got to my room where the door was ajar, I kicked it open with my foot and brought her to the bed where I sat her on the end.

"I've missed you," she said, reaching to undo my pants.

"I've missed you too, baby." I ran my hand through her hair as she licked her lips, taking out my cock.

Before I could make a move, she had me in her mouth, and it felt so warm and good that I felt my head spinning. I rocked my hips a little, and she relaxed her throat to take me deeper.

"Fuck, baby, that's good. You've got the sexiest mouth." I pulled away and leaned down to kiss her.

"I love to pleasure you."

"But there's only one problem," I said, meeting her eyes. She got a look of concern until I smiled. "You're not naked, and I really want to see you naked."

She grinned as I reached for her top and pulled it up over her head.

"Lay back and slip your skirt off for me."

She did as I asked, and I had to love that she was willing to entertain me in that way. She lay back, then slipped off the skirt, kicking it aside. "Do you want me to take off my panties too?"

"No, those are mine, but you can take off your bra for me." I liked to see her topless in her panties, and there was something about it that had always turned me on.

As she undid her bra and tossed it aside, I cupped her breast and kissed her nipple, sucking and nibbling as I teased it with my tongue. Then I stood up, pushed my pants that were still slung low on my hips, and dropped them to the floor.

I gripped my cock, giving it a tug, and ran my other hand up her thigh. "You look so beautiful," I said, dropping to my knees. I kissed her mound through her panties, where she had a freshly trimmed little peach just waiting to be tasted.

I moved her panties to the side and slipped a finger beneath the elastic, parting her lips to find a warm wet spot that was waiting for me.

I pushed my finger in deep, caressing her walls, and inserted another one, working her little clit with my thumb until she moaned and bucked.

"I've missed this," she said. "I never knew it was possible to miss this feeling. I want more Zane. I need you inside me." She closed her eyes, and I could see the blush in her cheeks. She was embarrassed by her words.

"I'll give you anything you want," I said. "But can I taste you first? I've missed the taste of you."

She nodded, her face flushed as her chest rose and quickly fell. I hooked my fingers in her panties and pulled them down and off, tossing them aside with the rest of the discarded clothing.

She was so fucking gorgeous like that, her body taut, her nipples peaked as she lusted for me. And strangely enough, I wanted nothing but to please her. I gave a hungry growl and moaned as I tasted her sex. She had a sweet taste that exploded in my mouth and made me ravenous.

I devoured her, fingering her hard as I lapped at her clit and teased it with my tongue.

I wanted to make her come, and it didn't take long until her first orgasm consumed her, and she writhed so much I had to grip her ass to hold her still against my mouth.

"Zane! Oh my. Oh yes." She was coming apart, unable to string together a complete sentence. "It's—that's—" She panted, giving another moan. "Amazing."

"Yes, it is," I whispered. I rose up, smiling at her. She had my cock so hard, I couldn't wait to come in her.

"You're laughing at me," she said with a giggle, putting her hand over her face.

"No, I'm not. I like it when you let loose. It's hot, baby. I want to make you lose all inhibitions and just let it consume you. I'd never laugh at you."

She gave me a sweet smile. "I feel safe with you," she said, and I knew I couldn't ever let that fail as her smile turned to concern. She was afraid I'd hurt her. I didn't want her to be afraid of anything with me.

"You are safe with me." I'd never want her to feel otherwise. I had to make sure I didn't ever do anything to ruin that.

CHAPTER 38

TARA

The look in his eyes said so much to me, and I knew in my heart that I was irrevocably in love. That was the scariest part of it all. And while he seemed sincere about me being safe with him, I wasn't sure if he understood the level of my feelings.

He rubbed my clit, and I was still feeling the aftershocks of pleasure from my first orgasm.

"Don't stop," I said.

He smiled. "Oh, don't worry, baby. I'm only getting started."

He inserted his fingers again, and after a few seconds, he pulled out and stroked himself. "Touch it and feel how wet you are."

I could feel the heat rising to my cheeks but did as he asked. I hadn't ever touched myself in front of anyone, and I hoped it turned him on.

His eyes seemed to darken with a look of lust as he watched me, and he took over, moving between my legs and rubbing his cock up my middle. "Don't stop," he said. "Tease that little clit for me."

I did as he instructed, and he leaned forward, kissing me hard on the mouth. When he pulled away, he rested his forehead on mine. "You're safe, and you can do anything and turn me on. Do you understand? I'm so turned on by everything you do."

I realized he was only trying to make me comfortable, and I relaxed and let the pleasure I was giving myself be enjoyed. While I had my eyes closed, my fingers slipping across my clit, teasing and flicking until I could feel another orgasm on the horizon of my pleasure, his cock parted my folds, and his wide head spread me open as it pushed inside of me.

I opened my eyes as he nudged his way in. "Does that hurt?" he asked.

"No, it feels so good."

He pumped his hips and fucked me, working my depths with a steady rhythm, and he lifted my legs up, my ankles landing on his shoulders as he thrust harder.

Zane stared into my eyes as if he was lost in them, and he closed his as the pleasure overtook him. I felt a certain sense of pride, knowing I was good for him, and it made me want to try new things and be everything I could for him.

He moved my legs, pushing them back towards my head, and just when I didn't think it could feel any better, the pleasure intensified as he hit a much more sensitive spot inside me.

My head swam, and I felt so far away all of a sudden, as if I had disconnected from my body and was floating above it, consumed with nothing but euphoric pleasure.

We were no longer two people but energy in motion and extreme sensation.

I didn't even realize I was being so loud until he spoke. "Come for me."

I did just as soon as he said it, as if his body had commanded it from my own. And the pleasure was so intense, my toes curled as my eyes rolled back in my head. And Zane didn't stop.

As I moved to sit up, he reached for me, and in a blink, I was in his arms, his strong arms holding me on his cock. He turned around and sat down, sitting me on his cock. "Ride me," he whispered in my ear. "Fucking own my cock, baby. Take all you want of it. It's yours."

He cupped my ass as I rode him, milking his cock with each

bounce, grinding hard on the rebound. I didn't even let the extra girth of his base stop me.

I put my palm against his chest and pushed him back, planting hands against his shoulders as I moved up and down, rolling my ass as I rode him.

"I'm going to come," he said, meeting my eyes as if it were a warning, but I wasn't about to move away from him. I wanted him, all of him. And I knew my bases were covered.

"Come for me, Zane," I whispered against his mouth before taking his lips with mine. And he brought his arms up around me, holding me down hard on him as he stilled. His cock was so big, taking over every part of me, that I could feel him twitch inside me as his cock erupted.

"You're fucking amazing, baby." He licked his lips and kissed me, still pumping his hips.

"You are," I said breathlessly. "I don't think I'm done."

"Good, because this is only the beginning." He slapped my ass, and I moved off of him, laying back on the bed.

"Come on," he said. "Let's take this party to the shower."

I felt a little self-conscious, even though I'd just been taught a lesson, but I was eager to be with him in the shower.

I offered him my hand, and we stood and went to the bathroom. He was still hard and ready, and my body was primed and ready.

But when we got in the shower, he surprised me. Instead of finding myself pinned against the shower wall with his sex driving into me, he held me in the shower spray and wet my hair, pushing it from my face. The he kissed me, holding me close.

As my chin quivered, he rubbed my arms and kissed my shoulder. "Touch it," he whispered.

I slipped my hand down and felt his cock was so hard, I could imagine it in me. "I want it," I said. "Warm me up."

"Are you ready?"

"Yes. Did you mean it when you said we could do anything?"

He smiled. "Yes, anything you want."

"Will you put me against the wall?"

He nodded, giving a small chuckle. "That's what I had planned." As if he had a new burst of energy, he pulled me close and walked me back to the wall. His shower was big, and there was even a bench in it, but that was of no use at the moment.

Zane moved on me so fast and took me in his arms. Before I knew it, my back and his hips were the only things keeping me off the floor. As we defied gravity, he put my arms up over my head and rocked his hips as he pinned them to the tile.

"Are you okay?" he asked. "If it's too rough, I'll stop."

"No, don't you dare." I got an arm free and held on to his shoulders. I wasn't going to let him go, not then and probably not ever. I didn't care if he broke me. I just wanted the pleasure to continue.

He worked me through the motions, and it was so good it was as if we were doing it for the first time again. And when I came at the moment of his second release, I felt as if we were one.

"That was intense," I said with a giggle.

Zane put me on the tile, and even though I found my feet, my legs were limp as noodles. He caught me. "Whoa, you might want to sit until you find your land legs."

"I don't have any strength," I said, feeling a little silly that I had no control over my own body.

Zane held me. "We can stand here as long as we need to." He reached for the soap. "I'll even make use of the time." He caressed my body, lathering me. He slipped his hand between my legs and cupped my ass as he kissed me.

I did the same for him, and in a way, it was so much more intimate than the sex. I felt connected to him on a whole new level and cared for in a way I never had before.

I loved him.

I felt the sting in my chest, knowing that too soon, I'd have to go back to my old life and my old responsibilities. "I don't want to leave," I said.

"Stay the night," he said, not understanding what I meant.

I didn't want to go home, and I wanted there to be a way I could stay in North Dakota, but instead of correcting him, I nodded. "I'd like that."

I was going to miss him so much. I hated that we had to say goodbye, but for the night, I was just going to enjoy being in his arms.

As we lay in bed, Zane holding me close until his breathing leveled off and he fell asleep, I looked around the room and wondered what it would be like to live with him and Mila. I imagined myself waking up on a Sunday morning to cook them a big breakfast and having a family gathering with his parents and fishing in the stream whenever we wanted.

I'd have a studio out back where all I did was paint, and I'd build a darkroom in it so I could take my own photographs. Maybe I'd figure out which one I wanted to do more and make a career out of it.

Those fantasies were nice, but I knew it wasn't going to happen. Zane liked having me around, but he had just come out of a very unhealthy relationship, and while he was probably content to stay long distance, I doubted he wanted more.

What was I going to do, be Mila's mother? Was I going to watch her while he went out in the fields and worked away from home? I'd miss him so much if he were gone too long. But then, maybe we could make it work somehow.

I kept the fantasy going until I fell asleep, and when I woke the next morning, I rolled over to find him awake and staring at the ceiling. "What are you thinking?" I asked.

"Just that you're going home today." He turned his head, and I nodded.

"Yeah, I really should get back. I know Ben is probably losing his mind without me there to hold down the fort."

He nodded. "Yeah, I guess he needs you." He seemed depressed but didn't say anything about me staying.

"I know Karen is going to be happy. She probably misses her extra income back home. Something tells me the men here aren't the kind to play games."

Zane shook his head. "Yeah, we're a special breed. We don't like games for sure. And I know I've had enough of that for one lifetime." He rolled away from me and got out of bed.

It felt so cold there without him. My heart ached, and I wasn't even gone yet.

"I should take you back to the hotel, I guess. I have to get Mila, and you have to pack."

"Oh, yeah, of course." I wondered if he'd come to see me off. "I'll call you on my way to the airport."

He nodded. "You do that, okay?" He turned, and I could tell that something in him had changed. He seemed colder, like he was angry.

All the way back to the hotel, he kept his head down and was quiet, and I couldn't tell if he was mulling over something or if he had just come back to his senses.

Maybe the night before wasn't all he had wanted it to be.

Before I got out, he gave me a kiss. "I had a good time last night. I'm glad you stayed."

"Me too. I'll call you later."

He nodded. "Later."

I got out and walked away, not knowing if I'd ever see him again. It was the hardest thing I'd ever have to do. But I knew I really had nothing to offer him. He had everything he needed. A loving family, a nice home, money, and a daughter who was everything to him. His love for her was probably all he'd ever need.

If not, he would have spoken up.

CHAPTER 39

ZANE

I let her walk away.

That haunted me as I went to pick up Mila from my parents' house. What the hell had been wrong with me? I couldn't just let her go, could I?

But who was I to ask her to stay? To give up her life to live in North Dakota with me and my daughter and my family? She would have been giving it all up for my life, and while I knew she hated Vegas, was that really fair?

The night before had been so special, and I realized just how much she meant to me. I was in love with her, and all I could hope for now was that somehow, we'd find a way back into each other's arms.

I got to my parents' house, and when I walked in, my father was lying on the floor, and Mila was walking on his back.

"You shouldn't let her walk all over you that way, Dad."

"Your father threw his back out, throwing her in the air," said my mother. "He forgets he's no spring chicken."

"I'm still the rooster around this house," he said, looking up to give my mother a wink.

"How was your night?" asked my father when Mila got down from his back and walked over to hug my legs.

"It's was fine." I looked down at my little girl, who was smiling up at me.

"Where's Tara?" she asked.

"She's at the hotel. She's packing her things."

"Why?" she said.

"She's going back home today, Noodle."

Mila frowned, and my parents went quiet.

"Am I missing something?" I asked them.

My father looked at my mother. "Honey, why don't you help her gather her things?"

Mom took Mila's hand and went to my old room, where she'd stayed the night before.

"What's going on?" I asked, concerned that something had happened with Mila.

"She might have her heart set on Tara becoming her new mom," he said.

"And what gave her that idea?"

"She must have overheard your mother and me. We thought she was in her room, and we were talking about how we liked Tara and how you shouldn't let her get away."

"You really feel that way?"

"She's the best thing that's happened to you since Mila. And you know for me to say that, it means something."

I sighed, wishing it were that easy. "She's got her own life in Las Vegas, Dad. I don't know if I can just ask her to move here just to date me. She doesn't have that kind of money, and I have Mila to consider. If I was a single man, it would be different."

"How? You'd move her in with you?"

"Well, yeah." I didn't think my parents would go for me having Tara move in unmarried with my daughter.

"So? What's the difference?"

"Mila."

"Have you asked her how she feels about Tara? She's told me and your mother she really likes her. It might not hurt to see what she thinks before you let that one slip away. Hell, just mention it to Tara and see what she thinks. If both Mila and Tara are good with it, then your mother and me will be."

"What about my work? I can't ask her to be a babysitter while I go off. I don't know. It doesn't seem fair."

"It's life. If she chooses it, you're not forcing her. And she wouldn't have to wait tables. Do you want the woman you love waiting tables in a Las Vegas hotel? Where men like you will be giving her big tips?"

I grew angrier just hearing him put it that way. "No, I don't want her to go." I couldn't let her go.

"Talk to your daughter, and then go and stop that girl from leaving. You're going to be miserable if you don't."

"Thanks," I said, knowing that if I had his blessing and my mother's, then I was already one step ahead. Of course, Mila would make the final decision.

My mother brought her out with her bags, and she still had a frown.

"Come on, Noodle. Let's get home." I had to talk to her in private. I didn't want my parents to influence our discussion.

I walked her out to the truck and put her in her seatbelt. She was quiet and remained that way, even when I put on her favorite music for the ride. "What's the matter, Noodle? You're quiet."

"You're quiet, too," she said.

"Yes, but why are you quiet? Do you have something on your mind?"

"I want Tara to stay," she said.

"Me too. But her home is in Las Vegas, and she wouldn't have a home here unless she stayed with us."

"Then she should stay with us, Daddy. I want her to stay. I want her to be my mom."

"You'd have to listen to her, Noodle. And it's not that easy to just say she can live with us and be a part of our lives."

"Why not?"

"You couldn't change your mind. If you get upset with her. And besides, I'm not sure she wants to stay, Noodle. It's a big decision."

"Couldn't you ask her to? She likes you, and she likes me too. She would stay if you asked. I know it."

I glanced back at her. Her arms were crossed, and she was pouting. She hadn't ever looked so upset. Like her little heart was breaking. Mine was breaking too.

I turned into the next road and made a loop back to the highway. I was going to the Heights, and I was going to ask her to stay.

I cursed when I saw the traffic backed up on the highway and wondered if I could take the next exit and make it past whatever was going on. Tara didn't have but another hour in town, and I had to make it to her before she called to go to the airport.

After ten minutes of slow-moving traffic, I cursed to myself, wishing little ears weren't in the truck so I could curse out loud. I had to drive responsibly too, and that was probably the only thing keeping me from road rage at that point.

When I finally made it to the next exit, I drove a little faster than the speed limit to make up for a lost time, and thankfully, I was at the Heights five minutes later.

"Why are we here, Daddy?"

"This is where Tara is staying, remember. We're going to ask her to stay." And yes, I was hoping she wouldn't be able to tell both of us no. I had never used Mila as an advantage, but she could still say no.

We pulled up to the front, and I told Mila to get out of her seatbelt by the time I came around to her door.

I took her hand, and we hurried, but when we finally made it up to her room, I found the cleaning lady there and the room empty. "What is going on?" I said.

"Can I help you?" she asked.

"No, it's okay. I was just looking for my friend." I took out my phone and tried to call her. I had hoped to show up and surprise her, but I'd been the one surprised.

The phone rang as I took Mila back to the elevators we had come up on, but no one ever answered. Not even her voicemail.

"Dammit," I swore.

"Daddy!" said Mila. "Nana said that's a bad word."

"You're right, Noodle. It is. But I don't think we're going to get to Tara in time. I think she's already on her way to the airport."

"Dammit," she mumbled, parroting what I'd said. I couldn't even get mad at her, and I'd have to have a talk with her about it later, but for now, we had to get back to the registration desk.

When the elevator opened, I went out to the front desk.

"Hello, how may I help you, sir?"

"Can you tell me if Tara Wright already checked out of the luxury suite?"

"Yes, she and her guest checked out about twenty minutes ago."

I breathed a sigh of relief. Twenty minutes wasn't that long of a head start, and I was hoping if I kept going, I'd be able to catch her.

"Thanks," I said to the woman. "Come on, Noodle. We have to catch her."

I hurried back out to the truck and put Mila in. I couldn't break traffic laws with her in the truck, but I could move fast on my feet to make up for it. I buckled her in and went around in a hurry, hoping the traffic had eased up so I could make it to a shortcut.

I drove out of the lot and headed back to the highway, where thankfully the traffic was moving, and I made the exit I wanted, taking an old dirt road that went to the oilfields as a cut through.

It shaved some time off of the trip, and soon, I pulled into the airport and drove around to the front. "Look for Tara," I told Mila, trying to call her again. I found a place to park, not seeing her anywhere on the way, and when no one answered again, I got a sick feeling. "Surely, she isn't up in the air.

What if that twenty minutes the woman said was more like half an hour?

As we walked by the row of windows, a plane took off in the distance. "Look, Daddy!" said Mila, pointing to it.

"I see Noodle." I stopped and let out a long breath, knowing I was defeated.

"No, Daddy! Look!"

I realized Mila was pointing over my shoulder. When I spun around, there was Tara and Karen standing at the airport coffee shop.

I felt the strongest sensation of relief in my life, and we hurried over. Karen saw us coming before Tara did.

She nudged her, and Tara spun around. I didn't waste any time talking. Still holding Mila, I pulled Tara close and kissed her.

After the quick peck, she glanced at her friend, who was equally surprised. "How did you know I was here? I was just about to call you."

"I tried to call." I thought she must have been avoiding me.

"We've been here, getting coffee." She glanced at her phone. "No service. That figures. This phone is cheap."

"Stay with us," I blurted.

Tara did a double-take. "What?"

"Stay here with us. We don't want you to go. You should stay here with us."

Karen smiled and pulled her lips in tight to hide it. She didn't have anything to say, but she was enjoying the show.

"I have a life back home, and no money to move here, Zane. Where would I stay?"

"With us."

"Your parents—"

"Already know. They want you to stay too." I searched her eyes, and she still looked unsure. "Please, Tara. I love you."

Tears filled her eyes as she moved to kiss me again. I put Mila down, and she hugged Tara's legs as we continued to kiss.

She pulled away, placing her hand against my cheek, and for the longest moment, I thought she was going to say no. Instead, she looked deep into my eyes. "I love you too."

Mila cheered, and Tara pulled away and turned to Karen. "Are you going to be okay going back alone?"

Karen grinned. Her eyes moved to a man across the room. "I'll be just fine. I overheard he's going my way." She winked at Tara and shook her head.

"Be careful," she told her friend. "And tell Ben I'm really sorry."

"No, you're not," said Karen. "I wouldn't give him the satisfaction."

"We'll come to get her stuff soon," I said. "You'll have to come back and see us."

"I might do that," she said. "You take care of my girl." Karen gave me a wink as they called her flight. "That's my ride." She hugged Tara again, and I gave her a minute to say her goodbyes.

She walked Karen over to the security line with Mila holding her hand the whole time, and my girls returned to me, both smiling ear to ear.

"Let's go home," she said. "If you're sure. There's still time to catch the—"

I pulled her close and kissed her. Mila giggled, but I didn't let it stop me from showing Tara that I wasn't letting her go.

EPILOGUE

TARA

One year later

Once I had settled into life in North Dakota with Zane and Mila, it was easy to see what I wanted to do with myself. Not only was I still holding out for a proposal and all the joys of marital bliss and motherhood to Mila, but I had also decided to go to art school and was just waiting for my final grades.

"When can you call and get your scores?" asked Zane, who had been out of bed for the past hour. He had let me sleep in since I was pulling crazy hours with school.

It had been his idea for me to go, and while I had wanted to get a job, he insisted my helping out with Mila was job enough.

"I'm going to try and do it now," I said, sitting up and rubbing my eyes. I took my phone from the bedside table and logged into the online app. "I'm only waiting on two more grades to see if I held on to my average."

"I'm sure you did," he said, shutting the bathroom door.

"Is that Mila in the kitchen?" I asked. I could hear pots and pans and the sound of the microwave.

Zane opened the door with a toothbrush in his hand. "Yeah, don't worry about it. She's fine."

I gave him a strange look. "Your daughter is using appliances, and I'm pretty sure I smell bacon frying."

"I just checked on her," he said. "She's fine."

"What are you up to?"

He took the toothbrush from his mouth and sighed. "Just trust me."

I could tell that they had something going on, but I pretended not to notice. I finally got my phone to cooperate and display my scores, and I nearly bounced out of the bed as I read them. "I did it!" I said. "I kept my average."

"That's my girl."

I was about to get out of bed when he walked back to the bed and kissed me with his minty mouth. "Don't get up yet."

"What are you going to do to keep me here?" I asked, wagging my brows. I pulled him closer, and he chuckled, but then he pulled away when Mila called him.

"Don't move," he said. "Promise?"

"I promise." I could hear the microwave timer going off as he walked away. He must have been helping her. They had something up their sleeve, and from the smell of it, it was breakfast in bed.

I tried to act surprised when they showed up with a tray. On it was a large bouquet of flowers, a card standing up against its vase, and a plate of eggs, bacon, and toast with fresh strawberries and cream. They had even fixed a glass of my favorite juice.

"Happy end of the school year," said Mila, who was finishing up her first year as well.

"It's your end of the year as well," I said. "We should all be celebrating that."

"We'll go out for ice cream later, but this is all for you."

"Wow, thanks."

"Open the card," he said, giving me a nudge.

"Yes, open the card. It's from both of us, and I drew you a picture."

She seemed just as excited as he did, and I could truly say over the past year, I had grown to love her like my own daughter.

When I opened the card, the picture was so special, and it was of all of us together by the stream. "Thanks, Mila. It's so beautiful, and you're really growing in your talent." Her art was better than some of the people I went to school with.

"Thanks. I used my new art set." She had already moved on to different media and was now exploring pastels.

"The flowers are pretty too," I said, leaning in to smell them. "Thank you both so much." I took a bite of the eggs as we chatted about the grades, and just when I thought the fun was over, Mila gave me a present she pulled up from the end of the bed.

"I guess that's why I couldn't get up?"

Zane smiled. "You almost blew it," he said.

"I feel like it's my birthday," I said.

I opened the box and found a spa package for Mila and me and another one that I could go to solo when I needed a break from it all. Not that I could see myself ever wanting one. Living with them had been great, and while Zane and I had tossed around getting married and joked with his mother about eloping in Las Vegas, that was as far as that conversation had gone.

I felt a little slighted when I pulled out a new blouse and a pair of earrings. "You're spoiling me," I said. It wasn't that I wanted more, but I would have been happy with a simple plastic ring from the bubble gum machine and a proposal.

"I haven't even begun to spoil you," said Zane. He sat on the edge of the bed, took a piece of my bacon, and offered it to me. I ate from his hand, and Mila rolled her eyes.

"She's not a baby, Daddy," she said.

"Why don't you go and see if there is something else in the kitchen?"

Mila took off, giggling the entire time.

"Thanks for this, Zane. It's really sweet."

"Well, you've been such a good sport, especially when I was gone on that last job. I know it's not easy taking on so much responsibility, but I'm glad you're here with us. I wanted to show you how much I love and appreciate you."

I took the diamond earrings from the box. "These are so pretty."

"Well, I knew you didn't want anything too flashy, but the salesman said they'd go with everything."

So would an engagement ring.

All of a sudden, Mila yelled for her father again. "Daddy! I need your help!"

He glanced at me. "Stay put?"

"I'm not going anywhere. I'm going to finish my breakfast." I took the juice and moved it to the bedside table, and I did the same with my flowers. I ate a couple of bites of my breakfast, and even though it had gotten cold, it was the best breakfast ever.

Finally, they came back into the room, and while Mila walked with her hands over her head, I could tell that Zane had the most weight from the huge box.

I sat up a little higher in bed. "What on earth?" Zane was barely able to hold the big box, and he winced, struggling.

"You got it, Noodle?" he asked.

"Zane, be careful!"

He stepped away, and Mila held the large box all on her own. I nearly screamed, but they both laughed.

"We tricked you," she said. "It's not heavy at all."

"Still be careful. You made my heart jump."

"Sorry, baby." Zane came and knelt down by the bed. He moved my tray aside, and Mila placed the box on the bed in front of me. "Go ahead. Open it."

I wondered what kind of trick they were playing as I unwrapped the bright red and white polka dotted paper.

But inside of that box was another box, and this one had striped paper. "What in the world?" I said as Mila giggled. "How many are there?"

"I'm not telling," said Zane. He stayed right there with me and knelt by the bed as I went through three more big boxes, each barely smaller than the last. The room was a mess of paper, and Mila ran around, wadding it all up in a big ball.

"You're teasing me," I said. "There's not anything in here is there?"

"No, there's something in there. I promise you. Would I lie?"

"No, but you'd prank me," I said. "You and your little miniature."

He laughed. "You love us," he said.

"You know I do." I was never more in love with anyone as I was the two of them. I just wanted it to be forever.

I continued to unwrap, and as the packages got smaller, Mila began to help me. "You're not going fast enough," she said.

"My hands are getting dry from all of this paper, and I'm pretty sure I've got a papercut."

Together, we had the box down to the size of a brick. Zane laughed as we both gave out. "I think my parents overdid the wrapping," he said.

"You mean you didn't do this?" I asked.

He shook his head. "It's from me, but they helped."

"Oh, they've helped, all right." I ripped off more paper, which they had taken the special care to alternate just to keep it colorful. I felt like I was drowning in it by the time I was to the smallest one.

"If there's another box in here, I'm going to cry," I said. I could tell it was a ring box once the paper was removed.

"Open it," he said, putting his hand on my leg.

Inside was the most beautiful ring I'd ever seen. It had one large cushion surrounded by smaller diamonds. It wasn't too large or flashy but more than I'd ever imagined. I put my hand to my mouth as tears pooled in my eyes.

"Do you like it?" he asked.

"Yes, I love it."

Zane looked at Mila, and she gave him a nudge. "Tara, you're an incredible woman, and you've been a fantastic mother figure and partner. We love you, and I'd love it if you'd be my wife."

"Will you marry my Daddy?" asked Mila. "And be my new mom for real?"

I was surrounded by love, and the ring felt like it was where it had always wanted to be. "Yes, I love you both so much, of course, I will marry you."

Mila cheered and ran around in circles as Zane hugged me and pulled me up out of the bed to spin me around in his arms. "I'm so happy," he said. "I've wanted to ask you for a while, but Mila wanted to make it special."

"It's special because you're both here, and you both want me."

"We love you, baby." He held me close, and I wiped away my tears. "Now, my mother can finally pull out all of those bridal mags she's been hoarding over the past year."

"She has magazines?"

"She bought the first one after you moved in. She's been hoping you'd let her help plan the wedding."

"Of course, I will."

"And me too," said Mila. "I want to be in the wedding too!"

"Of course, you can," I said.

"Looks like we have some plans to make," said Zane. "Are you happy?"

"I'm more than happy." It was the best time of my life. Not only did I have a beautiful daughter to be, but Zane's love was everything.

The End.

ABOUT THE AUTHOR

Chloe is a hometown girl from Tennessee who loves a great short romance, drinking coffee most of the day, and hanging out with family. When she's not writing, she can be found playing the piano or surfing Facebook!

Having been a reader all her life, she's hoping that you'll find yourself lost to time, laughing and falling in love all over again with her books.

OTHER BOOKS BY C. MORGAN

Take Me Back
My Uptown Girl
Tell Me No Lies
Ringing in New Years
Stealing His Sister
Santa's Favorite Elf
Opposites Attract
Keeping Score
Drive Me Crazy
Hometown Hotshot
Your Secret is Safe
Make Me An Offer
Singles Retreat
Accidentally On Purpose
Dating Dr. Wright
Hot Summer Nights
Model Student
Guarding Her Assets
Accidentally In Love
Romance Rivals
Don't Walk Away
Wash Over Me
Whatever it Takes
Mountain Man's Secrets
Mountain Man's Girl
Mountain Man's Fake Fiancé

Mountain Man's Baby
Mountain Man Crush
Keep Me Warm
Professionals with Benefits
Too Hot To Handle
Finding Real Love
The Sweet Stuff
Model Behavior
Mad In Love
My Little Secret
Reasons to Breathe
The Fix Up
Pick Me, Handsome